Wee Macgreegor ~
Wee Macgreegor *Again*

by

J. J. BELL

With an introduction

by

J. J. BELL

Birlinn

The Publisher would like to dedicate this volume
to David Blaikie and Allan Boyd – companions in
the spirit of the Hebrides, the spirit of literature
and the spirit of whisky – for all their help
and support.

© Birlinn Ltd, 1993
13 Roseneath Street, Edinburgh

Typeset in Monotype Plantin by
ROM-Data, Falmouth, Cornwall
and printed and bound by
Cox and Wyman Ltd, Reading

A CIP record for this book is available
from the British Library

ISBN 1 874744 09 2

Contents

Introduction
The Story of the Book

EVERY book, even the least important, holds a story not printed on its pages. It may be an interesting and illuminating story, worth telling for its own sake, though generally, we may suppose, it could matter only to the author and those who care for him.

The story of the present little book has a certain oddity, but that alone would be a far from sufficient reason for its appearing in print; and I should say at once that I am setting it down mainly because, when my friend, Robert D. Macleod, suggested my doing so, I saw an opportunity to record my acknowledgments, as I had often wished to do, to certain friendships, without which there could have been nothing to make a story about. In a way, it must be a fine thing for an author to be able to hold up his book and say: "Alone I did it !" Yet I reckon myself as more to be envied, with my memories of those who helped me, or made it possible for me, to do it.

Imagine, then, if you please, the case of a young man who, in the midst of a Science course at the University, took, as it were, the wrong turning, and with no literary equipment, save pen, ink, paper, some postage stamps and a little imagination, determined to become an author.

At the beginning of a new century, after five years of industry, his achievements amount to some hundreds of pieces of light verse scattered – many of them freely, in both senses of the word – among several dozens of periodicals; two little books of nursery rhymes, some scores of short stories, mostly in Scottish journals; two years' experience as sub-editor and book-keeper on a Glasgow illustrated weekly, and the privilege of filling a column, once a week, in the *Glasgow Evening Times*.

The last is his stand-by, and sometimes he feels that it is his limit. His parents kindly conceal, as they suppose, their doubts; his brothers and sisters admire everything he writes – which, of course, is very bad for him; his older relatives, having picked up the phrase somewhere, murmur "How precarious!" – and feel the better, no doubt, for having so delivered themselves. Still, he goes on, ever seeking, in particular, to improve his "English." Swinburne for verse and Anthony Hope for dialogue are among his models ... But you never can tell.

My connection with the *Evening Times* began in this way. In those earlier years I had been writing short stories for one of its associated papers, the *Glasgow Weekly Herald*, and then, one day, the Editor of the latter, Mr A. Dewar Willock, invited me to come to his office. I had never beheld an Editor, nor had anybody I knew done so, and it is no exaggeration to say that I entered his room in an extremely highly strung condition. I was received by a young man, Mr George C. Porteous, then sub-editor – afterwards Editor – who did something to mitigate the strain till his chief appeared, a dark, bearded man, with the kindliest of eyes behind glasses, a humorist in the finest sense. He talked about my work and advised me where to send certain stories which had not been suitable for his journal – advice which I took, with fortunate results.

After that I called on him occasionally, without invitation; yet my self-confidence was not such that I could have introduced myself to any other editor.

One night I wrote a small poem. None of those early efforts have been preserved, but I have a vague recollection that it dealt with Spring, a Girl and, possibly, some Daffo-dils, or, maybe, a Dicky-bird. That does not suggest material for a sober newspaper, but in a daft moment I sent

it to Mr Willock, asking whether he thought it would be of
any use to the *Evening Times*. Two nights later my brother
pointed it out – not without embarrassment, the thing being
so sentimental – on the editorial page of that paper, whose
circulation, within the next hour, I increased by six copies
– why, I do not know, since they lay in my cupboard till long
after.

On my next visit to Mr Willock he took me to another
room, and kindly introduced me to Mr Michael Graham,
thereby opening the door to a fairly long and entirely happy
association with the *Evening Times*. For a year or so my
contributions were confined to verse, and then, greatly
daring, I sent in about half a column of prose. I have never,
I am sorry to say, kept a diary, but trivialities may become
landmarks in our lives, and I can still see myself writing
those light paragraphs about Glasgow on a "Fair Saturday,"
and labelling them: "A Young Man's Fancies," not, of
course, dreaming that here was the beginning of a long
series of articles and sketches under that heading.

I have heard brother-writers remark that the older one
grows the harder it is to come by fresh ideas, and I can well
believe that it may be so where one's writing is confined to
a certain subject, or subjects. But ought it to be so with the
general journalist and the imaginative writer? Is there no
inspiration in experience? As the old Devon saying has it:

> *A woman, a spaniel, a walnut-tree –*
> *The more you beat'em, the better they'll be.*

I would except at least the spaniel, and insert the mature
brain, which, I am assured by a man of science, will respond
to almost any amount of flogging, provided the blood be in
fair condition. In other words, the thing we importantly call
mental exhaustion is really physical. At all events, this brings
me to my point – namely, that with all the advantages of
youth, and its energy, and with all the world to choose from
there were occasions when I got "stuck" – and "stuck" far
more badly than in later years – for an idea on which to build
my article, or sketch, for the next Friday's *Evening Times*,

which I usually wrote on the Saturday, revised on the Monday, and delivered on the Tuesday.

Pardon, please, another triviality. Came a Saturday, when I felt I was going to be beaten. The family was from home for the week-end. Late in the day I left my own corner and came down to my father's library. A last resort – something serious. There was an early edition of *Hakluyt's Voyages* in beautiful binding, and I took down a volume.

I should be glad if a friendly psychologist would inform me as to the association of ideas between anything in Hakluyt and a working man, with his wife, baby and small boy, in Argyle Street, on a Saturday afternoon. The only lead I can give him is this. Ten years earlier, on board a Firth of Clyde excursion steamer, on a Glasgow "Fair Saturday," I had heard a distracted mother of five address her eldest in these words: "Macgreegor, tak' yer paw's haun', or ye'll get nae carvies to yer tea!"

Anyway, on a page of Hakluyt, I "saw" the little family, and that was the beginning. It was necessary, of course, to employ the vernacular, which I had done only once before, in a very short and rather sentimental sketch of a young working man and his wife inspecting a showcase of won-drous jewels in the Glasgow Exhibition of 1901.

I am well aware that I have been suspected of eavesdrop-ping on tramway cars and elsewhere, and of furtively lurking in close-mouths, and in sundry other places, in order to gain my knowledge, such as it is, of the Glasgow, or Lowland, dialect; but the truth is that, just as I have never deliberately "studied" a fellow-creature, I had never made any effort to "learn" the speech of the people of the period. While I was familiar with the older men in my father's factory, who used the vernacular as a matter of course, I feel certain that I acquired little or nothing there. Indeed, I cannot doubt that from the lips of my paternal grandmother, a lady of the old school, who died when I was seven, fell all the quaint words and phrases – many of them embodied in nursery rhymes – into my memory, there to lie quiet till the years should bring a use for them.

So I sat down to write the first "Macgreegor" story, and, when it was finished, it struck me as pretty poor stuff. It certainly did not strike me as particularly funny – nor has "W. M." ever done that, while much of him has seemed to me rather pathetic. On the Monday it did not appear any brighter, but there was not time to try all over again, and at the last moment I sent it off to Mr Graham, with an apologetic note, and prepared myself for its rejection.

Yet, on the Friday afternoon there it was, in all the comfort and encouragement of print, though I still expected a letter, saying it had been allowed, for once, to pass, but must not happen again.

On the following Monday I went in to see Mr Willock, pretending that it was about another matter. Mr Willock laid one hand on my shoulder, gave me a hearty shake with the other, and said, in effect: "That's the stuff to give 'em, my boy! Do it again!" And presently Mr Graham said something almost as nice.

Any young writer who may do me the honour to read this will guess what that meant, and what the memory of those two men stands for in my life.

Letters from readers began to come to the office and direct to myself – kindly messages, though there was one, I recall, bitterly abusive, which, I confess, hurt me very much, though, no doubt, it was good for me.

The sketches did not appear in the *Evening Times* every Friday – Mr Graham and I saw the risk of overdoing it – but by the beginning of the following year I had accumulated fifteen or sixteen of them. Somebody – I am sorry I do not remember who it was – suggested collecting them into a cheap volume. I was going to be married in the autumn, and, while I had no illusions as to any rich reward, I thought it would be fun to have such a little book in being. However, it seemed that even the fun was to be denied me.

The publishers to whom, in turn, I submitted the material were quite unanimous. They generously admitted that the little sketches were amusing, but pointed out that their appeal was too local to justify the risk of publication. I offered the copyright to one firm for £10, to another for £15; but no, they were not tempted.

The idea of a book would have been dropped and forgotten had not I, by chance, mentioned it to my friend, J. A. Westwood Oliver, whose assistant I had been on the *Scots Pictorial*. He was, as always, sympathetic. He told me that his little company could not venture on the risks of book publication; then added that he thought *Macgreegor* might have a modest sale in Glasgow and the West, and that if I cared to guarantee £50, against possible loss, he would himself see it through the press. One of my brothers then sportingly offered to put up the £50.

There was so little material that the ordinary size of page had to be rejected, and we chose a format already made popular by Barry Pain's *Eliza* – 6 by 3½ inches. I wanted the price to be sixpence, but deferred to Mr Oliver's theory that anyone who would rashly give the smaller coin for such a book would just as rashly part with the larger. The title was to be simply *Macgreegor*, and the early editions were printed with the solitary word at the top of the pages. At the last moment, however, as the cover was going to press, Mr Oliver suggested the addition of the "Wee," which, I cannot doubt, made a big difference in the popularity of the title.

Almost at the last moment, too, it was decided to have a picture on the cover. Some drawings were hurriedly obtained, but all were rather commonplace, if grotesque, representations of the conventional "bad boy," and it was through the good offices of Mr William Hodge, head of the printing firm, that we got the John Hassall drawing, which undoubtedly drew many an eye to the book. Then Mr Oliver gave an order for 3000 copies, though I had almost implored him to confine it to 2000.

And by now you will be agreeing that I had not very much to do with *Wee Macgreegor*.

I was married in October, and my wife and I went to live in a quiet place on the Clyde, some five-and-twenty miles from

the city. The book was published on 23rd November, and
we wondered anxiously what was happening to it. A week
passed; then came a telegram from Mr Oliver. The first
printing was exhausted; a second was on the machines. By
the end of the year the sales were 20,000.

The Press notices were extraordinarily generous. One in
the *Glasgow Evening News*, by Neil Munro, whom, though
he lived just across the water, I was not to meet till ten years
later, must have been very helpful. Later, when the circulation had got to 50,000 or so, he wrote me a letter,
threatening to come over with the family dirk. Another
notice, by William Archer, in the *Morning Leader* was the
book's best London introduction.

There was much pleasant correspondence from all parts
of the world, even from remote corners, some from children, which was the pleasantest of all. Traders seemed to
see a virtue in the title and the Hassall drawing, for presently
appeared "Wee Macgreegor" lemonade, matches, china,
"taiblet," picture postcards, sardines, and so forth. Sober-
minded persons called it a "craze," and I should be the last
to contradict them, for its favour from the English reader
has always been inexplicable to me.

When the sales in this country had reached 60,000 news
came over that the book was being "pirated" in America,
where I had never thought of taking out copyright. The
score or so of "pirated" editions were mostly cheap and
crude productions. For some reason, best known to themselves, the publishers did not use the Hassall drawing;
possibly they felt it was not "Scotch" enough. Most of them
displayed effigies of little boys – in one instance, I believe,
of a little girl – in full Highland costume, obviously copies
from outfitters' catalogues. We had a copyright published
edition printed in Canada, but these American productions
swamped it. Messrs Harper & Brothers, New York, published an "authorized edition," making a beautiful little
book of it, and recognized myself in the matter, which was,
of course, an act of grace on their part.

On this side, in 1903, Mr Oliver's company issued

editions in cloth and leather, with illustrations by A. S. Boyd, but, naturally, the big demand was for the original little paper-covered volume. This is not the place for figures – though I have quoted some already – but, having heard so many extravagant estimates, I may take this opportunity of stating that the sales of the book in its original form did not pass the quarter-million. I do not suppose that many of those flimsy copies are in existence to-day. When Mr Oliver's company went out of business, the publishing of *Wee Macgreegor* was transferred to Messrs Mills & Boon, London, who by including its sequel made a sizable shilling book. For a time, too, it had considerable prosperity as one of *The Daily Mail* "Sixpennies." Then, in 1913, Messrs Thos. Nelson & Son took it into their remarkable series of "Sevenpennies," which, however, was checked by the rising costs of war-time, and later they put it into exceedingly neat forms, 1s. 6d. and 2s., in which they have kept it alive ever since.

I must not neglect to say that in its first months the little thing was greatly helped by the proprietors and managers of the Glasgow railway station bookstalls, who not only displayed it most lavishly, but kept their boys shouting up and down the platforms, with copies. Some of those boys were wonderful young salesmen. They could sell the book to its author.

In 1911, Mr Alfred Wareing, Director of the Glasgow Repertory Theatre, conceived the idea of putting *Wee Macgreegor* on the stage, and in December presented a play, or rather series of episodes, adapted from the book. It was produced by Harold Chapin, the brilliant young playwright and fine soldier lost to us early in the War, and myself. The big difficulty at the outset was to find a boy to play the name part, and I still wonder what we should have done but for my friend, the late R. J. Maclennan, of the *Evening News* – the helping hand again, you see! – who took trouble to discover a likely lad for us. Willie Elliott, a messenger-boy, was fourteen, little for his age, nice-looking and intelligent.

He had no ambition to become an actor, but the job, I suppose, seemed worth his while. It was my duty to take him through his part, and for a time he fairly baffled me by turning the vernacular into fairly good English. Eventually, thanks to the untiring patience of the chief producer and the principals, he did very well, being little troubled by self-consciousness. As far as I know, it was the only part he had ever played. When the War came he enlisted in the Gordons, was three times wounded, and is now, I believe, raising a family in Canada. The play ran for seven weeks at the Royalty, and was afterwards taken on a short tour. As drama, it was without merit; its dialect alone would have prevented its going far afield; but the players made the most of it, and the author confesses that it did him good to hear the audience laugh.

Wee Macgreegor – as small boy – has not been screened. In the old "silent" days a contract for its filming was signed, and a sum was paid, but the producing company did not survive to make the picture. Nor has it been translated into any foreign language, though I have a record, dated 1904, of a gallant but misguided Frenchman who threw down the pen – and perhaps threw up the inkpot – about the middle of the second chapter. German philologists have written pleasant letters about some of the words, such as "toorie" and "peely-wally," but have shown no interest in the tale. Numerous persons wrote asking the meaning of "jaw-box." A gentleman in South Africa has, I believe, done a chapter or two into English, for use in schools. Two letters I particularly prize: one from a little girl in Ross-shire, who asks me to write "some more," tells me she is seven, and signs herself "Yours very truly"; the other from the granddaughter of Dr Samuel Smiles, the famous author of *Self-Help*, who informs me that "the old gentleman" always carries a copy in his dressing-gown.

With the present edition, issued primarily to meet the need for a library size of the book, *Wee Macgreegor* is certainly in the handsomest dress he has had since he was born.

Whether he deserves it is not for his author to say, more especially as his coming into the world and his continued (miraculous) existence therein have been – as has been shown – so largely due to sheer friendliness; none the less his author is grateful to the publishers, to whom the idea of the present edition belongs.

The earlier editions are dedicated to A. Dewar Willock and to Michael Graham, and to their Memories; and now I am happy to be allowed to dedicate this new edition, as seems right and fitting to do, to the son of the one and successor of the other – James Willock, Editor of the *Glasgow Evening Times*.

J. J. B.

ABERDEEN,
October 1933.

Glossary

A', all
ABIN, above
ABLOW, below
AULD, old
AVA' at all
AWA', away

BA', ball
BASS, a door mat
BAIKIE, rubbish receptacle
BAUN', band
BAWBEE, halfpenny
BAWR, jest, "lark"
BEGOOD, began
BEW, blue
BLATE, backward, ashamed
BLETHER (TO), to talk
  nonsense
BRAW, fine, handsome
BREID. bread
BREITH, breath
BUITS, boots

CA' (TO), to call
CA' (TO), to drive, to force
CAIRRIT, carried
CANNY, careful
CARVIES, sugared caraways
CALLER, fresh
CHEUCH, tough
CHEUCH JEAN, a toffy sweet
CHIEF, friendly, "chummy"

COME BEN, come in
COORIE DOON (TO), to
  crouch in sitting position
CLAES, clothes
COUP (TO), to upset, to fall
CRACK, conversation

DAFT, silly stupid
DAIDLEY, pinafore
DAUNER, stroll
DOO, dove
DOUR, stubborn
DROOKIT, drenched

EEN, eyes
ERNED, ironed

FASH (TO), to worry
FA' (TO), to fall
FECHT, fight
FILE (TO), to soil
FIN (TO), to feel
FIT, foot
FLY, sly, sharp
FRAE, from
FREEN', friend
FRICHT, fright
FRIT, fruit
FURBYE, also
FURRIT, forward

GAB, mouth

GAR (TO), to induce, compel

GAUN, going, go on!

GEY, rather ("pretty")

GLAUR, mud

GREET (TO), to weep

GRUMPHY, pig

GUID-SISTER, sister-in-law

HAP (TO), to cover cosily

HASSOCK, stuffed foot-stool

HAUD (TO), to hold

HAVERS, nonsense

HOAST, cough

HOGMANAY, New-Year's Eve

HUNNER, hundred

HULLABALOO, noise, disturbance

HURL, ride (in a vehicle)

INGIN, onion

INTIL, into

JAWBOX, sink in kitchen

JOOG, jug, mug

KEEK (TO), to peep

KIST, chest

KEP (TO), to catch

KIST, cheat

KITLY, tickly

KIZZEN, cousin

LET BUG (TO), to show, to inform

LEEVIN', living

LOUSE (TO), to loosen, to unlace

LUG, ear

LUM, chimney

LYIN' BADLY, lying sick

MAIRRIT, married

MAUN, must

MUCKLE, great, big

NAB (TO), to seize

NEB, nose

NE'ERDAY, New-Year's Day

NICK, policeman

NICK (TO GET THE), to be "run in"

NICKIT, caught, captured

NOCK, clock

OARIN', rowing

'OOR, hour

OOSE, OOSIE, wool, woolly

OOTBYE, out of doors

OWER, over, excessively

OXTER, arm

PARTINS, crabs

PECHIN', panting

PEELY-WALLY, sickly, feeble-looking

PEERY-HEIDIT (TO BECOME), to "lose one's head"

PICKLE (A), a few

PLUNK (TO), to play truant

POOSHUN, poison

POKE, a (paper) bag

POTTY, putty

PREEN, pin

PUIR, poor

QUATE, quiet

RID, red

RIPE (TO), to pick (one's pocket)

SAIR, sore

SARK, shirt
SCALE (TO), to spill
SCART (TO), to scratch
SCLATES, slates, scales
SCLIM (TO), to climb
SHAIR, sure
SHIN, soon
SCOOT (TO), to squirt
SCUD, to smack, to whip
SHOOGLY, shaky, insecure
SKELP (TO), to whip
SIC, such
SILLER, (silver) money
SOJER, soldier
SOOM (TO), to swim
SOOPLE, supple
SLITHERY, slippery, slimy
SNASHTERS, dainties (cakes)
SPEIR (TO), to enquire
SPELDRON, a small dried fish
STAUN' (TO), to stand
STAIR-HEID, stair landing
STEERIN', restless, energetic
STRACHT, straight
STRAVAYGIN', wandering
STRIPPIT, striped
STROOP, spout
SUMPH, a lout
SURREE, soiree
SYNE, ago
SYNE (TO), to wash out
SWEIRT, unwilling

TAE, toe
TATE, a small portion

TAURRY-BILER, tar-boiler
TAWPY, a "softy"
TAWTIE, potato
TEWKY, a chicken
THOLE (TO), to bear, to
    endure
THAE, these
THUR, those
THON, THONDER, yon,
    yonder
THRANG, busy, occupied
TIL, to, unto
TIM (TO), to empty
TOORIE, ornament on bonnet
TOOSIE, untidy
TOSH UP (TO), to tidy up
TWAL, twelve

UNCO, very, extremely

WANNERT, wandered
WAUR, worse
WARL', world
WEAN, child
WHEEN, some
        WHAUR, where
WHUMLIN' tumbling, rolling
WULKET (TO TUM'LE THE),
    to throw a somersault
WICE, wise
WINDA-SOLE, window-sill
WULK, whelk
WUR, our

YIN, YINST, one, once

Wee Macgreegor

I

"MAW!" said the small boy for the twenty-third time since the Robinson family began their perambulations in Argyll Street, "Maw!"

"Whit is't ye're wantin' noo, Macgreegor?" asked his mother, not without irritation in her voice.

"Maw, here a sweetie shope."

"Weel, whit aboot it? Ye'll get yer gundy the morn, ma mannie."

"I want it noo, Maw."

"Deed, then, ye'll jist ha'e to want. Ye micht think shame o' yersel', wantin gundy efter ye've ett twa aipples an pie furbye."

"But I'm hungry yet."

This seemed to amuse his mother, for she laughed and called to a big man in front of her, who was carrying a little girl, "John, Macgreegor's sayin' he's hungry."

"Are ye hungry, Macgreegor?" said John, halting and turning to his son, with a twinkle in his eye. "Ye'll be wantin' a scone, maybe."

Macgregor looked offended, and his mother remarked, "No' him! It's thae sweetie shopes that's makin' him hungry. But I've tell't him he's to get nae gundy till the morn's mornin'."

"D'ye hear whit she's sayin', Macgreegor?" said his father. Then, suddenly, "Come on, Lizzie, an' we'll get him a bit sweetie to taste his gab."

"Ye jist spile the wean, John," said Lizzie, moving, however, with a good-natured smile to the shop window. "But mind, it's to be baurley sugar. I'll no ha'e him filin' his stomach wi' fancy things. See an' get baurley sugar, John, an' wee Jeannie 'll get a bit o' 't. Wull ye no', ma daurlin'?" she demanded sweetly of the child in her husband's arms. Wee Jeannie expressed delight in sounds unintelligible to anyone but her mother.

"I want taiblet," said Macgregor to his father, in a whisper rendered hoarse with emotion at the sight of the good things in the window.

His mother was not intended to hear him, but she did. "Taiblet!" she exclaimed. "Weans that gets taiblet gets ile efter."

The boy's nether lip protruded and trembled ominously.

"Och, Lizzie," said John, "ye're aye thinkin' aboot the future. A wee bit taiblet 'll dae the laddie nae hairm. Deed, no! An' fine I ken ye like a bit taiblet yersel'."

"Ay, that's a' richt, John. But ye've shairly no' forgot whit the doctor said when Macgreegor wis lyin' badly efter ye had him at the Exhibeetion. He said Macgreegor had a wake disgeestion, and we wis to be awfu' carefu' whit he ett. An' I wis readin' in the 'Companion' jist the ither nicht that there wis naethin' waur fur the disgeestion nor nits, an' thon taiblet's jist fu' o' nits."

"Aweel," said her husband, evidently overcome by her reasoning, "I'll get baurley sugar. Haud wee Jeannie." And he entered the shop.

When he rejoined his family, he handed the "wholesome sweetmeat" to his wife, who first of all extracted a short stick for wee Jeannie, wrapping one end of it in a scrap of paper torn from the "poke." Macgregor accepted his share in gloomy silence, and presently the party resumed their walk, John again carrying his daughter, who from time to time dabbed his countenance with the wet end of her barley-sugar in a filial desire to give him a taste.

Having proceeded west about one hundred yards, they were called to a halt by Lizzie at the door of a big warehouse.

"I'm gaun in here, John," she said. "I'm wantin' a bit rid flannen fur a goonie fur wee Jeannie."

"Naethin' fur yersel', Lizzie?"

His wife looked at something in one of the windows rather wistfully. "It's ower dear," she murmured.

"It's no' that dear," said John, thoughtfully.

"Weel, it's guid stuff. But I'm gey sweirt to pey sae muckle fur whit I micht dae wi'oot. An' Macgreegor's needin' a new bunnet."

"His bunnet's fine. Jis you gang in, Lizzie, an' buy whit ye've got yer e'e on. We'll see aboot a bunnet efter. Dod! ye maun ha'e yer Ne'rday, wumman, like ither folk. Awa' wi' ye!"

"I'll tak' wee Jeannie in wi' me," said Lizzie, looking pleased. "I'm shair yer airm's sair wi' haudin' her. She's gettin' a big lassie – are ye no', ma doo?" She stepped into the doorway, but returned for a moment. "See an' keep a grup o' Macgreegor, John," she said.

"Oh, ay! Him an' me'll jist tak' a bit daunner up an' doon till ye come oot." Having wiped from his face the sticky traces of his daughter's affection, and set his pipe going with several long breaths of satisfaction, he held out his hand to his son, with "Come on, Macgreegor."

Macgregor slipped his small fist into the big one, and they set off slowly along the crowded pavements, stopping frequently to see the sights of the street and the windows, while the youngster asked innumerable questions, mostly unanswerable.

"Ha'e ye ett yer baurley sugar?" asked his father, during a pause in the childish queries.

"Ay; I've ett it … It's no' as nice as taiblet, Paw."

"But ye'll no' be carin' fur taiblet noo?"

"Taiblet's awfu' guid," returned Macgregor guardedly, with a glance upwards at his parent's face. "Wullie Thomson's paw gi'es him taiblet whiles."

"Aweel, Macgreegor, I'm no' gaun to gi'e ye taiblet… But if ye wis pittin' yer haun' in ma pooch ye micht – Ye're no' to let on to yer Maw, mind!"

The enraptured Macgregor's hand was already busy, and a moment later his jaws were likewise.

"Ye've burst the poke, ye rogue," said John, feeling in his pocket. "Noo, ye're to get nae mair till the morn. Yer Maw wud gi'e't to me if she kent ye wis eatin' awmonds."

"I'll no' tell," said Macgregor, generously.

As they approached the warehouse once more, John carefully wiped his son's mouth, and vainly endeavoured to assume an expression of innocence.

However, when Lizzie joined them she was too pleased and proud for the moment to suspect anything.

"Gi'e Jeannie to me," said John.

"Na, na; I'll cairry her a wee. I got a sate in the shope. But I'll gi'e ye ma paircel. It'll maybe gang in yer poket."

"Jist," said her husband, as he stuffed in the long brown-paper package. "Did ye get whit ye wantit?"

"Ay, John, an' I bate them doon a shullin'."

"Ye're a rale smairt wumman! Come, an' we'll gang an' see the waux-works."

"Paw," put in Macgregor, "I wudna like to be a waux-work when I wis deid."

"Haud yer tongue, Macgreegor," said his mother. "John, ye maun check him when he says sic awfu' things."

"Aw, the wean's fine, Lizzie… Macgregor, ye're no' to say that again," he added, with an attempt at solemnity.

"Whit wey is folk made intil waux-works?" inquired his son, not greatly abashed.

"Oh, jist to amuse ither folk."

"But whit wey – " Macgregor's inquiry was interrupted by his colliding violently with a bag carried by a gentleman hurrying for his train.

"Ye see whit ye get fur no' lukin' whaur ye're gaun," said his mother. "Pit his bunnet stracht, John… Puir mannie, it wis a gey sair dunt," she added gently.

"I'm no' greetin', Maw," said Macgregor in a quavering voice, rubbing his eyes with his cuff.

"That's a braw lad!" said Lizzie.

"Never heed, Macgreegor! Ye'll be a man afore yer mither!" said John.

Thus consoled, the boy trotted on with his parents till they reached the gaudy entrance of the waxworks.

"Noo, I'll tak' Jeannie," said the husband.

"Ay; that'll be the best wey fur gaun in. An' I'll tak' the paircel, fur it'll be in yer road." So saying Lizzie handed her charge to John. Then she pulled the parcel from his pocket; and lo and behold! it came out accompanied by sundry fragments of taiblet, which fell on the pavement.

John would have dropped anything else but his present burden. Macgregor gazed at the dainties at his feet, but did not dare attempt to secure them. Lizzie looked pitilessly from one to the other. It was a tableau worthy of wax.

But who can follow the workings of the childish mind? Two tears crept into Macgregor's eyes as he raised them fearfully to his mother's face.

"Paw never ett ony," he mumbled.

The expression on Lizzie's face changed to astonishment.

"Whit's that ye say?"

"P-p-paw never ett ony," the boy repeated.

And then of a sudden, Lizzie's astonishment became amusement.

"Deed, ye're jist a pair o' weans!" And she laughed against her will.

"It wis a' ma fau't, Lizzie," said John.

"Ay; ye sud ha'e pit the taiblet in yer ither pocket! Eh? ... Na, na, Macgreegor, ye'll jist let the taiblet lie," she exclaimed, as the boy stooped to seize it.

"There nae glaur on it, Maw."

"Ay, but there is. Come awa'!"

And away Macgregor was pulled to see the waxworks.

But why did Paw wink at his son and point stealthily to his "pooch"?

II

"PAW," said Macgregor, as the family party turned out of Sauchiehall Street into Cambridge Street, "Paw, whit wey dae they ca' it the Zoo?"

"Deed, Macgreegor, ye bate me there," returned his father. "Lizzie," he said to his wife, "Macgreegor's speirin' whit wey they ca' it the Zoo."

"Macgreegor's aye speirin'," said Lizzie. "If they didna ca' it the Zoo, whit wud they ca' it?"

"Weel, that's true," observed her husband. "But it's a queer word, Zoo; an' the mair ye think o' 't the queerer it gets. I mind I yinst – "

"Paw, wull we shin be there?" inquired his son, whose philological craving was apparently neither very severe nor lasting.

"Ay, ye'll be there in a meenit Lizzie, are ye shair it's a' richt aboot takin' wee Jeannie in to see the beasts? I doot she'll be frichtit."

"Frichtit? Nae fear, John! Wee Jeannie's no' that easy frichtit. Losh me! When the meenister wis in the hoose on Wensday, wee Jeannie wisna a bit feart – wis ye, ma doo? She jist laucht til him, an' played dab at his e'e wi' the leg o' her auld jumpin' jake. Mr. Broon wis fair divertit, an' gi'ed her yin o' his cough lozengers. Na, na, John; she's no' that easy frichtit."

"Aweel, ye ken best, Lizzie. See, gi'e her to me."

"Oh, I'll haud her till we get inside. She'll shin be walkin' her lanesome – wull ye no', honey? Jist keep a grup o' Macgreegor, John, or he'll be fleein' awa' an' gettin' rin ower or wannert."

"Paw," said Macgregor, "I see the Zoo."

"Ay, thon's hit. Ye never seen wild beasts afore, Macgreegor?"

"I near seen wild beasts in the shows at the Lairgs, Paw."

"Aw, ay; ye wis bidin' wi' yer Aunt Purdie then. She wud be feart to gang in whaur the beasts wis."

"Aunt Purdie's an auld footer," said Macgregor.

"Whisht, whisht!" interposed his mother. "Ye're no' to speak that wey aboot yer Aunt Purdie. She's a rale dacent wumman... John, ye sudna lauch at Macgreegor's talk; ye jist mak' him think he's smairt."

"Aw, the wean's fine, Lizzie. Weel, we'll get across the road noo."

"Whit wey – " began the boy.

"Macgreegor, tak' yer Paw's haun'. I'm no' wantin' ye to be catched wi' yin o' thae electric caurs," said his mother.

The street was crossed without mishap, and presently the quartet found themselves within the Zoo. For a couple of minutes, perhaps, they paused on the threshold, uncertain which direction to take. Then the announcement made by an official in a loud voice to the effect that a performance by the lions and tigers was about to take place on the west side of the building sent them hurrying thither with the crowd, Macgregor for once in his life being too overcome for speech.

Beyond sundry ejaculations, little conversation took place while the trainer exhibited his pluck and wonderful command over the brutes; and it might have been observed that Macgregor never once made the slightest attempt to withdraw his fingers from the fatherly clasp.

"Mercy me! It's maist wunnerfu'!" exclaimed Lizzie, when it was all over.

"Dod, it bates a'!" said John, as he took wee Jeannie from her arms.

And a small voice at his side whispered hoarsely, "I wisna feart, Paw!"

"Macgreegor's sayin' he wisna feart, Lizzie," said John to his wife.

"Maybe he wisna," returned Lizzie, "but I can tell ye I wis a' shakin' when thae muckle brits wis loupin' aboot the man. I wis wunnerin' whit I wud dae wi' wee Jeannie if ony o' the beasts wun oot the cages an' commenced fur to pu' the heids an' legs aff the folk."

"Och, wumman, there's nae fear o' that."

"If a beast wis gaun fur to pu' ma heid aff," remarked Macgregor, who had grown suddenly bold, "I – I – I wud – I wud gi'e't a kick!"

"Ye're the boy!" said his father.

"Ye sudna let him boast like that, John," said Lizzie reprovingly.

"Whit wud ye dae, Macgreegor," asked John, with a grin, "if a beast wis efter yer Maw?"

" I – I – wud pu' its tail," replied the valiant Macgregor. "And then I wud – " A loud roar from one of the lions interrupted him and caused him to clutch at his parent.

"Aw, Macgreegor," said his mother, "I doot ye wud jist rin awa' an' leave yer Maw to be ett."

The boy's under lip trembled. "I wudna dae that, Maw," he said solemnly.

"Wud ye no', ma dearie?" said Lizzie, her voice softening. "Weel, weel, we'll say nae mair aboot it. Whit's yer Paw an' wee Jeannie efter noo?"

"It's an ephelant, Maw," said Macgregor, as they over-took the father and daughter, who were admiring the stuffed carcase of a huge elephant.

"He's no leevin'," John explained. "He's the yin that had to be shot a while syne."

"Whit wey wis he shot, Paw?"

"He wis dangerous."

"Whit wey wis he dangerous?"

"I'm no jist shair, but a man yinst tell't me the beast wis trampin' on his keepers, an' eatin' the bunnets aff the folk's heids."

"Paw, whit's thon big white oosie beast?"

"Thon yin? Dae ye ken, Lizzie?"

"I've seen picturs like it, John. It's a – oh, ay, it's a Polish bear."

"Dod, ay! It wud gey shin polish aff you an' me, wum-man," said John, laughing heartily.

"Dod, ay!" echoed Macgregor.

"Ye're no' to say that," said Lizzie.

"Whit, Maw?"

"Ye're no' to say 'dod.' "

"Paw says it, Maw."

"Weel, yer Paw sudna say 't."

"Whit wey, Maw?"

"Ha'e, Lizzie," said John, handing his wife a catalogue which he had just purchased, "that'll tell ye the names o' the beasts. Whit dae they ca' thon strippit – "

"Maw, whit's the name o' thon spotit yin?" cried Macgregor.

"They're baith Hyaenies," replied Lizzie, after consulting the numbers on the cages and the booklet. "Thon big black beast wi' the awfu' tae-nails is the Aswail or Sloth Bear."

"Ay, it's jist Aswail it's in its cage," remarked her husband with a chuckle.

"My! ye're rale smairt the day, John, wi' yer bit jokes. But whaur's Macgreegor?"

The youngster was discovered, after some search, at the other side of the building, gazing with an expression of awe at a couple of camels.

"Paw, the wee yin's face is unco like Aunt Purdie," he observed.

His father guffawed.

His mother frowned. "John, I've tell't ye afore no' to lauch when Macgreegor says impident things. I wunner at ye!"

"But, Lizzie, I cudna help it this time. Dod, I thocht it wis gey like yer brither's guidwife masel'!"

"John!"

"As shair's daith! It's jist the face she pits on when she's comin' oot the kirk on a wat Sawbath."

"Weel, she canna help her face, puir thing!" said Lizzie.

"I never cud unnerstaun' hoo yer brither Rubbert cud mairry sic an auld bogle, an' him wi' sic a braw sister."

"Hoots, John! Ye're fair aff at the nail the day!" said Lizzie, trying not to smile.

"Paw, whit wey ha'e the caymels nae trunks like the ephelants?"

"Macgreegor," remarked Lizzie, "ye wud turn Solyman hissel' dementit! Jist luk at the humphs on their backs, an' dinna fash yer – "

"Paw, whit wey ha'e the caymels got humphs?"

"Man, ye're a fair divert, Macgreegor," said John. "Maybe it's because they ha'e nae trunks. See, there a penny fur ye. Awa' to the stall ower thonder, an' get a wheen biscuits fur the beasts."

"I'm gaun to feed the ephelants," Macgregor announced on his return.

"That's richt! See, there the big yin haudin' oot his trunk... Dod, a biscuit's naethin' to him. Gi'e yin to wee Jeannie an' she'll feed the ither yin."

"Is the ephelant's trunk jist the same as a man's neb, Paw?" inquired Macgregor.

"Ay, jist the same."

"Whit wey dae folk no' pick up things wi' their nebs, Paw?"

"Aw, haud yer tongue, Macgregor," said his mother. "John, bring wee Jeannie ower to see the paurrits."

The birds having been duly admired and commented upon, Macgregor was again discovered to be missing. This time he was found engaged in making faces at a family of monkeys.

"Come awa' frae the nesty things!" cried Lizzie. "I canna thole monkeys, John. Whit'll thon beast be in the watter?"

"The number's wan-twinty-nine."

"Oh, ay. Common Seal, frae the German Ocean. Ah, but that'll be the wee yin. The big yin's a Californian Sea Lion. Macgreegor, here a sea lion!"

"It's no vera like a lion, Maw... I see its whuskers! Whit wey has it nae oose on its feet?"

"Thae things isna feet. Thae's fins."

"Whit wey has it nae oose on its fins, Paw?"

"Maybe it cudna soom wi' oose on its fins."

"Whit wey cud it no' soom wi' oose on – "

"Come awa' an' see this extraornar beast, Macgreegor," said Lizzie. "The book says it's ca'ed a tapir."

"Whit wey is't ca'ed a tapir, Maw?"

"Gi'e't a bit biscuit," returned his mother evasively. "Puir beastie, it's lukin' gey doon i' the mooth, is't no, John?"

"It's a' that. But I wid be doon i' the mooth, masel', Lizzie, wi' a neb like that on me. See an' no' let it nip yer fingers, Macgreegor."

"Whit wey is its neb sae shoogly, Paw?"

"Dod, Macgreegor, I'm thinkin' it kens ye. It's wagglin' its neb at ye fur anither bit biscuit."

"John," said his wife, "I'll tak' wee Jeannie an' ha'e a sate fur a wee."

"Are ye wearit? Wud ye no' like a dish o' tea?"

"Och, I'm no' needin' tea, John."

"Plenty folk tak' tea when they're no' needin' it. Come on, Lizzie!"

Lizzie shook her head and muttered something about "gentry" and "wastry."

"I – I got a rise in ma pey the day, Lizzie," said her husband suddenly.

"Did ye that, John?"

"Ay! Hauf-a-croon."

"Deed, I wis thinkin' it wis mair nor naethin' that wis makin' ye sae jokey-like," said Lizzie with a laugh.

"Come on, then, Lizzie. Here, Macgreegor!"

"Paw, whit wey – "

"Aw, ye'll see the beasts again in a wee. Cud ye eat a pie?"

Macgregor drew a long breath. "Cud I no'?" he exclaimed, beaming.

III

THE Robinsons were on their way to tea at Aunt Purdie's, and the anxious Lizzie was counselling her son regarding his behaviour at the table of that excellent lady.

"Noo, Macgreegor," she said, "ye're no' to affront me. Yer Aunt Purdie's rale genteel, an' awfu' easy offendit."

"Dod, ay!" said John, "ye'll ha'e to mind yer Q.P.'s the day, as the sayin' is."

"Dod, ay!" said Macgregor.

"I've tell't ye dizzens o' times, Macgreegor, ye're no' to say that," said his mother.

"I furgot, Maw."

"If yer Aunt Purdie wis hearin' ye speak that wey she wud be sair pit oot. An', John," turning to her husband, "ye sud be mair carefu' whit ye say afore the wean. He's jist like a paurrit fur pickin' up words."

"Dod, ay!" said John seriously, "I'll ha'e to be carefu', Lizzie."

"Ye're an awfu' man," said his wife, frowning and smiling.

"Wull I get a tert at Aunt Purdie's?" inquired Macgregor.

"Ye'll see whit ye'll get when ye get it," replied his mother. "An' mind, Macgreegor, ye're no' to be askin' fur jeely till ye've ett twa bits o' breed an' butter. It's no' mainners; an' yer Aunt Purdie's rale parteeclar. An' yer no' to dicht yer mooth wi' yer cuff – mind that. Ye're to tak' yer hanky an' let on ye're jist gi'ein' yer neb a bit wipe. An' ye're no' to scale yer tea nor sup the sugar if ony's left in yer cup when ye're dune drinkin'. An' if ye drap yer piece on the floor, ye're no' to gang efter it; ye're jist to let on ye've ett it. An' ye're no' – "

"Deed, Lizzie," interposed her husband, "ye're the yin to think aboot things!"

"Weel, John, if I dinna tell Macgreegor hoo to behave hissel', he'll affront me. It's maybe a sma' maitter to a man, John, but a wumman disna like to be pit oot afore her guid sister. An', John, ye're to try an' be discreet yersel', an' think afore ye mak' a bit joke, fur she's a rale genteel wumman, an' awfu' easy offendit."

"But yer brither likes a lauch, Lizzie."

"Ay, Rubbert's a herty man; but a' the same, John, ye're no' to gar him lauch abin his breith. An' yer no' to lauch yersel' if Macgreegor tries to be smairt."

"A' richt, Lizzie," said her husband good-humouredly. "Dod, I'm thinkin' ye're jist aboot as feart fur me as fur the wean."

"Havers, John! I'm no' finnin' fau't wi' you. It's jist that ye whiles furget yer – "

"Ma Q.P.'s."

"Ay, ye're Q.P.'s, as ye ca' it. I aye thocht Q.P.'s wis a kin' o' fit-ba'."

Her husband was about to explain when Macgregor exclaimed that Aunt Purdie's dwelling was in sight.

"Ay, it's the third close," remarked John, proceeding to plug his pipe with a scrap of newspaper. After that he pulled up his collar, tightened his tie, cocked his hat a little over one eye, winked at his wife, and chucked wee Jeannie under the chin.

"I wud just as shin be at hame, Lizzie," he observed, as they turned into the close.

"Whisht, John! Mrs. Purdie's a rale dacent wumman, an' – an' we needna wait ower lang. See if ye can gi'e Macgreegor's hair a bit tosh up. It's awfu' ill to lie... Noo, John, ye'll gang furrit an' ring the bell. Mind, ye're to speir if Mrs. Purdie is in afore ye gang ower the doorstep."

"But she wudna ha'e askit us to wur tea if she had been fur gaun oot," said John.

"Tits, man! Mrs. Purdie keeps a wee servant lass, an' ye maun speir at her if her mistress is in. Mind, yer no' to say 'it's a fine day,' or onythin' like that; ye're jist to speir if Mrs. Purdie's in. D'ye see?"

"Weel, weel, wumman, onythin' fur peace." And John pulled the bell-handle. "I ken she's in," he whispered. "I hear her roarin' at somebody."

"Sh! John. Jist dae whit I tell't ye."

The door was opened and John bashfully repeated the formula.

"Will you please step in?" said the domestic, a small, rosy-cheeked girl, who still showed her ankles though she had put her hair up.

"Dicht yer feet, Macgreegor, dicht yer feet," said Lizzie in a quick, loud whisper. "See, dicht them on the bass."

Macgregor obeyed with great vigour, and followed the others into the lobby.

"Paw, we've a brawer nock nor that yin," he remarked in a husky undertone, pointing at a grandfather's clock in a corner.

"Whisht!" said his mother nervously.

"Wull I pit ma bunnet in ma pooch, Maw?" asked the boy.

"Na, na! John, pit his bunnet up aside yer ain."

Just then Mrs. Purdie appeared and bade them welcome; and presently they were gathered in the parlour, the table of which was already laid for tea. Mr. Purdie was getting on well in the world – his grocery establishment was gaining new customers daily – and Mrs. Purdie was inclined, alas! to look down on her homely relatives, and to regard their manners and speech as vulgar, with the result that her own manners were frequently affected, while her speech was sometimes a strange mixture.

"And how are you to-day, Macgregor?" she asked the boy as they sat round the fire.

"I'm fine," replied Macgregor, glancing at the good things on the table.

"Fine what?" said Aunt Purdie.

"Ye sud say, 'Fine, thenk ye,' " whispered his mother, giving him a nudge.

"Fine, thenk ye," said Macgregor, obediently. "I wis at the Zoo."

"Oh, indeed. And what did you see at the Zoo?"

"Beasts, thenk ye," said Macgregor.

"An' hoo's Rubbert?" asked Lizzie with some haste.

"Robert is keeping well, thank you; but he's sorry he

cannot leave the shope this evening. His young man was unfortunately rin over by an electric caur yesterday."

"Oh, thae caurs!" said Lizzie, "I'm aye feart fur Macgreegor gettin' catched, an' comin' hame wantin' a leg."

"Robert's young man got conclusion of the brain," said Aunt Purdie with great solemnity. "He was carrying a dizzen of eggs an' a pun' of the best ham when the melancholy accident occurred."

"Dae ye tell me that?" exclaimed Lizzie. "An' wis the eggs a' broke?"

"With two exceptions." And Aunt Purdie went on to describe the accident in detail to Lizzie, while John and Macgregor looked out of the window, and wee Jeannie, who had been put on the floor to "play herself," found amusement in pulling to pieces a half-knitted stocking which she discovered in a basket under the sofa.

Soon the little, rosy-cheeked maid entered with the teapot, and they all took their places at table, wee Jeannie being lifted on to her mother's knee and warned not to touch the knife.

"Mr. Robison," said Aunt Purdie, looking very hard at John, "kindly ask a blessing."

John turned red and mumbled something, at the end of which he wiped his brow and loudly blew his nose.

The hostess, after looking for a moment as if she thought it rather an inferior "blessing," commenced her duties.

"I'm no' wantin' a joog, Maw," said Macgregor to his mother, as he observed Aunt Purdie filling a mug with milk and hot water.

"It's fur wee Jeannie," whispered Lizzie. "But ye're jist to tak' whit ye get."

Conversation flagged for the first five minutes. Then Mrs. Purdie broke the silence.

"Have you been going out much this winter, Mr. Robison?" she inquired in her best style.

For an instant John gaped. "Dod, Mrs. Purdie, I'm gled to say I've no' been aff ma work a day since the New Year."

"I mean out to entertainments, parties, and conversonies," said Mrs. Purdie with a pitying smile.

"Oh, ay. Aweel, Lizzie an' me likes the fireside, but we've
been to the Zoo an' the pantymine an' twa-three surees."

"I like surees," observed Macgregor, digging into a pot of
jam. By a strange mischance he had already dropped two
pieces of plain bread and butter on the floor, but to his credit
it must be recorded that he had remembered his mother's
injunction not to attempt to recover them.

"Ay, Macgreegor's the yin fur surees," said John. "He
cam' hame frae the Sawbath-schule suree the ither nicht wi'
fower orangers an' guid kens hoo mony pokes o' sweeties."

"An' he had to get ile i' the mornin'," said Lizzie, whose
time was chiefly occupied in feeding wee Jeannie.

"Do you like oil?" said Mrs. Purdie, smiling sourly at
Macgregor.

"Naw," returned the boy, with his mouth full. "Dae you
like ile, Aunt Purdie?"

"Whisht!" said his mother reprovingly.

"Assist yourself to a cookie, Mr. Robison," said Mrs.
Purdie, a trifle confused. "And pass your cup. Mrs. Robison, is your tea out?"

"Thenk ye," said Lizzie. "This is rale nice cake, Mrs.
Purdie."

"It was recommended to me by Mrs. M'Cluny, the
doctor's wife. Mrs. M'Cluny is very highly connected, quite
autocratic, in fact. Her and me is great friends. I expect to
meet her at the Carmunnock conversonie on Monday night –
a very select gathering. Her an' me – "

"Paw, I want a tert."

"Na, John," said Lizzie, "he's had yin."

"I want anither, Maw."

"Ye canna ha'e anither, Macgreegor. Weel, Mrs. Purdie,
ye wis sayin' – "

"I was observing – "

"Paw, gi'e's a curran' cake," said Macgregor in a whisper.

John winked at his son, and stealthily moved the dish of
dainties in his direction.

The two ladies were discussing the coming "conversonie," and appeared oblivious to what was going on. The plate came nearer and nearer, and at last Macgregor's eager paw went cautiously towards it. The currant cake was secured, but as the boy drew back his hand his mother detected him.

"Macgreegor!" she exclaimed.

The hapless youngster started guiltily. Over went the jam-pot, spreading its contents on the cloth; over went Macgregor's teacup, which was smashed to atoms on the floor. Wee Jeannie, with a gurgle of delight, evidently under the impression that something in the way of entertainment was expected of her, tipped her mug after the cup, while her father, rising in confusion, sent a plate and five cookies to swell the wreckage.

John stood helpless; Lizzie sat speechless and pale; wee Jeannie, discovering that it wasn't a joke after all, set up a dismal wailing; and Macgregor, with quivering lip and misty eye, stared at the ruin he had wrought. No one dared to look at Aunt Purdie. Her expression was grim – very grim indeed. When she did speak, her words were few but incisive. They had reference to the bringing-up of children, of which, she thanked Providence, she had none. Poor Lizzie apologised for her son, expressed herself "fair affrontit" at his conduct, and declared that she would "sort" him when they got home. The hour following tea was an uncomfortable one, and John did not conceal his relief at being out of the house.

"She'll no' ask us back," he observed.

Lizzie said nothing.

"Macgreegor's sayin' he's gey an' sorry," said John presently.

"Muckle need," muttered Lizzie.

"He's sayin' he'll tak' ile if ye like," went on her husband.

"He'll get mair nor ile!"

"Aw, wumman, the wean cudna help it. It wis a' an accident. Let him aff this time, Lizzie. I broke a plate masel', ye ken, an' wee Jeannie broke a joog. Are we a' to get ile an' – an' the ither thing, dearie?" …

"Och, John, ye aye get ower me."

And so peace reigned again.

Ten minutes later John noticed that Macgregor was lagging behind. He went back a couple of steps and took his son's hand.

"Whit's that ye're pittin' in yer gab, Macgreegor?" he asked suddenly.

Macgregor drew something from his pocket. "I'll gi'e ye a bit, Paw," he said generously. "It's a curran' cake."

IV

"JIST you gang oot an' dae yer messages, Lizzie, an' I'll mind Macgreegor," said John when he had finished his tea.

"Ye'll no' let him speak, John," said Lizzie, rising and beginning to remove the dishes from the table to the jaw-box with as little noise as possible. "Ye ken he didna sleep a wink a' nicht, an' he had jist a wee doze at denner-time. He's needin' a guid sleep, puir mannie, sae ye maun keep him as quate's ye can, John." Husband and wife talked in whispers.

"Dae ye think he's better the nicht?" asked the former anxiously.

"Oh, ay; I ken he's a bit better, but he's no' near ready fur the turkey's egg ye brocht hame the day, John."

"I thocht it micht gi'e him strength, Lizzie."

"Deed, ay. But, ye see, his inside's ower wake yet. He'll get the egg as shin as he can disgeest it."

"Ay," said John agreeably, but looking disappointed.

"Ye hivna ony sweeties in yer pooch?" said Lizzie suddenly and interrogatively, glancing at him as she dried a saucer.

John pretended he did not hear, and his wife repeated the question quietly but firmly.

"Och, jist a wheen joojoobs, wumman," he replied at last.

"Aweel, John, I'll jist tak' chairge o' them till the wean's ready fur sweeties."

"I'll no' gi'e Macgreegor ony the nicht, Lizzie," he said, looking uncomfortable.

"I ken that."

"Tak' them oot o' ma pooch," said John, smiling ruefully, and pointing to his jacket hung behind the door.

"Tak' them oot yersel'," returned his wife, "an' pit them in the wee drawer in the dresser."

"Ye're an awfu' wumman!"

"Ye're an awfu' man!"

"Maybe ye're richt."

"Weel, John, ye've plenty o' whit they ca' common sense

in maist things, but ye're jist a wean aboot Macgreegor,"
said Lizzie.

"Ay," said John humbly.

"An' I've got to keep an e'e on ye, dearie," she added more
gently. "Noo, I'm dependin' on ye to keep Macgreegor
quate," she said a little later. "I'll no' be lang. An' I'll get
wee Jeannie on ma wey back. It wis rale kind o' Mrs. Thomson
to tak' the wean the day, fur she's gettin' a steerin' lassie, an'
wudna unnerstaun' that Macgreegor wis lyin' badly."

Presently Lizzie, after bending for a minute over the bed
where the small patient lay, prepared to leave the house.
"He's sleepin', John," she said, with a pleased smile.

Left to himself, John smoked his pipe before the fire and
meditated. Two minutes passed, and then –

"Paw!"

"Are ye waukin', Macgreegor?" John sprang up, laid
down his pipe, and went to the bedside.

"Paw, whit wey am I no' to get a joojoob?"

"Aw – weel, ye see, it wudna be guid fur yer inside."

"But ma heid's sair, Paw."

"Yer Maw said I wisna to let ye speak. Whisht noo, ma
wee man, an' try an' gang to sleep."

"I canna sleep. Ma heid's sair. I want a joojoob."

John stroked his son's head and patted his shoulder
tenderly. "Puir laddie, wud ye like a drink?"

"I want a joojoob, Paw."

Somehow the man's eye, leaving the boy for a moment,
roved round the kitchen. The wee drawer in the dresser had
been left partly open.

"I canna sleep. I want a joojoob," said Macgregor again.

John sighed. He gazed longingly at the wee drawer. Then
he pulled himself together and looked back at his son. "Ye
canna get a joojoob, ma wee man," he said sadly. "Wull I
tell ye a story?" he asked almost despairingly.

"Ay," replied the patient, without much enthusiasm. "I
want a – "

"Whit'll I tell ye?" inquired the father hastily. "Aboot a
draygon?"

"Ay," languidly assented Macgregor. "Tell's aboot a draygon, and gi'e's a – "

"There wis yinst a draygon," began John, without delay, "an' it leeved in a den."

"Hoo big wis the draygon, Paw?" inquired Macgregor with faint interest.

"It wis bigger nor the biggest beast ye seen in the Zoo. An' it wis a' covered wi' sclates, an' fire an' reek cam' oot its mooth, an' when folk wis gaun by its den it played puff! puff! at them, an' roastit them wi' its breith, an' then it ett them."

"Whit wey did the folk no' scoot watter at it, Paw?"

"Dod, Macgreegor, ye may weel speir that. But, ye see, the folk didna scoot watter; an' at last the king o' the place begood to get feart he wud ha'e nae folk left to pey him taxes an' cry 'hurray!' when he gaed ootbye, an' he got dizzens o' bills prentit an' pastit up a' through the toon tellin' the folk that he would gi'e hauf his riches an' the haun' o' his bewtiful dochter til the man that killt the draygon. An' then a lot o' young lauds said they wud kill the monster or dee in the attemp'; an' they dee'd, an' wis ett up."

"Whit wey did they no' shoot the draygon, Paw?" asked Macgreegor, with some animation.

"Aw, ye see guns wisna inventit."

"Ay. Whit else, Paw?"

"Keep yersel' ablow the claes, ma mannie. Weel, efter hunners o' fine braw lauds wis roastit an' ett up, there wis a young fairmer cam' furrit, an' said he wis gaun to ha'e a try. An' the folk lauched at him, fur the lauds that wis ett up wis a' rale sojers that kent hoo to fecht. But the young fairmer didna tak' the huff. He jist askit fur a sword an' a shield, an' when he got them he gaed awa' hame to his tea, singin' wi' a licht hert. Fur, ye see, he had made a plan. An' i' the mornin' he got thegither a' his coos an' sheeps an' hens an' jucks, an' chased them a' doon to the draygon's den. An' the draygon wis awfu' hungry that mornin', fur it hadna ett ony braw lauds fur near a week; an' when it seen the coos an' sheeps an' hens an' jucks comin', it lickit its lips, an'

cam' oot its den, an' played puff! puff! an' roastit them a',
an' ett them up. An' when it wis feenished it wis jist as fou's
a wulk, an' it warstled intil its den to ha'e a bit nap. It hadna
been sleepin' lang afore it wis waukened wi' the young
fairmer cryin' 'Come oot, ye auld draygon! Come oot till I
stab ye!' It never let bug it heard him speakin', an' in a wee
while the young fairmer keekit intil the den an' gi'ed it a gey
sair jag i' the e'e wi' his sword. An' then – "

"Did he pit oot its e'e, Paw?"

"No' exac'ly, but it wis a gey sair jag. An' then it begood
to play puff! puff! at the young fairmer, but it wis unco short
o' breith efter eatin' a' the coos an' sheeps an' hens an' jucks.
An' the young fairmer kep' awa' the fire and reek wi' his
shield an' gi'ed the draygon a jag in its ither e'e, an' cried –
'Come oot, ye auld taurry-biler till I ca' the heid aff ye!' Wi'
that the draygon, no' likin' to be ca'ed an auld taurry-biler, let
oot a roar, an' tried fur to catch the young fairmer. But it wis
jist as fou's a wulk, an' hauf-blin' furbye, an' as shin as it
pit its heid oot the den the young fairmer stud up on his
taes an' brocht doon the sword wi' a' his micht, an' cut aff
the draygon's heid, an' the draygon wis deid. An' then – "

"Wis it bleedin', Paw?" asked Macgregor eagerly.

"Dod, ay! An' then the young fairmer got hauf the king's
riches an' mairrit his dochter, an' wis happy ever efter. An'
that's a' aboot the draygon."

"Tell's anither story, Paw."

John told two more stories, and at the end of the second
Macgregor said –

"I likit the draygon best. I want to be cairrit noo."

"Na, na, I daurna tak' ye oot yer bed."

"Hap me weel, an' cairry me, Paw," said the boy.

Eventually his father gave in, rolled him in a blanket, and
began to pace the kitchen floor.

"Mairch!" commanded Macgregor. "An' whustle tae," he
added; "whustle like a baun'!"

John obligingly began to whistle "The girl I left behind
me," and marched up and down the kitchen till Macgregor
expressed himself satisfied.

"Sing noo, Paw."

"Is yer heid no' bad?"

"No' sae bad as it wis. Sing, Paw!"

"Vera weel," said John, sitting down with his burden at the fireside.

"I want to see ootbye," said the burden.

So John went over to the window, and they looked into the street below, where the lamps were being lit.

> "Leerie, leerie, licht the lamps,
> Lang legs an' crookit shanks,

sang John softly.

Then –

> "I had a little powny,
> Its name wis Dapple Grey.
> I lent it til a leddy
> To ride a mile away.
> She whuppit it, she lashed it,
> She ca'ed it through the mire –
> I'll never lend my powny
> Fur ony leddy's hire!"

"Sing anither," said Macgregor.

> "Wee Jokey-Birdy, tol-lol-lol,
> Laid an egg on the winda-sole.
> The winda-sole begood to crack –
> Wee Jokey-Birdy roared an' grat."

"Sing anither," said Macgregor.

John sang another half-dozen rhymes, and then Macgregor expressed himself willing to leave the window for the fireside. "Sing 'A wee bird cam',' Paw," he murmured, putting his arm a little further round his father's neck. It was probably the old tune that appealed to the boy, for he lay very still while John hummed the verses, swaying slightly from side to side, and gently beating time with one hand on his son's shoulder. When the song was ended there was a short silence, and then Macgregor sighed lazily, "Sing 'Leerie' again, Paw."

"Leerie," so far as John knew it, was a poem of two lines set to a tune made out of three notes, but he sang it over

and over again, softly and soothingly –
>"Leerie, leerie, licht the lamps,
>   Lang legs an' crookit shanks" –

and, having repeated it perhaps thirty times, he ceased, for Macgregor had fallen sound asleep.

When Lizzie, with wee Jeannie slumbering in her arms, came in ten minutes later, John was sitting alone by the fireside in the semi-darkness.

"Is he sleepin'?" she asked anxiously.

"Dod, ay!" said John.

"That's guid. He wisna wauken when I wis oot?"

"Aw, jist fur a wee while. I didna gi'e him ony joojoobs, Lizzie," said John with a quiet laugh, pointing to the wee drawer in the dresser, "but I wis gey sair temptit."

V

"WHEN I'm a man," observed Macgregor, leaning against the knees of his father, who was enjoying an evening pipe before the kitchen fire, "when I'm a man, I'm gaun to be a penter."

"A penter," echoed John. "D'ye hear whit Macgreegor's sayin', Lizzie?" he inquired of his wife.

Lizzie moistened her finger and thumb, twirled the end of a thread, and inserted it into the eye of a needle ere she replied. "Whit kin' o' a penter? Is't pictur's ye're wantin' to pent, Macgreegor?"

"Naw!" said her son with great scorn. "I'm gaun to ha'e a big pot o' pent an' a big brush, an' I'm gaun to staun' on a ladder, an' pent wi' white pent, an' rid pent, an' bew pent, an' – "

"Aw, ye're gaun to be a hoose-penter, Macgreegor," said his father.

"Ay. But I'm gaun to pent shopes tae. An' I'm gaun to ha'e big dauds of potty fur stickin' in holes. I like potty. Here a bit!" And Macgregor produced from his trouser pocket a lump of the greyish, plastic substance.

"Feech!" exclaimed Lizzie in disgust. "Whaur got ye that? Ye'll jist file yer claes wi' the nesty stuff."

"Wullie Thomson whiles gets potty frae his Paw. Wullie's Paw's a jiner."

"I thocht you an' Wullie had cast oot," said John. "Ha'e ye been makin' freens wi' him again?"

"Naw. But I seen him wi' the potty, an' I askit him for a daud."

"It wis rale nice o' the laddie to gi'e ye a bit," remarked Lizzie, looking up from her seam.

"He didna gi'e it, Maw. I tuk it frae him."

"Aw, Macgreegor!" said Lizzie, shaking her head reproachfully.

"Wullie's bigger nor me, Maw."

"Ay; but he's gey wake i' the legs."

"I hut him, an' he tummilt; an' I jist tuk hauf his potty," said Macgregor unconcernedly.

John was about to laugh, when he caught his wife's eye.

"An' hoo wud ye like," she said addressing her son, "if yer Paw gi'ed ye potty, an' anither laddie cam' an' – "

"Paw hasna ony potty."

John sniggered behind his hand.

"Weel," said Lizzie, casting her husband a severe look, and turning again to her son, "hoo wud ye like if yer Paw gi'ed ye taiblet an' anither laddie cam' an' tuk hauf o' 't awa'?"

"I wud gi'e him yin on the neb twicet!" said Macgregor boldly, going over to the window to see the lamps being lighted.

"But if he hut ye an' knockit ye doon?"

"I wudna let him. Paw hasna gi'ed me taiblet fur a lang while," said the boy over his shoulder.

"Macgreegor," said his mother solemnly, "I'm thinkin' ye're gettin' waur every day."

"Aw, the wean's fine, Lizzie," interposed John, softly.

"Haud yer tongue, John," retorted Lizzie quietly. "The wean's no fine! An' instead o' lauchin' at him an' makin' a pet o' him, ye ocht to be gi'ein' him a guid skelpin'."

"I've never skelpit a wean yet, an' – "

"It's easy seen ye've never skelpit Macgreegor, John. Ye jist let him get his ain wey, an' he disna ken when he's misbehavin' hissel'. Weans needs to be checkit whiles."

"Aweel, whit dae ye want me to dae, Lizzie?"

"I want ye to punish Macgreegor for hittin' that puir speldron o' a laddie, Wullie Thomson, an' stealing his potty," said Lizzie in an undertone.

Macgregor came back from the window with the putty plastered over his nose.

"Paw, see ma neb!" he said gaily, unaware of the conversation which had just passed concerning him.

John laughed loudly. "Dod, but ye've a braw neb the nicht, Macgreegor!"

"Tak' it aff this meenit!" cried Lizzie. "John, ye micht

think shame o' yersel' to sit there lauchin' at his nesty tricks! D'ye no' mind hoo Mrs. Cochrane's man tell't us his neb wis aye bew wi' him pittin' potty on't when he wis a wean? ... Tak' it aff, Macgreegor, or I'll sort ye!"

Macgregor, but little abashed, returned to the window, removed the offending plaster, rolled it into a ball, and proceeded to squeeze it through his fingers with undisguised relish.

"John," whispered Lizzie, "dae whit I tell't ye."

"I canna," returned John miserably. "It micht wauken wee Jeannie," he added a little hopefully.

"I didna exac'ly say ye wis to – to wheep the laddie," said his wife, "but ye maun gi'e him a lesson he'll no' furget. I'm no' gaun to ha'e him boastin' an' ill-usin' ither weans. D'ye see?"

"But whit am I to dae, Lizzie?"

"I'll tell ye, John. Ye'll gang ower to the dresser an' open the wee drawer, an' ye'll tak' oot the taiblet ye brocht hame fur Macgreegor the morn – Are ye listenin'?"

"Ay, wumman."

"An' ye'll tell Macgreegor ye bocht the taiblet fur his Setterday treat, thinkin' he deservit it, but ye've fun' oot he disna deserve it, an' ye canna gi'e him ony."

"Aw, Lizzie!"

"An' ye'll tie up the paircel, an' gar him tak' it roon the corner to Wullie Thomson, an' gi'e it to Wullie Thomson, an' gi'e him back his potty furbye."

"Aw, Lizzie!"

"An' it'll be a lesson to Macgreegor no' to strike laddies waker nor hissel'. Ye wud be gey sair pit aboot, John, if a muckle laddie wis strikin' Macgreegor."

"Deed, wud I! But – but Macgreegor's that fond o' taiblet."

"Man, man, can ye no' think o' whit's guid fur Macgreegor? That's the wey ye spile him, John. Ye wud gi'e him the cock aff the steeple if he cried fur't!"

"Maybe ye're richt, Lizzie. But it's a hard thing ye're askin'. Wud it no' dae to gi'e him hauf the taiblet to tak' to Wullie Thomson?"

"Na, na," said Lizzie firmly. "Here, Macgreegor," she called to her son. "Yer Paw wants to speak to ye... Noo, John!"

With a huge sigh, John rose, went to the wee drawer in the dresser, and returned with the poke of "taiblet."

"Paw," said Macgregor absently, "I like taiblet better nor potty."

The father glanced appealingly at the mother, but she was adamant. She had resumed her needle, but was keeping an eye on the twain.

"Macgreegor," said John with a painful effort, "whit wey did ye strike puir Wullie Thomson?"

"I wantit a wee daud o' potty."

"Ay," murmured John, and paused for a moment. "Are ye sorry ye hut him?"

"Naw. I got the potty, Paw."

"But ye sud be sorry, Macgreegor."

"Whit wey, Paw?"

"Wis he greetin'?"

"Ay; wis he!"

John looked across at Lizzie for aid, but she was sewing diligently.

"Weel," he said, haltingly, "yer Maw an' me's no' vera pleased wi' whit ye done to Wullie Thomson. It wisna fair to strike the likes o' him."

Macgregor's visage began to assume an anxious expression.

"Yer Maw," continued John, "yer Maw says ye canna – "

"John!" murmured Lizzie, warningly.

"Yer Maw and me thinks ye canna get ony taiblet the morn."

Macgregor's under lip shot out quivering.

"An' – ye've got to gi'e the taiblet to Wullie Thomson, an' gi'e him back his potty, furbye, an' – an' – oh, Lizzie, I canna say ony mair!"

It took a few seconds for the dire truth to dawn upon Macgregor, but when it did, a low wail issued from him, and the tears began to flow.

John was about to lift him on to his knee, but Lizzie interposed.

"Pit on yer bunnet, Macgreegor," she said quietly, "an' tak' the taiblet an' potty roon' to Wullie Thomson. It's no' dark yet," she added, glancing out of the window.

"I'm no' wantin' to gi'e the taiblet to Wullie Thomson," sobbed the luckless youngster.

"Ye've jist to dae whit ye're tell't," returned his mother calmly, but not unkindly. "Ye're no' to be a tawpy noo," she went on, endeavouring to dry his eyes. "Ye're to be a man. Whit wud Wullie Thomson think if he seen ye greetin'? Eh, Macgreegor?"

Lizzie had struck the right note. The sobs ceased, though the breath still came gustily. He mopped the tears with his cap, and replaced it on his head.

"Am I to gi'e him a' the taiblet an' the potty furbye?" he inquired plaintively.

"Ay. An ye're to say ye're sorry fur hurtin' him. He's no' a fine, strong laddie like yersel', Macgreegor – mind that! Yer Paw an' me wudna like if ye wis wake i' the legs like puir Wullie. Noo, jist gang roon' an' gi'e him the taiblet an' his potty, an' see if ye canna mak' freen's wi' him again."

"I'm no' wantin' to be freen's," said Macgregor, rebelliously. "I'm no' wantin' to gang."

"Are ye feart fur Wullie Thomson?" asked Lizzie. Another clever stroke!

"I'm no' feart! I'll gang!"

"Fine, man!" cried John, who had been listening in gloomy silence. "I kent ye wisna feart."

Macgregor began to feel himself rather a hero. In dignified silence he took the poke of "taiblet," which his mother had tied securely with a piece of tape from her work-bag, and departed on his errand.

John looked anxiously to Lizzie.

She sat down to her seam again, but her fingers were less deft than usual. They both eyed the clock frequently.

"He sudna be mair nor five meenits," remarked John. "I doot we wis ower hard on the wean, wumman."

Lizzie made no response, and ten minutes dragged slowly past.

"Did ye expec' he wud dae't?" asked John presently.

"Och, ay!" she answered with affected carelessness.

"I wisht I had went wi' him," said John.

Lizzie put in half-a-dozen stitches in silence. Then she said – "Ye micht gang roon an' see whit's keepin' him, John."

"I'll dae that, Lizzie... Dae ye think I micht buy him a bit taiblet when I'm ootbye?" He asked the question diffidently.

His wife looked up from her seam. "If ye like, John," she said, gently. "I'm thinkin' the laddie's had his lesson noo. He's unco prood fur to be a wean, is he no'?"

"Ay," said John. "There's no mony like Macgreegor." He nodded to his wife, and went out.

About twenty minutes later father and son re-entered the house together. Both were beaming.

"I cudna get Macgreegor awa' frae Wullie Thomson, Lizzie," said John, smiling.

"Weel, weel," said his wife, looking pleased. "An' did ye gi'e Wullie the taiblet an' the potty, Macgreegor?"

"Ay, Maw."

Whereupon his mother caught and cuddled him. "Gi'e him a bit taiblet, John," she said.

John did so right gladly and generously, and Macgregor crumped away to his heart's content.

"An' whit kep' ye waitin' at Wullie's a' this time?" inquired Lizzie, pleasantly.

"He gi'ed me a big daud o' potty, Maw," said the boy, producing a lump the size of an orange.

"Oh!" exclaimed Lizzie, trying not to look annoyed.

"An' him an' me ett the taiblet," added Macgregor.

VI

"HECH! Macgreegor, ye're gaun ower quick fur me," gasped Mr. Purdie, as the youngster whose hand he held hurried him along the Rothesay Esplanade in the early afternoon sunshine.

"I cud gang quicker, Granpaw."

"Deed, ay! Ye're fine an' soople! But the boat'll no' be in fur mair nor hauf-an-'oor. Sae we'll jist tak' a sate fur a wee. I'm gettin' auld, Macgreegor, I'm gettin' auld."

"Ay, ye're gey auld," said Macgregor agreeably.

"But I'm no' that auld," said Mr. Purdie hastily.

They took a seat facing the bay. Macgregor proceeded to haul in a tin steamboat which he had been dragging after him since they started on their walk, while his grandfather drew from its case a well-seasoned meerschaum, removed the newspaper plug and "dottle," laid the latter on the top of a fresh fill, and, at the expense of seven or eight matches, lit up.

"I see a boat comin'," exclaimed Macgregor, ere they had been seated for five minutes.

"Whaur? ... Oh ay. But that's no' the richt boat. Wait till ye see a boat wi' twa yella funnels."

"I like rid funnels better nor yella yins. Whit wey is Maw comin' in a boat wi' yella funnels?"

"Yer Maw disna like the watter, an' the boats wi' yella funnels dinna come sae faur as the boats wi' rid funnels. That's jist the wey o' 't, Macgreegor. Ha'e! Pit thae in your gab."

"I like peppermint lozengers," observed Macgregor, drawing in his breath to get the full effect. "I like leemonade, furbye," he added presently.

"Are ye dry?"

"Ay."

"Aweel, ye'll maybe get a botle afore we gang to the pier. Whit ha'e ye been daein' to yer steamboat? It's a' bashed, see!"

"A laddie trampit on it," said Macgregor, holding up his
toy. "But the string gaed roon' his leg an' coupit him an' he
gaed awa' greetin'. Whit wey is there no' a baun'?" he
inquired, looking round at the bandstand.

"It's no' the season yet."

"Whit wey is't no' the season? I like a baun' wi' a big drum.
Wull there be a baun' the morn, Granpaw?"

"Na, na. No' till the simmer. If ma hoast's no' better I'll
maybe bide in Rothesay till the simmer, and then ye'll come
back an' stey wi' yer granny an' me, an' gether wulks, an'
dook, an' hear the baun'.'"

"Is yer hoast bad the noo?"

"Ay; it's gey bad at nicht, Macgreegor."

"I yinst had an awfu' sair hoast," said Macgregor thoughtfully. "I got code-ile. If you wis takin' code-ile ye micht be
better afore the simmer, Granpaw."

Mr. Purdie smiled. "Wud ye like ma hoast to be better
afore the simmer, Macgreegor?"

"Ay. I – I wud like to bide in Rothesay tae. I dinna like
wulks, but I like pickin' them oot awfu'. I dinna like dookin',
but I like paidlin'.'"

"I'm thinkin' I'll try the code-ile, Macgreegor."

"It's rale nesty to tak'… But it micht mak' yer hoast better
afore the simmer… Rothesay's a nice place; is't no'? … I'm
gaun ower to luk at the watter." Macgregor slipped off the
seat, and dragging his steamboat behind him, went over to
the railings of the esplanade.

"Ye're no' to sclim up," cried Mr. Purdie, rising in alarm.
"If ye wis fa'in' in there ye wud be droondit."

"There's an awfu' lot o' watter the day," remarked the
boy as his grandfather put an arm round him.

"Ay, ye see the tide's in."

"Oh, there a wee fish! D'ye no' see it, Granpaw? There
anither!"

"Ye've better sicht nor me. Noo, noo, ye're no' to lean
ower that wey. Ye canna soom, ye ken. An' whit wud yer
Maw say if ye fell in?"

"She wud gi'e me ile – no' the code-ile, but the ither ile.

It's faur waur. I'm gaun fur to sail ma boat noo."

"Ye canna sail it there."

"Ay, can I! See!" Macgregor lowered his toy with the string till it touched the water a yard beneath them. After several partial swampings it was induced to float on a comparatively even keel. "It's soomin'!" he exclaimed in triumph as he jerked it about. And then the string slipped from his fingers. He turned to his grandfather in dire dismay.

"Puir laddie," said Mr. Purdie, looking about for help in the shape of a rowing craft.

"Ma boat, ma boat!" wailed Macgregor, softly.

Old Mr. Purdie went down on his knees, suppressing a groan as he did so, laid his pipe on the ground, and, leaning over the edge, endeavoured to secure the string with his walking-stick. For several minutes he wrought, but all in vain, and then Macgregor cried out that his boat was sinking. It was too true! Damaged, doubtless, by many a stormy passage on dry land, and also by being tramped upon, the luckless vessel had gradually filled, and now it was being slowly but surely submerged. Mr. Purdie, in great distress, endeavoured to save it with his stick by getting a hold of the metal rigging, but his sight was poor and his hand shaky, and he only succeeded in giving it a prod amid-ships, which precipitated the disaster. Down, down, in ten feet of clear water it quietly sank, while its owner could do nought but watch and wail, "Ma boat, ma boat!"

Mr. Purdie rose, rubbing his knees and coughing. "I'm rale vexed, Macgreegor," he began.

Crunch!

"Ma pipe, ma pipe!"

Alas! troubles never come singly. Macgregor had lost his beloved boat; Mr. Purdie had trod upon and reduced his dear old pipe to atoms.

"Ma boat, ma boat!"

"Ma pipe, ma pipe!"

The boy gazed despairingly into the depths; his grand-father stared gloomily at the ground.

"Dinna greet, laddie," said Mr. Purdie at last.

"I'm no' greetin'," returned Macgregor, rubbing his eyes with his sleeve and sniffing violently. Then he perceived the trouble which had befallen his companion.

"Whit wey – " he began, and stopped, stricken dumb by the distress in the old face.

"Macgreegor," said Mr. Purdie, taking out a shabby purse, "ye'll maybe get yer boat when the tide gangs oot. I'll tell the man ower thonder to keep his e'e on it. An' – an' ye're no' to greet."

"I'm no greetin', Granpaw."

"Aweel, I'm rale vexed fur ye. An' I wudna like ye to be meetin' yer Maw wi' sic a lang face. Ha'e! There a saxpence, Macgreegor. Jist rin ower to the shopes an' buy onythin' ye ha'e a fancy fur, an' I'll wait fur ye here. Noo, ye dinna need to gang faur – jist ower the road. An' haste ye back, fur it's near time fur yer Maw's boat." Having thus delivered himself, Mr. Purdie heaved a big sigh and looked once more at the wreckage at his feet. The meerschaum had been a presentation, and he had valued it exceedingly. "It wis gettin' auld like hissel', but it wisna near dune yet," had been the substance of a frequent remark of his friends to him during the last five or six years. And now – now it was "dune."

"Are ye no gaun to the shopes?" he asked his grandson, who was still looking at the sixpence.

"Ay. I'm gaun," said Macgregor. "Thenk ye, Granpaw," he added, remembering for once his mother's good instructions. And, his small visage wreathed in smiles of joyful anticipation, he ran off.

Mr. Purdie saw him disappear into a fancy goods emporium, and then stooped down and gathered the fragments of his pipe into a large red handkerchief, which he carefully deposited in a side-pocket of his coat. After that he marked the place where Macgregor's toy had sunk, and toddled along to tell the nearest boat-hirer to look out for the wreck at low water. He was beginning to get anxious when Macgregor reappeared jubilant, dragging behind him a clattering object.

"Did ye buy anither boat?" inquired Mr. Purdie, feeling rather disappointed, for the boat-hirer had assured him that the wreck could easily be recovered.

"It's no' a boat," said Macgregor, smiling. "It's a beast."

"A beast?"

"Ay, Granpaw. A aggilator."

"A whit?"

"Aggilator! That's whit the wife in the shope said it wis. Luk at its taes! It can soom, but I'm no' gaun to pit it in the sea."

Mr. Purdie examined the new purchase. "Oh, I see," he said at last. "It's whit they ca' a – a – a crocidile, Macgreegor."

"Naw, it's no' a crocidile, Granpaw, it's a aggilator."

"Weel, weel, it's a queer like thing to buy onywey; but if ye're pleased wi' it, that's a' aboot it. Noo, it's time we wis gaun to meet yer Maw."

Macgregor gave his disengaged hand to his grandfather, and they proceeded pierwards. Silently they went for a minute, at the end of which Macgregor remarked – "I didna spend a' my saxpence on ma aggilator, Granpaw."

"Did ye no'? Whit did ye pey fur't?"

"Fowerpence. I bocht a wheen strippit ba's."

"Did ye?"

"Ay, but I didna spend a' the tippence on them."

"Ye wud keep a penny fur yer pooch, like a wice laddie."

"Naw. I bocht ye a pipe, Granpaw," said Macgregor grinning. He released his hand and dived into his pocket.

"Weel, I never!" said Mr. Purdie, receiving a small paper parcel from his grandson. "To think the wean mindit me!" he murmured to himself. He patted Macgregor on the head and removed the paper.

"It's an awfu' nice kin' o' pipe, Granpaw," said Macgregor. "Ye pit watter intilt, an' then ye blaw, an' it whustles like a birdie!"

Mr. Purdie fairly gaped at the instrument of torture in his hand. For a moment he seemed to be stunned. Then he exclaimed, "It bates a'!" and went into a fit of chuckling, which was only stopped by the advent of a "hoast."

"Dae ye like it, Granpaw?" asked Macgregor.

"Fine, laddie, fine!" said Mr. Purdie when he had recovered his breath. "Dod, ye're Paw'll ha'e a guid lauch when he sees ma new pipe. Ye'll ha'e to learn me to play on't, though."

"Ay, I'll learn ye," said Macgregor graciously, and he looked much gratified at the prospect.

"Can ye see the boat comin'?" inquired the old man a little later.

"Ay. It's comin' frae the licht-hoose."

"Weel, it'll no' be in fur a wee yet. We'll jist tak' a sate on the pier."

"Ay, Granpaw... I'm gey dry."

"Tits! I near forgot yer leemonade. But we'll shin pit that richt, Macgreegor."

VII

IT was evident that the Robinson family, as it tramped along Argyll Street that Saturday afternoon, was bent on business of importance. Lizzie and wee Jeannie were dressed in their best, which would take rather long to describe; Macgregor had on his Sunday suit and a new glengarry bonnet; and John wore his pot hat a little to one side, and suffered from a high, tight collar, the points of which nipped his neck every time he moved his head.

"Are we near there, Paw?" inquired Macgregor, looking up to his father's face.

John looked down at his son, smothered an exclamation of agony, and replied in the affirmative.

"Whit wey dae folk get likenesses tooken?" asked the boy.

"Dod, ye may weel speir, Macgreegor! It's yer Maw wants a pictur' fur to gi'e to yer Granpaw Purdie."

"I'm no' wantin' to be tooken, Paw."

"Are ye no', ma man? Deed I'm gey sweirt masel'. But yer Maw wants the pictur'."

"Whit's that ye're sayin' to Macgreegor, John?" said Lizzie.

"Aw," replied her husband, turning to her, and wincing as the collar bit him, "Macgreegor an' me wis thinkin' we wis feart fur the photygrapher."

"Oh, ay," said Lizzie with a good-humoured smile. "Aweel, wee Jeannie an' me'll no' let him hurt ye – wull we, ma doo? But whit's wrang wi' ye, John? Ye're makin' maist frichtsome faces!"

"It's the collar, wumman. Ye wud ha'e me to pit it on."

"It luks rale nice. Is't a wee thing ticht?"

"Dod, it's like to nip the neck aff me!"

"Never heed, John. It'll come oot fine in the photygraph. Mercy me! whaur's Macgreegor?"

They retraced their steps anxiously, and discovered their son standing on the kerb, gazing longingly at the barrow of a vendor of hokey-pokey or some similarly elusive dainty.

"Macgreegor, tak' yer Paw's haun', an' dinna let me catch ye stravaygin' awa' again, or ye'll get nae carvies to yer tea," said Lizzie, glad enough to have found the youngster so speedily.

"John," she added, "fur ony sake, keep a grup o' the wean."

"Come on, Macgreegor," said John, holding out his hand. "We're jist comin' to the photygrapher's."

Presently they began to climb a long, narrow stair.

"Gi'e wee Jeannie to me, Lizzie," said John.

"Ay; ye'll manage her better nor me. I'm no' wantin' to be photygraphed wi' a rid face an' pechin'," said Lizzie, handing over her burden, on receipt of which John suffered fresh torments from his collar.

"Maw, wull I get ma likeness tooken wi' ma greengarry bunnet on?" asked Macgreegor, as they toiled upwards.

"Ye'll see whit the man says," returned his mother.

"I'm no' wantin' him to tak' it aff."

"Weel, weel, ye'll see whit he says."

"Wull ye tak' aff yer ain bunnet, Maw?"

"That's a daft-like thing to be askin'."

"Whit wey – "

"Whisht, whisht!" said Lizzie, who was evidently anxious to save her breath.

At last they reached the top flat, and were accommodated with seats in the reception-room. Lizzie took wee Jeannie on her knee, and proceeded to make the child as neat as a new pin, conversing with her the while.

"Paw," inquired Macgreegor, staring at a number of photographs on the wall, "whit wey dae folk mak' faces when they get their likenesses tooken?"

"Thae's jist real faces," said John laughing, and putting his hand to his throat.

"Can I get makin' a face when I'm gettin' ma likeness tooken?"

"Yer Maw wudna like that."

"Whit wey, Paw?"

"Och, jist – jist because she wudna. See, Macgreegor, yer Maw's wantin' ye."

Lizzie beckoned the boy to her. "Macgreegor, pu' up yer stockin', an' dinna screw yer face like that... Oh, laddie, whit wey did ye gang an' mak' yer heid sae toosie? Staun' till I get yer hair to lie." She fished a comb from her pocket and used it till she had reduced the unruly locks to order. "Noo, sit doon on that chair, an' dinna stir a fit till the man's ready fur us. John!"

"Weel, Lizzie?"

"Come ower here till I pu' doon yer jayket. It gars ye look fair humphy backit."

"Hoots, wumman, I'm no' gaun to get ma back tooken," said John, coming over nevertheless.

"Ye never ken hoo ye'll get tooken," said Lizzie sagely. "I wis lukin' at some o' the pictur's here, an' some o' them's no' jist whit I wud ca' inchantin'."

"Ye better no' let wee Jeannie see them, or she'll be gettin' frichtit. Eh, wee Jeannie, whit dae ye say, ma duckie?" he said, laughing and chucking his daughter under the chin.

"Paw!" exclaimed wee Jeannie. "Paw-aw-aw!"

"Fine, lassie, fine!" cried her father. He was in great form now, his collar stud having given way a minute previously.

"Noo, yer jayket's lyin' better, John," said his wife. "But yer tie – oh, man, yer tie's awa' up the back o' yer heid!"

"I canna help it, wumman. If I pit on yin o' thae masher collars, ma tie slips ower it, as shair's daith!"

"But whit wey dae ye no' use the tabs?"

"Och, I'm fur nane o' yer tabs! Never heed, Lizzie. I'll pu' it doon masel'."

"Tits!" exclaimed Lizzie, "I near had it that time! Noo – noo I've got it. There!"

At the word of triumph the tie slipped into its place, but the collar flew open.

"Whit's ado wi' ye, John?" she cried a little crossly. "Whit wey did you unbutton it?"

"The stud's broke!"

"The stud's broke? Oh, John, an' you gaun to ha'e yer photygraph tooken!"

"Ach, it's a' richt, dearie. I'll jist button my jayket, an'
that'll haud it thegither. See, that's fine!"

"Oh, John," she began, but just then a voice requested
the family to step into the adjoining room.

"Mind, John, it's to be a caybinet growp," whispered
Lizzie, as she took a last survey of wee Jeannie and
Macgregor.

John explained his wishes to the photographer, and presently the group was arranged – Lizzie with wee Jeannie on
her knee, Macgregor standing beside her with his toes
turned well out, and John behind with one hand resting
affectionately on her shoulder. Then the photographer
dived under the black cloth.

"Whit's he daein', Paw?" inquired Macgregor in a hoarse
whisper.

"Whisht!" murmured Lizzie.

"He's spyin'," said John, softly.

"Whit wey is he spyin', Paw?"

"Jist to see hoo we're a' behavin'," returned his father
jocularly. "Eh, Lizzie?"

"Be quate, John!" whispered Lizzie severely. She was
sitting very stiff and dignified. Wee Jeannie began to show
signs of restlessness, but ere long the photographer reappeared. He suggested that the little boy should remove his
hat, and that the gentleman should open his jacket.

"I'm dune fur noo," muttered John with a wry smile.

"Macgreegor, tak' aff yer bunnet," said Lizzie miserably,
fearful of what would shortly happen behind her.

"I'm no' wantin' to tak' aff ma bunnet, Maw," said
Macgregor.

"Dae whit ye're tell't. Ye can haud it in yer haun'."

"Yes, just so. Hold your bonnet in your hand, my little
man," said the photographer pleasantly.

Macgregor obeyed sulkily.

"Kindly undo all the button – all the buttons, please,"
said the photographer to John with great politeness, and
turned to the camera.

With a feeble snigger John undid the last but one. Lizzie's

head had been sinking lower and lower. She felt she was about to be affronted.

"Maw," said Macgregor suddenly, "I – I've toosied ma heid. Wull I pit on my greengarry bunnet again?"

Lizzie looked up quickly, and whipped something from near her waist. "John," she said, " gang to the ither room, an' see if I left ma caim on the table." Her voice sank to a whisper. "An' – an' – here twa preens." She turned to the photographer. "Ye'll excuse me keepin' ye waitin' a meenit, sir?" she said to him. "This laddie's a rale wee tease," she added softly.

The photographer smiled good-humouredly, and immediately she discovered that the comb was in her pocket after all. She tidied her son's hair carefully, and said, "I think I wud like him tooken in his bunnet, if ye've nae objections."

"Oh, very well," replied the man agreeably. "His expression was certainly happier with it than without."

John entered grinning, his jacket thrown open. "I cudna fin' yer caim onywhere, Lizzie."

"Och, I had it in ma poket efter a'. Noo, we're ready, if you please, sir," she said to the photographer, who, without delay, set about his business.

He waited till the smiles had died down somewhat, when he instructed them where and how to look, and made an exposure, which Macgregor spoilt by scratching his nose at the critical moment.

"I cudna help it, Paw. Ma neb wis that kitly," said the boy.

"Weel, ye maun jist thole the next time, Macgreegor. Noo he's gaun to tak' anither yin."

"Whit's that wee thing he scoots wi'?"

"Whisht!"

"Steady, please," requested the photographer.

Wee Jeannie began to wriggle on her mother's knee.

"Oh, see! oh, see!" said Lizzie, pointing to the camera. "Oh see a boney wee winda!"

"Paw, whit's inside the boax?" asked Macgregor.

"If you please," said the photographer. "Now when I say three, – One – two – th – "

"Am I tooken, Paw?"

"No' yet, Macgreegor, no' yet. Ye near spilet anither photygraph. Keep quate, noo."

"Noona, noona," said Lizzie, dandling wee Jeannie, who was exhibiting fractious symptoms. "Wee Jeannie's gaun to ha'e her likeness tooken i' the boney wee winda! (My! John, I wisht I had brocht her auld jumpin'-jake.) Oh, see! oh, see!"

A lull at last occurred, and the photographer took advantage of it; and, after another period of unrest, he secured a third negative, which he assured Lizzie would prove highly successful. John had expected to have the photographs away with him, but his wife informed him in a whisper that he mustn't think of such a thing. "Caybinet growps" took time. Matters, having been settled, the family departed from the studio.

"Maw, wull my greengarry bunnet ha'e a rid toorie in the likeness?" inquired Macgregor.

"It'll no' be rid, onywey, dearie."

"Whit wey, Maw?" He was obviously deeply disappointed.

"Speir at yer Paw, ma mannie."

Macgregor repeated the question.

"Aweel, if it disna come oot rid," said John, "I'll ha'e it pentit rid fur ye. Dod, I wull, fur ye're jist a jool! Is he no, Lizzie?"

"Oh, wee toosie heid!" cried his mother with a laugh and a sigh.

VIII

"RIN to the door, Macgreegor, an' see wha it is," said Mrs. Robinson, who was engaged in feeding wee Jeannie with tit-bits from the Saturday dinner-table.

Stuffing half a potato into his mouth, the boy slipped from his chair and obeyed orders.

"It's maybe Mrs. M'Ostrich," remarked Lizzie to her husband.

"Whit wud she be wantin'?" inquired John, who was leaning back in his chair, looking perfectly satisfied with life, and idly whittling a match into a toothpick.

"I wis expec'in' her to bring back the things she got the len' o' yesterday."

"Whit things?"

"Did I no' tell ye? Aweel, Mrs. M'Ostrich wis ha'ein' comp'ny last nicht, an' she speirt if I wud len' her the twa bew vazes, an' the mauve tidy wi' the yella paurrit on it, an' the cheeny mulk-joog, an' a wheen ither things."

"Dod, she's no blate!"

"Aw, puir wumman, she hasna muckle in her hoose, an' she's that fond o' comp'ny."

"Deed she micht ha'e askit us yins til her pairty!" said John, laughing good-naturedly.

"Ye ken fine ye wudna gang til her pairty if she askit ye a thoosan' times. But whit's keepin' Macgreegor? ... Macgreegor, whit's keepin' ye?"

"I'm comin', Maw," replied a choked voice.

"Weel, haste ye! ... It's no' been Mrs. M'Ostrich efter a'. 'Deed, I hope she hasna chippit the bew vazes... Here, Macgreegor, wha wis at the door?"

"It wis postie, Maw."

"Whit kep' ye?"

"He's gied me a cheugh jean, an' I've ett it, an' here a letter fur Paw."

"Tits, laddie! Ye're ower chief wi' the postman. Whit's the big letter aboot, John?"

"Whit dae ye think, Lizzie?" asked her husband grinning.

"I ken whit it is," put in Macgregor, "fur I keekit in. It's ma likeness!"

"John! is't the photygraphs?"

"Ay, is it!"

"Aw, John, quick! – let me see! My! I thocht they wis never comin'. Mind ye dinna file them, John, an' dinna let Macgreegor tich them till he's washed his hauns... Oh, wee Jeannie, ye're gaun tae see yer boney likeness! – eh, ma doo? ... Macgreegor, mak' a clean plate, and then wash yer hauns... John, John, yer fingers is a' thoombs! Can ye no' open it?"

"Ye're in an awfu' hurry, Lizzie," said John, teasingly, pretending to fumble with the packet. "Maybe ye'll shin be wishin' I hadna opened it."

"Ach, awa' wi' ye! I ken the pictur's is first-class. Come on, John. Nane o' yer palavers."

So John opened the packet, which contained six very highly polished cabinets, and after a moment's inspection, burst into a great guffaw.

"Man, ye're jist a big wean!" said his wife, a little impatiently. "Let me see yin o' them."

"There ye are, wumman. Dod, it's rale comic!"

"I want yin, Paw," said Macgregor.

"An' ye'll get yin, ma mannie. Ha'e! Whit dae ye think o' that?"

Macgregor studied the photograph for half a minute, and then looked up at his father with an expression of disappointment.

"Whit wey is ma toorie no' rid, Paw?" he demanded.

John stopped smiling, and looked uncomfortable.

"Ye said it wud be rid," said the boy.

"Ay, I mind I said I wud tell the man to pent it rid, but – but I clean furgot. It's a braw likeness, though – is't no', Macgreegor?"

"I wantit ma toorie to be rid, an' it's black," said Macgregor, coldly.

"I'm rale vexed I furgot to tell the man... Lizzie, did ye hear whit Macgreegor wis saying?"

"Eh?" said Lizzie, who had been delightedly occupied in examining the details of the family group and pointing out some of them to wee Jeannie.

"Macgreegor's no' pleased at his bunnet no' ha'ein' a rid toorie," said John. "Ye see, I furgot to tell the man to pent it rid."

"It's jist as weel, John, fur it wud be a daft-like thing to ha'e a rid toorie in a photygraph."

"But ma bunnet's toorie's rid, Maw," said her son.

"Ay, dearie. But rid an' bew an' yella an' ither colours canna be tooken in a likeness."

"Whit wey can they no'?"

"I canna tell ye that. An' it wudna be vera nice to pit pent on a photygraph."

"Whit wey, Maw?"

"Aw, it jist wudna be nice ... Dis wee Jeannie ken her Paw? Dis she?" Lizzie cried, returning to the photograph and her daughter. "Ay, fine she kens her Paw!"

"It's mair nor her Paw dis," observed John, a trifle dejectedly. "I'm lukin' as if I wis a toff gaun to be chokit, wi' that masher collar."

"Ye're lukin' fine, John," said his wife. "An' I'm rale gled I got ye to pit on the collar. Ye're a wee bit solemn; but I dinna care to see a man ower jocose-like in a photygraph; it gars me think o' the likeness in the papers o' folk that ha'e been cured o' indisgeestion... Ah! ye wee cutty!" – this to wee Jeannie – "ye're no' to pit the boney pictur' in the gravy!"

"I dinna think it's a boney pictur'," observed Macgregor, who was nursing his chagrin. "It's a nesty auld pictur'!"

"Haud yer tongue, Macgreegor," said his mother.

"It's an ugly auld pictur'! I dinna like it a wee tate! I wudna – "

"Sh-h-h! Ye're no' to talk that silly wey. Yer Granpaw Purdie'll be weel pleased wi'it – wull he no', John?"

"I hope he wull, Lizzie. It's no' bad, takin' it a' thegither, but – "

"I tell't Granpaw Purdie it wud ha'e a rid toorie, an' – an' it hasna," said Macgregor.

"Och, whit's aboot a rid toorie?" said his mother, laughing.

"But I'm rale vexed aboot it," said his father gravely. "I promised Macgreegor the toorie wud be pentit rid, an' – "

"Weel, Macgreegor canna ha'e it rid noo, an' that's jist a' aboot it."

"An' I tell't Wullie Thomson it wud be rid, and Wullie Thomson tell't a' the ither laddies," said the youngster, with a quaver in his voice.

"Ye sudna ha'e tell't onybody it wud be rid till ye wis shair o' 't," remarked Lizzie.

"But I wis as shair's onythin'. Paw said it wud be rid!"

The unintentional reproach rendered John dumb with misery.

"Ye best gang oot an' play fur a wee," said Lizzie.

"I'm no' wantin' to gang oot," replied her son sulkily.

"Ye'll jist dae whit I bid ye, Macgreegor. Wee Jeannie's gaun to ha'e a nap, for she wis restless last nicht, an' she wudna sleep i' the forenune. Sae aff ye gang, ma mannie, an' ye'll get carvies to yer tea. But dinna gang faur, mind."

"Maybe Macgreegor's no' wantin' to gang ootbye," said John with an effort.

"That wud be somethin' new. Awa' wi' ye, Macgreegor, an' play wi' Wullie Thomson."

Very unwillingly Macgregor departed.

"John, ye sudna interfere when I'm tellin' Macgreegor to dae this or that," said Lizzie softly, as she patted her daughter, who was nearly asleep.

"Weel, I daursay I'm wrang, dearie. But I'm rale vexed fur Macgreegor. Did ye no' see hoo sweirt he wis to gang ootbye?"

"He's whiles gey dour, ye ken."

"Ay, but it wisna a' dourness. The puir laddie wis feart o' bein' whit ye wud ca' affrontit."

"Affrontit?"

"Ay, jist that. Fur whit wis he to say if Wullie Thomson an' the ither laddies askit him aboot his likeness? Ye see, Lizzie, I've nae doot he's been boastin' a wee aboot gettin' a pictur' o' hissel' wi' a rid toorie – an' noo – "

"Hoots, John! It's no sic a serious maitter as a' that."

"It's gey serious to the wean. Macgreegor's unco prood, an' it'll be a sair job fur him to tell the laddies aboot his pictur' no' ha'ein' a rid toorie efter a'."

"He sudna ha'e boastit."

"Aw, Lizzie!"

"He needna tell the laddies."

"But that's jist whit he'll dae, fur they'll no' furget to ask him, an' he'll no' tell a lee."

"I ken that, John."

"Weel, then, the laddies 'll lauch at him an' mak' a mock o' him fur guid kens hoo lang aboot his rid toorie."

"I'll sort them if they mak' a mock o' ma laddie," exclaimed Lizzie indignantly.

"Na, na. Ye canna dae that, wumman. The wean's jist got to suffer, an' it's a' ma fau't – a' ma fau't."

Lizzie rose without replying, and, having deposited wee Jeannie in bed, set about clearing the dinner table. When she had finished washing-up she turned to John, who was smoking "up the lum" in a melancholy fashion.

"I wis wonderin' if ye cudna get a rid toorie pentit yet," she said.

"Dae ye mean that, Lizzie?" he exclaimed, starting up.

"Ay. It wud please the wean, an' yersel' furbye. An' cud ye no' jist dae't yersel'?"

"But I've nae pent. An' it wud be gey difficult to pent on that glossy stuff unless ye kent the wey," said John, thoughtfully regarding the photograph.

"It jist wants a wee tick o' rid, dis it no'?"

"Ay, jist a wee tick, an' – dod, wumman, I ken whit'll dae!" cried John, in sudden ecstasy.

"Whisht, whisht! Mind wee Jeannie. Weel, whit is it?"

"Whit d'ye think?"

"I cudna guess."

"Jist a wee tick o' a penny stamp," replied the husband in a triumphant whisper.

"Noo, if that's no' clever!" murmured Lizzie, admiringly. "An' I've a stamp in ma purse, fur I wis gaun to write to

Mrs. Purdie to tell her we cudna gang to wur tea on Wensday. My! John, ye're a faur-seein' man, and Macgreegor'll be that pleased."

A minute later the twain were seated at the table with a photograph between them.

"I'm thinkin' ye're a braw wumman, Lizzie," said John.

"Yer jist a blether," said Lizzie, without looking the least offended.

Presently she handed over her scissors, and John cut "a wee tick" from the stamp which she had already given him.

"Canny, noo, John," she muttered. "It wud be a peety to spile the photygraph."

"I'll manage it," he returned ... "Dod, but I've swallowed it!"

"Tak' anither wee tick, John."

Another "wee tick" was taken from the stamp and successfully affixed to the tiny "toorie" of Macgregor's bonnet as it appeared in the photograph. Then John sat up, regarding his handiwork with no small satisfaction.

"Eh, Lizzie?"

"Fine, John!"

"The wean 'ill be pleased?"

"Deed, ay."

The twain beamed upon each other.

When Macgregor came in he found them still beaming, and he beamed also.

"Weel, ma mannie," said John gaily, "wis ye playin' wi' Wullie Thomson?"

"Ay, Paw. I wis playin' wi' Wullie an' the ither laddies at tig, an' I never wis het!"

"Ye didna say onythin' aboot rid toories, did ye?" inquired his father, with a surreptitious wink at Lizzie, who had the photograph under her apron.

"Ay. I tell't them I wisna gaun to ha'e a rid toorie in ma likeness, because a black yin wis finer."

"An' whit did they say to that?" asked Lizzie.

"They a' said it wis finer excep' Tam Jamieson, an I hut him on the neb, an' then he said black wis finer nor rid."

"But, Macgreegor," said John, motioning to Lizzie to keep silence, "wud ye no' like a pictur' wi' a rid toorie on yer bunnet?"

"Nae fears!" returned Macgregor, with sublime contempt. "I'm no' fur rid toories ony mair, Paw."

John and Lizzie looked helplessly at each other.

IX

"OCH, wumman, I'm no' heedin' aboot Mrs. M'Ostrich an' her pairty," said John, as he folded a strip of newspaper with which to light his pipe.

"Aw, but ye'll gang, John," said Lizzie persuasively.

"Are ye wantin' to gang yersel'?"

"Weel, ye see, it's no' as if I wis oot every ither nicht, an' – "

"Dod, then, we'll jist gang. I doot I whiles furget ye're in the hoose a' day; an' ye've had a gey sair time wi' wee Jeannie fur twa-three weeks. Ay, we'll jist gang."

Lizzie looked pleased. "When Mrs. M'Ostrich wis in this mornin' to get the len' o' ma bew vazes, an' the mauve tidy wi' the yella paurrit on it, an' a wheen ither things, she says to me, says she – 'Mrs. Robinson, ye're weel aff wi' yer man'; and then she says – "

"Hoots!" interrupted John, "I'm thinkin' Mrs. M'Ostrich is an auld blether."

"Auld blethers whiles say a true word," observed his wife. Then, fearing perhaps she was expressing too much in the way of sentiment, she became suddenly practical. "I've a braw sark ready fur ye. I done it up the day."

"Am I to pit on ma guid claes?"

"Oh, ay, John."

"But no' a staun'-up collar?"

"Aw, John! An' I've a beauty jist waitin' fur ye. Ye luk that smairt in a staun'-up collar. I wis thinkin' o' that when I wis ernin' it, an' if ye had jist seen hoo carefu' – "

"Ach, Lizzie, ye get ower me every time! If ye wis tellin' me to gang to Mrs. M'Ostrich's pairty wi' yin o' wee Jeannie's rid flannen goonies on, I wud jist ha'e to dae't!"

"Havers!" cried his wife, laughing the laugh of a woman who gains her point. "We'd best be gettin' ready shin."

"But whit aboot the weans?" asked John.

"Macgreegor's comin' wi' you an' me. Mrs. M'Ostrich said we wis to bring him, fur I tell't her I wis sweirt to leave him in the hoose."

"That's guid!" said her husband with a smile of satisfaction. "Macgreegor likes pairties."

"I hope he'll no' affront us, John."

"Aw, the wean's fine, Lizzie. An' whit aboot wee Jeannie?"

"She'll sleep soon', an' Mrs. M'Faurlan's comin' to sit in the hoose till we get back."

"I see ye've arranged it a'," he said good-humouredly. "Whit wud ye ha'e dune if I had said I wudna gang?"

"Ah, but I kent ye wud gang... Ye micht rin doon the stair the noo an' get a haud o' Macgreegor. He's ootbye playin' wi' Wullie Thomson. They've baith got sookers, an' they like fine when the streets is kin' o' wat. I dinna think sookers is vera nice things to play wi'."

"I yinst had yin masel', an' I near got the nick for pu'in' the stanes oot the streets... Weel, I'll awa' an' see efter Macgreegor."

Later in the evening the trio set out for the abode of Mrs. M'Ostrich, who, as Lizzie was wont to remark, "hadna muckle in her hoose, puir thing, but wis that fond o' comp'ny." Mrs. M'Ostrich, however, never had the least hesitation in borrowing from her friends any decorative article she did not possess, so that her little parlour on the occasion of one of her parties was decorated in quite gorgeous style. Her chief trouble was her husband, who, being a baker, retired to the kitchen bed early in the evening, and snored with such vigour and enthusiasm that the company in the other room heard him distinctly. Mrs. M'Ostrich had tried many devices, including that of a clothes-pin jammed on the snorer's proboscis, but all without avail. In the case of the clothes-pin, Mr. M'Ostrich, who had meekly submitted to its being fixed, had shortly after suffered from a sort of nightmare, and, half-awake, had startled a party in the parlour by frantic beatings on the wall and weird yellings to the effect that someone was trying to suffocate him. After that he was allowed to snore in peace, and Mrs. M'Ostrich had to explain to any new visitors the meaning of the disturbance. This she did to John and Lizzie immediately on their arrival.

They were the last of the guests to appear, the six others being already seated round the parlour, doing a little talking and a good deal of staring at the decorations, the number and glory of which seemed to have quite paralysed a little woman who sat in the window.

"Maw," whispered Macgregor, who had been accommodated with a hassock at his mother's feet, "thon bew vazes is awfu' like oor yins."

"Whisht!" said Lizzie... "As ye wis sayin', Mrs. M'Ostrich – "

"Maw, there a tidy wi' a yella paurrit on thon – "

"Whisht, Macgreegor!" said Lizzie, giving her son a severe look.

"He's a shairp laddie," observed Mrs. M'Ostrich, who did not really mind, so long as her guests recognised only their own particular contributions to the grandeur of her surroundings.

"Awa' an' sit aside yer Paw, Macgreegor," said Lizzie... "John, see if ye can keep Macgreegor quate."

The boy dumped his hassock over the feet of two of the company, and squatted beside his father. He felt rather out of his element among so many adults, most of them elderly, and he was disturbed at seeing his father looking so stiff and solemn.

A dreary half-hour went by, at the end of which he could keep silence no longer.

"Paw," he said to his parent, who was listening conscientiously to the long story of a Mrs. Bowley concerning her husband's baldness, "Paw, whit's that noise?"

"Aw, never heed, ma mannie," replied John, aware that the noise proceeded from the slumbering Mr. M'Ostrich. "It's jist a noise."

"It's awfu' like a big grumphy, Paw."

"Sh! Ye're no' to speak the noo."

"If I had a big grumphy – "

"Whit's the laddie sayin'?" inquired Mrs. Bowley, smiling so kindly that Macgregor accepted her as a friend there and then.

"It's a grumphy," he explained, confidentially. "Dae ye no' hear it?"

Mrs. Bowley laughed, and patted his head. "Ye mauna speak aboot grumphies the noo, dearie," she whispered. "Here a bit sweetie fur ye."

Macgregor put the dainty in his mouth, and drew his hassock a trifle nearer to Mrs. Bowley. "Ye're awfu' kind," he said in a hoarse undertone, and he and the good lady entertained each other for quite a long time, much to John's relief.

About half-past nine the company drew as near to the oval table as their numbers permitted, and did justice to the light refreshments which the hostess had provided. Macgregor, ignoring his mother's warning glances, and evidently forgetting there was such a fluid in the world as Castor Oil, punished the pastry with the utmost severity, and consumed two whole bottles of lemonade.

"It's an awfu' nice pairty, Paw," he whispered, when the chairs had been put back to the walls. "Are we gaun hame noo?"

Before John could reply, Mrs. M'Ostrich requested the attention of the company to a song by Mr. Pumpherston. All eyes were turned on a large, middle-aged man in one corner of the room, who wiped his brow repeatedly, and appeared very uneasy.

"Comeawa', Mr. Pumpherston," said Mrs. M'Ostrich encouragingly. "Jist ony sang ye like. Ye needna be feart. We're nane o' us musical crickets."

"Ay, come awa', Mr. Pumpherston," murmured several of the guests, clapping their hands.

"Is he a comic, Paw?" inquired Macgregor.

"Whisht!" said Lizzie, sighting danger ahead, and giving John, beside whom she was now sitting, a nudge with her elbow.

Mr. Pumpherston shuffled his chair an inch forward, fixed his eyes on the ceiling, and hummed, "Do, me, soh, do, soh, me, do."

"Ay, he's a comic!" said Macgregor in a delighted whisper.

Someone sniggered, and John gently but firmly put his hand over his son's mouth.

"He's jist lukin' fur the key, as it were," observed Mrs. Pumpherston, the little lady who had been overcome by Mrs. M'Ostrich's parlour decorations. "He's whiles gey slow at catchin' the richt key, but he'll be gettin' it in a wee," she added, as her husband continued his "Do, me, soh, do, soh, me, do," to the intense enjoyment of Macgregor, who quaked on the hassock in enforced silence.

At last Mr. Pumpherston started "Ye Banks and Braes," but when half through the first verse was compelled to stop and make search for a lower key.

"It's aye the wey wi' him," explained his wife. "But when yinst he get the richt key he sings it weel enough, if he disna furget the words... Ha'e ye got the richt key noo, Geordie?"

"I wis near it – but ye've pit me aff it. But I'll get it yet," quoth Mr. Pumpherston determinedly. And he did get it eventually, and regaled the company in a voice surprisingly small for such a large man.

Macgregor was much disappointed, if not indignant, at being deceived, as he believed, by Mr. Pumpherston; but presently, feeling drowsy, he climbed into his father's arms and dropped into a peaceful little doze. So he rested while several guests contributed songs, not all, by the way, such efforts as that of Mr. Pumpherston.

Lizzie and John were congratulating themselves upon their son's good behaviour during the evening, and Mrs. Bowley and another lady had just finished telling them what a "braw laddie" they were so fortunate as to possess, when Macgregor awoke, rubbed his eyes, and stared about him.

"Puir mannie, he's jist deid wi' sleep," remarked kindly Mrs. Bowley.

"He is that," assented the other lady. "Are ye wearit, dearie?"

"There's no' mony weans wud behave theirsel's like him," observed Mrs. M'Ostrich.

Mrs. Pumpherston said nothing, but smiled sourly. Probably the youngster's opinion that her husband was a "comic" still rankled.

"It's time ye wis hame, Macgreegor," said Lizzie, rising.

But Macgregor heard none of the foregoing observations. With a dreamy look in his eyes, he was listening intently. "I hear it, I hear it," he muttered.

"He's no' hauf wauken yet," said Mrs. M'Ostrich.

"Whit dae ye hear, daurlin'?" inquired Mrs. Bowley.

Macgregor rubbed his eyes again. "I hear it! ... It's in the hoose! ... It's ben the hoose! ... Paw, tak' me ben till I see the big grumphy!"

For a moment there was a dead silence. But laughter was inevitable. Poor Mrs. M'Ostrich, her face crimson, had to join in, but as Mrs. Bowley remarked to a friend next day, she was evidently "sair pit oot."

As for Lizzie, after a hasty apology and goodbye, she hurried John from the house, and never opened her mouth till they were in their own kitchen. On the departure of Mrs. M'Farlane, who had taken good care of wee Jeannie, Macgregor, three parts asleep, was put to bed with scant ceremony, after which Lizzie collapsed into a chair and looked long at her husband.

"Weel?" she said at last.

"Weel, Lizzie?" he returned, trying to smile. "Ye've had yer nicht oot."

"Ay. An' it's the last!"

"Toots, havers!"

"John, I've been affrontit afore, but never like the nicht. Macgreegor – "

"Aw, the wean didna mean ony hairm. He sud ha'e been tell't aboot Mrs. M'Ostrich's man."

"Oh, ye've aye an excuse fur Macgreegor. I'm – I'm naebody!"

"Lizzie, wumman!" He got up and went beside her. "Ye're jist a boney wee blether."

"Ah, I'm no' to be cajoled that wey, John."

John said nothing; but he tried several other ways, and did

succeed in "cajoling" her at last. She heaved a great sigh and smiled back to him.

"But, dearie, whit are we to dae wi' the wean?" she asked.

"Guid kens," said John.

And suddenly they both fell a-laughing.

X

"I DINNA think I'll gang oot the day, John," said Lizzie. "Wee Jeannie's that girny. I doot I'll ha'e to gi'e her ile, puir doo. Ye sudna ha'e gi'ed her thon bit kipper last nicht."

"Och, Lizzie, it was jist a tate the size o' yer nail."

"Weel, ye ken fine she's ower wee fur kippers, John. An' ye ken I wudna gi'e her that kin' o' meat masel'. I'm shair ye micht ha'e mair sense nor to gi'e her everythin' she cries fur. But it canna be helpit noo."

"I'm rale vexed, wumman," said John. "I think I'll bide in the hoose. I'm no' heedin' aboot gaun oot the day."

"Na, na, John. Ye've got to tak' Macgreegor to the baun', fur ye promised the wean."

"Tak' Macgreegor yersel', Lizzie, an' I'll mind wee Jeannie."

"Toots, havers! Ye see I'm no' jist shair if it wis the kipper that done it, sae ye needna be blamin' yersel' aboot wee Jeannie."

"Dae ye think it wisna the kipper?" said John eagerly.

"Maybe it wisna. Onywey, I ken whit to dae; sae aff ye gang wi' Macgreegor... Macgreegor, ha'e ye washed yer face?"

"Ay, Maw."

"Weel, bring ower the brush till I pit yer hair stracht ... Staun' quate noo! Tits, laddie! hoo can I mak' a shed when ye're wagglin' yer heid? ... There, noo! ... Let me see yer haun's. Did ye wash them?"

"Ay, Maw."

"Awa' an' wash them again. An'tie yer lace... Here, John, keep yer e'e on wee Jeannie till I get Macgreegor's new hat." Lizzie dived under the bed, opened a box, and brought out a parcel.

"Whit kin' o' bunnet's that?" inquired her husband.

"Wait an' ye'll see," returned Lizzie, smiling as she undid the paper. "The man said it wis an Alpine hat, an' vera genteel. Macgreegor's needin' a new hat. His glengarry's gettin' kin' o' shabby fur the Sawbath, sae he'll wear it every day an' ha'e this yin fur his guid yin. See? There the hat, John. It'll be a fine surprise fur Macgreegor... Here, Macgreegor, come an' see yer new hat."

"It's a queer kin' o' hat fur a wean," remarked John. "It's liker a man's. Dod, it's jist like auld Mackinky's – him that used to write til the newspapers efter he gaed daft. A Macalpine hat, did ye say? Macgreegor, let's see ye in yer Macalpine hat!"

But Macgregor, who had been gazing dumbly at the headgear for fully half a minute, suddenly exclaimed, "I'll no' wear that thing."

"Noo ye've done it!" said Lizzie in a sharp undertone to her husband. "Ye've pit the wean aff it wi' yer stupid talk... Macgreegor, ma mannie," she said to the boy, "yer Paw wis jist jokin'. See, pit on yer braw new hat, an' then ye'll gang to the baun'."

"I'll no' wear it," said her son, retreating a step. "I want ma greengarry bunnet."

"Ah, but this yin's faur nicer nor yer glengarry... Is't no'?" she demanded of John, giving him a warning glance.

"Aw, it's a vera nice hat," he replied evasively. Then, feeling that he was failing in his duty, he gently recommended his son to submit. "Come awa', Macgreegor, an' dae whit yer Maw bids ye."

"I'll no' wear it," said Macgregor stolidly.

"Ye'll no', wull ye no'?" exclaimed Lizzie. "If ye'll no', ye'll jist!" And taking the boy by the arm she gently but firmly placed the hat upon his head.

At this indignity tears sprang to his eyes; but he cuffed them away, and stood before his parents, an exceedingly sulky little figure.

"It's the brawest hat he ever had," said Lizzie, regarding her purchase with intense satisfaction. "Is't no', John?"

"Ay; it's a vera braw hat," replied John, with feeble enthusiasm. "Dae ye think it fits him, though?" he inquired.

"Fits him? Deed, ay! It's like as if his heid had been made fur 't! ... Is it no rale comfortable, Macgreegor?"

"I dinna like it," replied the boy. "I like ma greengarry."

"Och, ye'll shin get to like it, dearie. Ye micht gang to see the King wi' a hat like that on yer heid... Noo, awa' wi' yer Paw to the baun', an' be a guid laddie, an' ye'll get somethin' nice to yer tea."

"Come on, Macgreegor," said John, holding out his hand. "You an' me'll ha'e a hurl on the caur, an' maybe ye'll fin' oot whit I've got in ma pooch."

Lizzie nodded pleasantly as they departed, and John looked back and smiled, while Macgregor, though subdued, was apparently becoming reconciled to his novel headgear. During the car journey the twain were perhaps quieter than usual, but by the time they reached the park where the band was playing, John had ceased casting covert glances at his boy's head, and Macgregor, with a portion of "taiblet" in each cheek, was himself again.

Macgregor greatly enjoyed the loud and lively passages in the music, but he was inclined to be rather impatient while the conductor waved his baton slowly and the instruments played softly or were partly silent.

"Paw, whit wey is thon man no' blawin' his trumpet?" he inquired during a lull among the brasses.

"I cudna say, Macgreegor."

"If I had a trumpet I wud aye blaw it. I wud blaw it hard, tae!"

John was about to assure his son that he fully believed him, when he heard someone behind say –

"Jist luk at that, Mrs. Forgie! Is that no' an awful daft-like hat to pit on a laddie?"

"It is that, Mrs. Bawr. I wudna let a laddie o' mines gang oot in a thing like that fur a' the gold o' Crusoes."

John's ears tingled, and he nearly bit the end off his pipe. "Macgreegor, I think we'll gang roon' and see the drummer," he said.

"Naw, I want to see thon man blaw his trumpet," said Macgregor, who, fortunately, had not heard his critics.

"Some folk," observed Mrs. Bawr, "is gey fond o' tryin' to be gentry."

"Ye're richt there," assented Mrs. Forgie, with a sniff. "I'm aye sorry fur weans that gets drest up like wauxworks, jist fur to please their sully faythers an' mithers."

"Macgreegor," said John, "I'm no gaun to wait fur the man to blaw his trumpet. I doot he jist cairries it fur show. Come awa' wi' me." And, much to his surprise, the youngster was dragged away.

From that moment John's pleasure was at an end. Every smile he observed, every laugh he heard, seemed to have a personal application. Before the band performance was finished he and his son were on their way home, himself in mortal terror lest the boy should suffer insult. His worst fears were soon realised.

On the roof of the car Macgregor was chattering gaily when an intoxicated party enquired with a leer if he were aware that his hat was bashed. Macgregor shrunk close to his father, whose wrath all but boiled over, and was very subdued for the rest of the journey.

As they walked along the street they were met by two small boys, who grinned at their approach, and laughed loudly behind their backs. John gripped the little fingers a thought closer, but held his peace.

Presently a juvenile voice behind them yelled, "Wha dee'd an' left ye the bunnet?" and another exclaimed, "Gentry pup!"

"Never heed, Macgreegor," whispered John.

"I – I'm no' heedin', Paw," said the boy tremulously.

Three little girls passed them, and broke into a combined fit of giggling. One cried "Granpaw!" after them, and the trio ran up a close.

But they were nearly home now, and surely the torment was at an end. But no! At the corner of the street appeared Willie Thomson and several other of Macgregor's playmates. They did not mean to be unkind, but at the sight of their little friend they stared for a moment, and then fled sniggering. And from a window above came a jeering hail – "Haw, you wi' the fancy hat!" followed by the impertinent exhortation – "Come oot the bunnet an' let's see yer feet."

Finally, as they hurried into the familiar entry, a shout came after them, in which the word "gentry" was cruelly distinct. Climbing the stairs, John wiped the perspiration of shame and wrath from his forehead, while his son emitted strange, half-choked sounds.

"Never heed, Macgreegor, never heed," whispered John, patting the heaving shoulders. "Ye'll no' wear it again, if I've to buy ye a dizzen bunnets."

They entered the house.

"Ye're early back," said Lizzie cheerfully.

"Ay, we're early back," said her husband in a voice she was not familiar with.

"Mercy me! Whit's a-do?" she cried. "Whit ails ye, Macgreegor?"

For a moment there was dead silence. Then Macgregor dashed his new hat on the floor. "I'll no' wear it! I'll no' wear it! I winna be gentry! I winna be gentry!" he moaned, and rushed from the house, sobbing as if his heart would break.

"De'il tak' the hat," said John, and, lifting his foot, he kicked it across the kitchen, over the jaw-box, and out at the open window.

Lizzie stared at her husband in consternation, and wee Jeannie, not knowing what else to do, started screaming at the top of her voice.

"Ha'e ye gaed daft, John?" gasped Lizzie at last.

"Gey near it," he replied. "See, Lizzie," he continued, "that hat's to be left in the street, an' yer no' to say a word aboot it to Macgreegor. Listen!" And he proceeded to supply her with details.

"But it's a bewtiful hat, an' that genteel, an' I peyed – " she began ere he had finished.

"I'm no' carin' whit ye peyed fur 't. I'd shinner loss a week's pey nor see Macgreegor in anither Macalpine hat, or whitever ye ca' it... Aw, Lizzie, if ye had jist seed the wey the puir laddie tried fur to keep frae greetin' when they wis makin' a mock o' him, ye wud – "

"Here, John, haud wee Jeannie," said Lizzie abruptly. "I

maun see whit's come ower him… Dinna greet, duckie. See if ye can keep her quate, John."

Lizzie was absent for a few minutes, and returned looking miserable. "I canna see him, John. Ye micht gang doon yersel'. He's maybe hidin' frae me," she said, with a sigh.

"Nae fear o' that, dearie. But he disna like folk to see him greetin'. That's why I didna rin efter him at first. But I'll awa' an' see if I can get him noo. An' – an', Lizzie, ye'll no' say onythin' aboot the hat? I'll bring it up, if ye want to keep it."

"Na. I'll no' say onythin', but it's a rale braw hat, an' that genteel, an' I doot somebody's rin aff wi'it."

Just then Macgregor walked in, looking rather ashamed of himself, and with the tears scarcely dry. Yet, at the tenderly solicitous expressions of his parents, he smiled as if he had been waiting permission to do so.

"Paw, there a – "

"Gi'e yer Maw a kiss," said John.

"Ye're an awfu' laddie," murmured Lizzie, cuddling him.

"Paw, there a wee – "

"Wud ye like a curran' cake to yer tea, Macgreegor?" inquired Lizzie, as she released him.

"Ay, Maw," he answered, beaming. Then – "Paw, there a wee dug ootbye, an' it's worryin' ma hat, an' it's pu'in' it a' to bits!"

XI

"CAN I get oarin', Paw?" said Macgregor from the stern, where he was sitting beside his mother and little sister.

"Dod, ay; ye'll get oarin'," replied his father, who was rowing leisurely and enjoying his pipe.

"Na; ye canna get oarin'," exclaimed Lizzie.

"Whit wey, Maw?"

"Jist because ye canna. Keep yer sate, noo, or ye'll ha'e the boat coupit."

"Aw, the wean's fine," said John. "If he wants to get oarin', let him – "

"Macgreegor maun bide whaur he is," returned Lizzie. "Near a' the accidents i' the papers comes o' folk changin' their sates. An' ye ken fine, John, I wudna ha'e come wi' ye the day if ye hadna tell't me there wud be nae cairry-ons in the boat."

"Och, ye're awfu' easy frichtit," remarked her husband good-humouredly.

"Ay; I'm easy frichtit. Whit wud I dae wi' wee Jeannie if the boat wis capsizin'? I'm fur nae wattery graves, thenk ye, John!"

"Havers, wumman! Come on, Macgreegor, an' I'll learn ye to – "

"Dinna stir a fit, Macgreegor, or I'll – "

"I want to get oarin', Maw."

"Weel, I'm tellin' ye ye canna get oarin'; an' that's jist a' aboot it! Luk at wee Jeannie, noo, an' her that nice an' quate. She's no' wantin' to get oarin' an' ha'e us a' droondit – are ye, ma doo?"

Wee Jeannie continued to apply herself to a stick of barley sugar, and said nothing.

"She's ower wee fur to oar," said Macgregor scornfully. "Whit wey can I no' get oarin', Maw?"

"Michty me! Can ye no' tak' a tellin', laddie? See the yatts thonder! See thon big yin wi' the yella lum!"

"It's no' a lum; it's a funnel," returned Macgregor coldly.

"Aweel, it's a' yin," said his mother agreeably. "See thon steamboat comin' to the pier! Whit a reek! It's got yella lums – funnels – tae."

"I like rid funnels better nor yella yins. Can I get oarin' noo, Maw?"

"Tits, Macgreegor! I wunner at ye gaun on aboot oarin' when I've tell't ye ye canna. A fine job it wud be if ye coupit the boat an' a whale got the haud o' ye!"

"There nae whales at Rothesay."

"Is there no'?"

"Granpaw said there was nane; an' he kens."

John chuckled. "He had ye there, Lizzie," he said. "Ye canna doot yer ain feyther's word."

"Aweel," said Lizzie, "there maybe nae whales as a rule, but nae man kens whit's in the sea, as Solyman says."

"Whales is feart fur folk," observed her son.

"The whale wisna feart fur puir Jonah, Macgreegor."

"If I had been Jonah – "

"Ye wud jist ha'e been ett up fur forty days and forty nichts."

"I wudna!"

"Ah, but ye wud! An' it wudna be vera nice in the whale's inside."

"I wud ha'e jaggit it wi' knifes an' preens till it let me oot," said the valiant Macgregor.

John laughed loudly, and Lizzie said reprovingly: "Ye sudna laugh when Macgreegor says sic daft-like things. Ye jist encourage him wi' his blethers an' boastin'... Macgreegor, I tell ye, if ye wis in the whale's inside ye wud jist be roarin' an' greetin' fur yer Maw."

"I wudna!"

"Ay, wud ye! Sae ye needna be boastin' aboot knifes an' preens."

"Wis Jonah roarin' an' greetin' fur his maw, Maw?"

"Ach, haud yer tongue! See thon wee boat wi' the sail."

"Whit wey has this boat no' got a sail, Maw?"

"It's got nae mast, ye see, Macgreegor," said his father.

"Whit wey has it no' got a mast, Paw?"

"Weel, ma mannie, it's jist a boat fur oarin'," said John.

"Can I get oarin' noo?" asked Macgregor.

"I'm shair I've tell't ye a dizzen times ye canna," cried his mother, who was engaged in fixing a fresh bit of paper to one end of wee Jeannie's barley-sugar.

"When 'll I get oarin'?"

"No' the noo, onywey."

"Wull I get oarin' in a wee while, Maw?"

"Ye'll no' get oarin' the day, sae ye needna be – "

"Wull I get oarin' the morn, Maw?"

"Oh, my! Wis there ever sic a wean! Deed, Macgreegor, ye wad spile the patients o' Job! Whit are ye wantin' to oar fur?"

"I jist want to oar."

"Let him oar, Lizzie," said John mildly.

"Na, I'll no' let him oar! An' I think ye micht ha'e mair sense nor to say 'let him oar' when I've tell't him fifty times he canna get oarin'.'"

"But the wean's that disappintit," urged her husband.

"Better disappintit nor droondit," quoth Lizzie shortly. "Whaur are ye gaun noo, John?" she suddenly inquired.

"Oot to get thon steamboat's waves," he returned, laying down his pipe and bending to the oars.

"Whit's that ye say?"

"I'm gaun to tak' ye oot to get a wee shoogy-shoo wi' thon steamboat's waves."

"I'm fur nane o' yer shoogy-shoos, John."

"Whit fur no'? Macgreegor likes a shoogy-shoo. Eh, Macgreegor?"

"Ay, Paw," replied Macgregor, roused from apparently gloomy reflections. "I like when the boat's whumlin' aboot."

"I'll whumle ye," cried his mother. "Noo, John, ye're no' to dae't. We'll get sookit into the paiddles, as shair's daith!"

"Nae fears, wumman."

"Ah, but there is fears! I'm no' wantin' to get ma heid an' ma airms an' ma legs ca'ed aff, an' droondit furbye!"

"Wud the paiddles ca'wur heids aff?" inquired Macgregor with interest.

"They wud that," said Lizzie, relieved to see her husband altering his course.

"An' wud wur heids gang intil the ingynes?" pursued the youngster.

"Oh, haud yer tongue, Macgreegor!" cried his horrified mother. "Whit a notion fur a wean!" she observed to John.

"Paw, wud wur heids gang – "

"Whisht, laddie!" said his father. "Yer Maw disna like it."

"Whit wey?"

Getting no answer, he relapsed into a thoughtful silence, which lasted for about three minutes.

"Can I no' get oarin' noo?" he inquired.

"Here a boat wi' a rid funnel comin'," said John.

"Can I no' get – "

"Dod, there an' awfu' crood on board her. D'ye see the folk, Macgreegor?"

"Ay. But can I no' – "

"Ha'e, Macgreegor," said Lizzie, who had been fumbling in her pocket, "there a lozenger fur ye."

"Thenk ye, Maw," he returned, and remained quiet for a little.

Then – "Ma fit's sleepin'!" he exclaimed. "I want to dance."

"Ye canna dance here," said his mother. "Rub yer leg an' dunt yer fit on the floor. But dinna get aff yer sate."

Macgregor rubbed and dunted for some time, but without obtaining relief. "It's fu' o' preens an' needles, an' it's gettin' waur," he complained.

"Weel, ye maun jist thole it, fur ye canna get up an' dance in the boat," said Lizzie, not unsympathetically. "Try wagglin' yer leg, dearie."

Macgregor waggled violently, but to little purpose. His countenance expressed extreme discomfort. "It's awfu' jaggy," he said several times.

"Puir laddie," said his father. "It's a nesty thing a sleepin' fit. Is't no', Lizzie?"

"Ay, I mind I yinst had it in the kirk, an' I wis near dementit. Is't no' gettin' better, Macgreegor?"

"Naw; it's gettin' waur, Maw."

The parents became quite concerned about the sufferer.

"I doot ye'll ha'e to gang to the shore, John," said Lizzie, "an' let him get streetchin' hissel'!"

"Ay, he's got crampit wi' sittin' there sae lang. Weans isna used to sittin' quate. Is't rale bad, ma mannie?"

"A' ma leg's jaggy noo," replied the boy.

"Lizzie," said John suddenly, "if the wean wis gettin' oarin' fur a wee, dae ye no' think – "

"Na, na. I canna thole folk gallivantin' aboot in boats. Mercy me! there folk droondit every day jist wi' changin' their sates."

"I cud creep to the ither sate, Maw," said Macgregor, who had suddenly ceased rubbing, dunting, and waggling.

"An' he's ower wee, furbye," objected Lizzie.

"I'm no', Maw. Wullie Thomson's wee'er nor me, an' he aye gets oarin'."

"Is yer fit better?" asked Lizzie.

"Naw," said her son, hastily resuming operations. "Wullie Thomson's maw lets him oar," he added.

"I suppose ye wud shinner ha'e Wullie's maw nor yer ain," she said, glancing at her husband.

Apparently Macgregor did not hear.

"D'ye hear whit yer Maw's sayin', Macgreegor?" said John. "She's speirin' if ye wud like Mrs. Thomson fur yer maw instead o' hersel'."

"Nae fears," said Macgregor promptly. "I like ma ain Maw best."

"Ye're an awfu' laddie," sighed Lizzie. "Wull ye be rale canny if I let ye get oarin'?"

XII

OLD Mr. Purdie placed his closed hands behind his back, and, with a twinkle in his eye, delivered himself of the ancient rhyme –

"Neevy, neevy, nick nack,
Which haun' will you tak'?
Tak' the richt, or tak' the wrang,
An' I'll beguile ye if I can!"

"I'll tak' the richt, Granpaw," said Macgregor.

Mr. Purdie extended the member mentioned, disclosing a slab of toffee done up in transparent paper. "Ye're a rale smairt laddie!" he observed with a chuckle. "Ye aye guess whaur the gundy is."

"Ay, I'm gey fly," returned Macgregor modestly, beginning an onslaught on the sweet.

Mr. Purdie chuckled again, and slipped the packet of toffee which had been concealed in his left hand into his pocket.

"I'm aye richt, am I no?" inquired his grandson.

"Ay, are ye, Macgreegor! It bates me to think hoo ye ken."

"Aw, I jist ken… It's awfu' guid!"

"Is it?"

"Ay, I'll gi'e ye a taste."

"Na, na," said Mr. Purdie, looking pleased. "I'll jist ha'e a bit smoke to masel'. Ye're no' to tell yer Maw I wis gi'ein' ye gundy, though; an' yer no' to let it spile yer tea."

"I'll never let bug, Granpaw," said Macgregor, as if to set his relative's guilty conscience at rest.

The twain had come down to the shore at low water, and Mr. Purdie was resting on a rock, while Macgregor hunted among the stones and sea-weed for small crabs, several of which he had secured already and confined in an old battered meat tin.

"Noo, dinna get yer feet wat, laddie," said Mr. Purdie when he had got his pipe, a highly-seasoned clay, well alight.

"Nae fears, Granpaw," returned the boy reassuringly. As

a matter of fact, his feet at the very moment were squelching in his boots. "Here anither!" he exclaimed, holding up a tiny crab. "It's awfu' kitly," he added, as he allowed it to run on the palm of his hand. "It's ower wee fur to nip. Wud ye like to fin' it in yer haun', Granpaw?"

"Deed, ay," said Mr. Purdie, with the desire to please his grandson. "Ay, it's gey an' kitly. An' whit are ye gaun to dae wi' a' thae partins?" he inquired, indicating the meat tin.

"I'm gaun to tak' them hame."

"No' to Glesca?"

"Ay, to Glesca!"

"Aw, but they'll jist dee, Macgreegor."

"Whit wey?"

"Partins winna leeve in Glesca."

"Whit wey wull they no'?"

"They need saut watter."

"I'll tak' saut watter hame tae. I'll tak' it in a botle, Granpaw."

Mr. Purdie shook his head, and the boy looked disappointed.

"Whit wud ye dae wi' partins in Glesca?" asked the former.

"Naethin'."

"An' whit wud ye tak' them hame fur?"

"It wisna fur masel'. I'm no' heedin' aboot partins. I wud be feart fur them growin' big an' creepin' intil ma bed. It wis wee Joseph wantit partins."

"Wha's wee Joseph?"

"He's a wee laddie. He's faur wee-er nor me, an' he's lyin' badly, an' his paw's deid, an' his maw washes."

"Ay, ay. An' sae wee Joseph wantit ye to bring him partins?"

"He wantit a monkey first; he thocht there wis monkeys at Rothesay, sclimmin' up the rocks an' rinnin' aboot the pier an' the shore. Wee Joseph never seen the sea."

"That's peetifu'. An' ye tell't him there wis nae monkeys?"

"Ay; an' he begood fur to greet. An' I tell't him aboot the partins, an' he said he wud like a wheen partins, an' – an' I thocht the partins wud leeve in Glesca, an' – an' – I'll jist tim them oot an' bash them wi' a stane."

"Na, na. Ye mauna dae that, Macgreegor," exclaimed Mr. Purdie hastily. "The puir beasties canna help no' bein' able to leeve in Glesca."

"I'll bash them," cried Macgregor, violently.

"Haud on, laddie, haud on. If you wis a wee partin, hoo wud ye like if a big laddie cam' an' bashed ye wi' a stane?"

"If I wis a partin, I wud leeve in Glesca." And the youngster's eyes moved in search of a suitable stone.

"Macgreegor," implored the old man, laying his pipe on the rock, and rising, "dae ye think wee Joseph wud like ye to bash the partins?"

"Ay, wud he."

"I'm shair he wudna. The puir wee partins never done onybody hairm."

Macgregor picked up a small boulder, remarking, "Partins nips folks' taes when they're dookin'."

"Ay; but no' wee partins like thur."

"Thae wee yins 'll shin be big," said Macgregor coldly. "I'll bash this yin first," he added, selecting a poor little specimen from the tin, and laying it on the rock.

Grandfather Purdie seized the uplifted arm. "Macgreegor," he said gently, "ye're no' to dae it."

"Whit wey?"

"Because," said the old man, searching for an argument that might appeal to the young savage, "because it's sic a wee bit thing."

"It's gey wee," admitted Macgregor, peering into the tin while the victim slid off the rock and escaped; "ay, it's gey wee. Here a bigger yin. I'll bash it!"

"Macgreegor," said Mr. Purdie solemnly, "ye mauna be crool. Ye wudna like if a muckle giant got a grup o' yersel', an' wis gaun to bash ye wi' his club."

"It's a' lees aboot giants. There nae giants!"

"Aweel, ye're no' to be crool onywey," said Mr. Purdie, at a loss. "Let the wee partins rin awa', an' dinna vex yer Granpaw. The wee beasties is that happy, ye ken, an' it wud be a sin to bash them. They're jist like weans doon at the coast fur the Fair, rinnin' aboot an' enjoyin' theirsel's, an' they'll be awfu' obleeged to ye fur no' bashin' them."

The old man had evidently struck the right chord at last, for Macgregor dropped the stone, and said – "Weel, I'll no' bash them, Granpaw."

"That's a fine laddie!"

"An' I'll let them awa'," he added, turning the tin upside down.

Mr. Purdie patted the boy's cheek. "I kent ye wudna be crool," he said tenderly. "Here anither bit gundy fur yer gab."

"Thenk ye, Granpaw."

"An' ye'll never think o' bashin' partins again, Macgreegor?"

"Naw. But – but wee Joseph 'll be unco sorry."

"Aha! But we'll ha'e to see aboot somethin' fur wee Joseph. Whit d'ye think he wud like?"

"He wantit somethin' that wis leevin'."

"Leevin'? Dod, that's no' sae easy," said Mr. Purdie, resuming his seat and pipe, and gazing thoughtfully across the bay. "I ken a man here that keeps birds," he remarked at last. "Wud wee Joseph like a bird, think ye?"

"Naw," Macgregor firmly and unhesitatingly replied.

"A bird wud be a nice pet fur a laddie that's lyin' badly. It wud cheep an' sing til him, ye ken."

"Birds is ower easy kill't. Ye canna play wi' birds in yer bed."

"Deed, that's true… Whit think ye o' a wee cat? Mrs. M'Conkie the grocer's got kittens the noo."

"Joseph had a wee cat, an' it scartit his neb, an' his maw pit it oot the hoose. He had white mice anither time, an' they had young yins, but his maw wudna let him keep them in the bed."

"Weel," said Mr. Purdie, "I'm shair I dinna ken whit to say, Macgreegor."

"The partins wis best, if they wud ha'e leeved. Wee Joseph wis fur keepin' them in a boax, an' him an' me wis gaun to mak' them rin races on the blanket. Maybe they wud catch their feet in the oose, though."

"I doot they wud, puir beasties... But I'm fear't we canna get Joseph onythin' that's leevin'."

Macgregor looked depressed, whereat his grandfather sighed helplessly, and let his pipe go out.

"Ye see, laddie, there's no' mony things ye can gi'e til a wean that's lyin' badly," said the old man. "Wull Joseph be better shin?"

"Naw. It's his back that hurts him. He's awfu' bad whiles. I wudna like to be him."

"That's maist peetifu'! I'll tell ye whit we'll dae, Macgreegor."

"Whit, Granpaw?"

"We'll ha'e a keek at the shopes afore we gang hame to wur tea, an' ye'll maybe see somethin' that wud please him."

"Wull we gang noo?" exclaimed the youngster, brightening.

Mr. Purdie consulted a fat silver watch. "Ay, we'll gang noo, an' see whit we can see. Gi'e's yer haun', Macgreegor... Hech, sirs! but ye're no' to gar me rin. I'm no' as soople as yersel', ma mannie. Mind yer feet, or we'll baith be tum'lin' on the slippy places."

Without mishap, however, they came to the road, and soon reached the town, Mr. Purdie "pechin' " and Macgregor beaming with anticipation.

At a window which seemed to be stocked with all the toys and trifles in creation they paused and gazed.

"Ha'e," said Mr. Purdie, producing his purse, "there a thrupny-bit. Jist tak' per pick, Macgreegor."

"Thenk ye, Granpaw. Oh, whit'll I buy?"

"Wud ye no' like to buy thon braw joog wi' the pictur' on it?"

"Naw."

"I'm thinkin' it wud be a nice kin' o' thing fur Joseph. Ye see it's got 'A Present frae Rothesay' on it; an' he wud like gettin' his tea oot o' 'it. Eh?"

"Naw."

"Aweel, ye maun please yersel'. There a pent-boax noo. Wud Joseph like to pent, think ye?"

"Naw. I like pentin' – I'm gaun to be a penter when I'm a man. But I'm gaun to ha'e pots o' pent an' big dauds o' potty."

"Weel, maybe wee Joseph – "

"Naw."

"There a pretty pictur' book," said Mr. Purdie. "Dae ye think – "

"Naw."

The old man gave up.

"I'll buy thon trumpet," cried the boy at last.

"I doot, when wee Joseph's lyin' badly, he'll no' be vera fit to blaw a trumpet."

"I cud blaw it fur him, Granpaw. I can blaw rale hard."

"Ay, but I'm feart wee Joseph michtna like that."

"Whit wey?"

Mr. Purdie was about to attempt explaining, when suddenly Macgregor gave vent to a cry of delight. "See – oh, see! there a monkey hingin' in the corner!"

"Haste ye an' buy it," said his grandfather, laughing.

Macgregor required no second bidding, and a couple of minutes later he was exhibiting his purchase. It was an earthenware monkey that bounded merrily at the end of a piece of elastic. "It's gey near leevin', is't no'?" he demanded. "See it loupin'!" And he continued to play with it until they were nearly home.

"Wee Joseph'll be unco gled to see it. It'll gar him lauch, puir laddie," said Mr. Purdie.

"Ay," assented Macgregor, without much animation. For the moment he had somehow forgotten all about wee Joseph. He wound the elastic carefully about the monkey's neck, and walked on in silence.

"Ye'll like gi'ein' it to the puir laddie," said Mr. Purdie, glancing down.

"Ay," answered Macgregor in a husky whisper.

XIII

THE Robinson family were spending the week-end at old Mr. Purdie's Rothesay residence, but, much to their disappointment, the weather had completely broken down an hour after their arrival. Macgregor stood at the window, gazing disconsolately at the misty bay, while his elders – wee Jeannie having been put to bed – talked of matters which seemed to him totally void of interest.

"Can I get gaun ootbye noo?" he inquired at last of his mother, who was busily knitting and talking to Grandma Purdie.

Lizzie glanced at the window. "Deed, Macgreegor, ye needna be speirin' aboot gaun oot the nicht."

"It's no' sae wat noo, Maw."

"I'm thinkin' it cudna be muckle waur, dearie. Ye wud be fair drookit in hauf a meenit. Jist content yersel' in the hoose, an' ye'll maybe get a fine day the morn."

"I want to gang to the pier an' see the steamboats comin' in, Maw."

"Aweel, I'm rale vexed fur ye, but ye're no' gaun ower the door the nicht. Whaur's yer graun' pictur'-book?"

"I seen a' the picturs."

"Puir laddie," said Grandma Purdie, "it's no' vera cheery fur him sittin' in the hoose a' nicht. John, can ye no' divert the wean a wee? Gi'e him a bit ride on yer fit, man."

"Come on, Macgreegor!" his father cried willingly. "Come awa' and ha'e a ride on ma fit."

"Ach, he's ower big fur that kin' o' gemm," said Grandpa Purdie, noticing that Macgregor did not appear to appreciate the invitation. "Are ye no', ma mannie?"

"Ay," muttered Macgregor.

"Wud ye like to build hooses wi' the dominoes?" inquired the old gentleman.

Macgregor shook his head.

"Weel, wud ye like to build castels wi' the draughts?"

Macgregor shook his head again, and looked gloomier and more ill-used than ever.

"I ken whit Macgreegor wud like," put in John. "Him an' me kens a fine gemm. I'll be a draygon, an' hide in ma den ablow the table, and Macgreegor 'll hunt me. I'll mak' him a spear oot o' ma 'Evenin' Times,' an' he'll stab me till I'm deid. Eh, Macgreegor?"

"Fine!" exclaimed Mr. Purdie.

"Preserve us a'!" cried Mrs. Purdie.

"Oh, John and Macgreegor whiles ha'e fine gemms at the draygon," said Lizzie, pleasantly. "But it's unco sair on John's breeks; an' he's got on his guid claes the nicht... Pu' them up a wee, John, sae as no' to spile the knees."

"A' richt, wumman," replied John, as he rolled his newspaper into a harmless weapon. Presently he handed it to his son, and disappeared under the table, where he covered his head with a red woollen tidy.

"Come on, Macgreegor; I'm ready fur ye noo!" he shouted, and immediately proceeded to emit fearsome noises.

"It bates a'!" Grandma Purdie cried, quite excitedly. "Whit a gemm!"

"John," said Lizzie, "did ye pu' up yer breeks?"

"Hoo can a draygon pu' up breeks?" returned her husband; and he resumed his growlings and groanings, while Macgreegor began to stalk his prey with great caution and stealth.

"See an' no' pit oot yer Paw's een," said old Mrs. Purdie, a trifle nervously.

"Gi'e the draygon a bit jab, an' gar him come oot his den," said Mr. Purdie. "Dod, if I wis jist a wee thing soopler, Macgreegor, I wud mak' ye anither draygon."

Just then the draygon made a claw at the leg of the hunter, who let out a piercing yell and lunged wildly with his spear, without, however, getting it home. The fun became fast and furious.

"Come oot yer den, ye auld draygon, till I bore a hole in ye!" yelled the bold Macgregor.

"Gurr – gurr!" said the dragon, suddenly appearing on the other side of the table.

At this point the door opened, and Aunt Purdie stepped
in. "What's ado, what's ado?" she inquired, rather sourly.
John rose from the floor, trying to look at his ease, and
Macgregor, the spirit of play being abruptly chilled, shook
hands dutifully with his relative and straightway retired to
the window.

Aunt Purdie, whose husband's grocery business was rapidly increasing, had taken rooms in Rothesay, not far from
the old folks, for July and August. She was much too
superior and proper a person for the Robinsons, and she
was Macgregor's pet aversion. As Lizzie was wont to say,
she was "rale genteel, but awfu' easy offendit."

"I was intending to go to the pier for to meet Robert," she
observed as she sat down, "but it was that wet I jist came in
to wait."

"Ye're rale welcome," said Grandma Purdie kindly.
"Whit boat is Rubbert comin' wi?"

"Robert is coming in the seven o'clock p.m. train from
Glasgow. He cannot leave the shope any earlier the now."

"Weel, he'll no' be compleenin' if trade's guid," said Mr.
Purdie brightly. "He'll ken to come here for ye the nicht,
nae doot."

"Yes," said Aunt Purdie. Then turning to Lizzie, but
speaking so that everyone in the room might hear, she said
– "I've jist received a letter from my friend, Mrs. M'Cluny."

"Ha'e ye?" returned Lizzie politely. She knew that she was
about to be treated to news of her sister-in-law's grand
acquaintances, in whom she had not the slightest interest.

"M'Cluny!" exclaimed old Mr. Purdie. "Dod, but that's
a queer-like name to gang to the kirk wi! It's liker Gart-
navel."

"It is very old Highland," said Aunt Purdie, with dignity.

"Ten year in botle," muttered John, with a snigger,
whereat Mr. Purdie slapped his knee and laughed loudly.

"Mrs. M'Cluny," went on Aunt Purdie, "informs me that
Dr. M'Cluny has got to leave Glasgow."

"Wha's he been killin'?" asked Mr. Purdie, and John
stifled a guffaw.

"Haud yer tongue, man," whispered old Mrs. Purdie, fearing lest her son's wife should take offence, as she had done too often before.

"Dr. M'Cluny," the visitor continued, "has received an appintment in England. It is a very good appintment, but I'm sure I don't know what we are to do wanting Mrs. M'Cluny when the winter season begins."

"Dis she gi'e awa' coals an' blankets?" inquired Mr. Purdie, with a serious face.

The lady glanced at him sharply. "I was referring to Mrs. M'Cluny's social – a – poseetion," she said stiffly. "We shall miss her greatly at our parties and conversonies. She was that genteel – I might even say autocratic. Her and me is great friends, and we have been often complimented for our arrangements at entertainments when we was on the commytee. Everybody says Mrs. M'Cluny is a capital organism."

"Deed, ye'll jist ha'e to tak' her place when she's awa'," said Mr. Purdie, winking at John.

"Well, I must do my best," returned Aunt Purdie modestly. "Of course, it has always been against Mrs. M'Cluny that her husband kep' a doctor's shope," she added.

"Bless me, wumman, whit's wrang wi' that? If a man's gaun to tell folk to tak' pooshun, he micht as weel sell it," cried the old man.

"It is nut conseedered the proper thing by the best people."

"Havers! Ye're ain man keeps a shope."

"A grocery establishment," said Aunt Purdie, "is a very different thing from a doctor's shope. I've never heard tell of a man with a doctor's shope getting a title from the hands of his Royal Majesty."

Mr. Purdie burst out laughing. "Ca' canny, wumman, ca' canny! I doot oor Rubbert's no' the lad to heed aboot titles. Hoots, toots! ... Come ower here, Macgreegor, an' gi'e's yer crack," he said, anxious to get Aunt Purdie off her high horse.

Macgregor came over from the window and leant against

the old man's knees. "Dae a recite, Grandpaw," he whispered.

"Eh? Recite?" The old man was pleased, however. "Weel, I'll gi'e ye a bit readin', if ye like, Macgreegor," he said, putting on his specs and taking an ancient and somewhat battered "Bell's Reciter" from a shelf at his elbow. "Whit'll I read ye, ma mannie!"

"Read aboot the man that wis lockit in the kist till he wis a – a – a skeletin, an' loupit oot on the ither man."

"The Uncle?"

"Ay. I like that yin awfu'!" said Macgregor, with a shudder of anticipation.

"Whit's that?" cried Lizzie. "Aw, yer no' to read him that yin, fayther. He had an unco bad nichtmare the last time."

"It wisna the skeletin done it, Maw," appealed the boy. "It wis the pease-brose I had to ma supper. I aye dream when I get pease-brose – an' ile."

"He's sleepin' wi' me the nicht," put in John. "Ye'll no' be feart wi' me, wull ye, Macgreegor?"

"Naw!"

After some discussion Lizzie reluctantly gave in, and Mr. Purdie proceeded with the reading, which, as a matter of fact, had little interest for Macgregor until the final tragedy was reached. Then, while the old man, short of breath, gasped the lines and gesticulated in frightsome fashion, did Macgregor stand with rising hair, open mouth, and starting eyeballs, quaking with delicious terror. And hardly had the words "a sinner's soul was lost" left the reader's lips when the boy was exclaiming –

"Dae anither recite, Granpaw, dae anither recite!"

"Na, na, laddie. Nae mair."

"Aw, ay. Jist anither. Dae the yin aboot the man that stabbit the ither man wi' a jaggy knife, an' hut him wi' a stane, an' pit him in the watter, an' wis fun' oot, an' got the nick. Dae that yin."

After a little rest Grandpa Purdie was prevailed upon to read "Eugene Aram's Dream," at the close of which he suggested that Macgregor should give a recitation.

"I'll gi'e ye a penny, Macgreegor," he said encouragingly.

"An' I'll gi'e ye anither," said John.

"An' I've a poke o' mixed ba's," added Grandma Purdie.

"Naw, I canna," said Macgregor.

"Come awa', ye can dae it fine," said his father. "Dae the recite yer Maw teached ye aboot the laddie on the burnin' boat."

"It wis an awfu' job gettin' him to learn it," remarked Lizzie.

"Weel, let's hear a' aboot it," said Mr. Purdie.

"Och, it's a daft recite, an' I canna mind it," returned Macgregor.

"Ah, but we're a' wantin' to hear it," said Grandma Purdie. "Come awa', like a clever laddie."

"Ye can mind it fine," remarked Lizzie. "Ye needna be sae blate."

"I've a thrupny bit in ma purse," said Mr. Purdie.

"Dod, I've yin, tae," said John.

The bribery was too much for Macgregor. "I'll dae't!" he exclaimed.

Everyone applauded, except Aunt Purdie, who muttered something about "bringing up children foolishly." Whereupon Lizzie murmured something about "talkin' o' bringin' up weans when ye hivna got ony!" – an observation which the other pretended she did not hear.

"I'll no' dae the yin aboot the burnin' boy," said Macgregor suddenly.

"Weel, dae anither," said his grandfather.

"He disna ken anither," his mother interposed. "It tuk me six month to learn him the – "

"Ay, I ken anither. I learnt it frae Wullie Thomson," her son interrupted.

"Whit's it aboot?"

"I'll no' tell till I recite it."

"Recite it then."

Macgregor put his hands behind his back, and after several false starts and giggles, delivered the following: –

"Yin, twa, three!
My mither catched a flea!
We roastit it, an' toastit it,
An' had it to wur tea!"

"That's a' I ken," he concluded, bursting out laughing.

His grandparents and his father laughed too, and Lizzie would have joined them had it not been for Aunt Purdie.

With a face of disgust, that lady, holding up her hands, exclaimed, "Sich vulgarity!"

Lizzie appeared to swallow something before she quietly said – "Micht I be as bold as to speir, Mrs. Purdie, if ye refer to ma son, Macgreegor, or to the words o' the pome he recitit the noo?"

"T – to the words, of course, Mrs. Robison," returned Aunt Purdie hastily.

"That's a' richt, Mrs. Purdie," Lizzie said, with disagreeable pleasantness. "I'm gled to hear ye referred to the words. H'm! Ay!"

Aunt Purdie opened her mouth, but fortunately the arrival of her husband just then prevented her speaking.

Robert Purdie was a big, genial man, and he had Macgregor up on his shoulder before he had been in the room a minute. The boy loved his uncle, and always associated him with large bags of what are known to some people as "hair-ile" mixtures – softish sweets with pleasing flavours, reminiscent of a barber's saloon.

"Ha'e ye been behavin' yersel', Macgreegor?" inquired Uncle Purdie presently.

"Ay," replied the youngster, while his aunt glowered.

"Aweel," said the big man, putting him gently on the floor, "awa' an' see whit ye can fin' in ma coat pooch oot in the lobby."

With a cry of rapture Macgregor fled from the parlour. He was sampling the "poke" when his mother joined him, having announced her intention to the company of seeing if wee Jeannie slept. "Dearie, ye're no' to say thon again," she said.

"Whit, Maw?"

"Thon pome, dearie."

"Whit wey, Maw?"

"Jist because I dinna want ye to say't."

"Weel, I'll no'," replied Macgregor, with his mouth full.

"That's ma ain laddie."

"Maw, d'ye ken whit I wud like to gi'e Aunt Purdie?"

"A pickle sweeties," suggested Lizzie, trying to smile.

"Naw. I wud like to gi'e her a daud on the neb twicet!"

XIV

"An' a' ye've got to dae," said Lizzie, laying the "Fireside Companion" in her lap and beginning another spell of knitting, "is jist to licht the wee stove, an' the eggs hatches theirsel's. Maist extraornar', is't no', John?"

"Dod, ay," returned John. "Whit did ye say they ca'ed it, wumman? Cremation o' chickens? Eh?"

"Incubation, John," his wife replied, after a glance at the page. "It's the het that gars the chickens come oot."

"Whit wey dae the chickens no' come oot when ye bile the eggs, Paw?" inquired Macgregor, quitting the square blocks of wood with which he had been building "wee hooses" on the kitchen floor, and advancing to his father's knee.

"Speir at yer Maw, Macgreegor," said John, laughing. "Ye're the yin fur questions!"

"Maw, whit wey – "

"I'm thinkin' it's aboot time ye wis in yer bed, dearie," his mother observed.

"But whit wey dae the chickens no' – "

"Aweel, ye see, if they wis comin' oot then they wud shin be droondit," she said hastily. "Gi'e yer Paw a kiss noo, an' – "

"Ay, but whit wey – "

"Bilin' watter wud be ower muckle het fur the puir wee tewkies," she added, seeing that the boy was persistent. "Ye've got to gar the wee tewkies think the auld hen's settin' on them, dearie."

"If I wis to pit an egg on the hob, wud a wee tewky come oot, Maw?"

"Na, na! That wud shin roast it. Ye've got to keep it nice an' cosy, but no' ower warm; jist like yersel' when ye're in yer bed. D'ye see?"

"Ay, Maw… But I'm no' wearit yet."

"Let him bide a wee, Lizzie," said the indulgent John. "Did ye ever hear tell," he went on with a twinkle in his eye, "o' the hen that fun' an aix an sat on it fur a fortnicht, tryin' fur to hatchet?"

"Hoots!" murmured his wife, smiling to please him.

"Did the hen no' cut itsel', Paw?" asked his son gravely.

"Dod, I never thocht o' that, Macgreegor," his father answered, grinning.

"It was a daft kin' o' hen onywey," said the boy scornfully.

"Aw, it jist done it fur a bawr," said John by way of apology.

"Noo, Macgreegor, yer time's up," his mother remarked, with a shake of her head.

"I'm no' wearit, Maw."

"Are ye no'? An' whit wey wis ye yawnin' the noo, ma mannie?"

"I wisna yawnin'."

"Whit wis ye daein' then?"

"I – I wis jist openin' ma mooth, Maw."

"Och, awa', wi' ye, laddie! Jist openin' yer mooth, wis ye? Deed, yer e'en's jist like twa beads wi' sleep! I seen ye rubbin' them fur the last hauf-'oor. Ay, fine ye ken it's Wee Wullie Winkie, ma dearie."

"Aw, Lizzie, the wean's fine," put in John, as he cut himself a fresh fill of tobacco. "Come here, Macgreegor, an' get a wee cuddle afore ye gang to yer bed."

"Na," said Lizzie firmly. "He'll gang to sleep on yer knee, an' then I'll ha'e a nice job gettin' him to his bed. Here, Macgreegor, till I tak' aff yer collar... Noo, see if ye can louse yer buits... Mercy me! if that's no' anither hole in yer stockin'. Luk at his heel, John! Ye're jist a pair the twa o' ye! Ye're baith that sair on yer stockin's. If it's no the heels, it's the taes, an' if it's no' the taes, it's the soles, an' if it's no' the soles, it's – Aweel, I've darned them afore, an' I daursay I'll darn them again," she concluded, with a philosophic smile, and stooped to assist Macgregor, who was struggling with a complicated knot in the lace of his second boot.

"John," said Lizzie two mornings later – it happened to be

Sunday – "I canna get Macgreegor to rise. He's sayin' he's no' weel."

"Eh!" exclaimed her husband, laying down his razor. "No' weel? I maun see – "

"No' the noo, John. I think he's sleepin' again. But – but wis ye gi'ein' him ony sweeties when ye tuk him ootbye yesterday efternune?"

"Naw, Lizzie. Ye seen a' he got yersel'. Jist thon wee bit taiblet. Is he feelin' seeck?"

"He said he wisna seeck, but jist no' weel. He's no' lukin' ill-like, but I'm no' easy in ma mind aboot him."

"I – I gi'ed him a penny yesterday," said her husband after an awkward pause.

"Aw, John!"

"But he said he wudna spend it on sweeties – an' I'm shair he didna."

"Maybe he bocht pastry. Whit fur did ye gi'e him the penny?"

"He askit fur it. Maybe he's jist a wee thing wearit, Lizzie."

Mrs. Robinson shook her head, and opened a cupboard door.

"Are ye gaun to gi'e him ile?" asked John.

"Ay, when he's wauken. Oh, John, John, ye sud be mair discreet, an' no' gi'e Macgreegor a' he asks fur. But get yer shavin' dune, an' come to yer breakfast. Ye didna see wee Jeannie's flannen petticoat, did ye? Her red yin, ye ken? I canna lay ma haun' on it, an' I'm shair it was aside her ither claes when we gaed to wur beds."

"Naw, I didna see it," John replied dully, and sadly resumed his shaving.

"It's maist aggravatin'," murmured Lizzie. "I doot I'm lossin' ma mem'ry… Did ma doo no' get on her braw new flannen petticoat?" she inquired of her daughter, who, however, appeared quite happy in her old garment, sitting on a hassock and piping on a horn spoon which had a whistle in its handle. "Wee Jeannie's breid an' mulk's near ready noo," she added, whereupon wee Jeannie piped with more zest than ever.

After breakfast Lizzie interviewed her son, who was again awake.

"Are ye feelin' better noo, dearie?"

"Naw."

"Whit's like the maitter?"

"I dinna ken. I dinna want to rise, Maw."

Lizzie refrained from referring to the penny that had done the harm. "I doot ye're needin' a taste o' ile," she said.

Macgreegor kept a meek silence.

"I'll gi'e ye a wee taste, an' then ye'll maybe try an' tak' yer breakfast."

"I'll try, Maw."

He took the dose like a hero, and afterwards made a meal the heartiness of which rather puzzled his mother. Then he said he was going to have another sleep.

"John," said Lizzie, "I canna think whit's wrang wi' Macgreegor. He's baith hungry an' sleepy. I wisht I kent whit he bocht wi' yer penny. I'm feart it wis some kin' o' pooshonous thing. I think I'll gang ower to Mrs. Thomson an' speir if Wullie's a' richt. Wullie an' Macgreegor wis oot thegither last nicht."

"Aye," said John. "Maybe he got somethin' tae eat frae Wullie."

"Maybe, John... If Macgreegor's wauken when I'm awa', ye micht get him to tell ye whit he dune wi' the penny. D'ye see?"

"Ay... I'm rale vexed aboot the penny, wumman."

"Weel, dearie, ye maun try an' be mair discreet. Ye canna expec' a wean to be fu' o' wisdom, as Solyman says."

Left to himself – Lizzie had taken wee Jeannie with her – John went over to the bed and gazed anxiously upon his son. Presently the boy opened his eyes.

"Weel, ma wee man," said John, with an effort to speak cheerfully, "are ye fur risin' noo?"

"Naw."

"Are ye no' ony better?"

Macgreegor languidly signified that he was not.

John cleared his throat. "Whit did ye dae wi' the penny I gi'ed ye?" he asked gently.

"I spent it."

"Ay. But whit did ye spend it on? Pastry?"

"Naw."

John felt somewhat relieved. "Aweel, tell me whit ye bocht."

"I – I'll tell ye anither time, Paw," said Macgregor, after considerable hesitation.

"Did ye get ony sweeties efter yer taiblet yesterday?"

"Naw… Can I get a wee tate taiblet noo, Paw?"

"Deed, I doot ye canna. Ye're no' weel."

"Ah, but I'm no' that kin' o' no' weel, Paw."

John shook his head sadly, and there ensued a long silence.

"Paw," said Macgregor at last, "hoo lang dae wee tewkies tak' to come oot their eggs?"

"Eh?"

The youngster's face was flushed as he repeated the question.

"I'm no' jist shair, Macgreegor," said John; "but I think the paper yer Maw wis readin' said it wis twa-three weeks."

"Oh!" cried Macgregor in such a tone of dismay that his father was startled.

"Whit's wrang, Macgreegor?"

"I think I'll rise noo, Paw," the boy remarked soberly.

"Are ye feelin' better?"

"Ay, I'm better."

"Whit's vexin' ye, ma wee man?" cried John suddenly, and with great tenderness.

Macgregor gave a small snuff and a big swallow as his father's arm went round him. "I – I thocht the – the wee tewky wud come oot shin," he murmured brokenly.

"The wee tewky?"

"Ay. But I – I canna bide in ma b – b – bed twa-three weeks." And then from under the clothes Macgregor cautiously drew a tiny red flannel garment, which he unrolled and laid bare a hen's egg. "I gi'ed ma penny fur it, Paw. The grocer tell't me there wis nae tewky in it, but – but I thocht there wis, an' I wis wantin' to – to keep it cosy, an' – an' – "

"Aw, wee Macgreegor!" exclaimed John, realising it all, but not even smiling.

When Lizzie returned and heard the tale she was sympathetic, but not sentimental.

"I'll jist bile the egg fur yer tea, dearie," she said.

"I wud like it fried, Maw," said Macgregor, who was rapidly recovering his spirits.

XV

"An' whit dae ye say to yer Granpaw fur the barra?" inquired Lizzie of her son, who was gazing with sparkling eyes at the small wheelbarrow which Mr. Purdie had just purchased for him.

Macgregor said nothing, but he suddenly flung himself upon the old gentleman and hugged him warmly.

"Hech, laddie!" cried Mr. Purdie, panting and chuckling, "ye'll squeeze a' the breith oot o' me. But I'm rale gled ye like yer barra. Yer Granny wis fur gettin' me to buy ye a pictur'-book, but – "

"I like the barra faur better nor a pictur'-book," said Macgregor. "Ye canna gi'e folk hurls in a pictur'-book."

"Deed, that's vera true. Maybe ye wud like to gang ootbye an' gi'e some o' yer wee freen's a bit ride."

"Ay, wud I!" said Macgregor eagerly.

"Aff ye gang then," said John, who was looking nearly as pleased as the youngster.

"Och, John," Lizzie put in, "Macgreegor maun bide a wee. It's no' every Setterday efternune his Granpaw comes up frae Rothesay."

"Hoots, toots!" exclaimed Mr. Purdie, patting his grandson's head. "The laddie's no' to bide in the hoose fur me. Him an' me'll ha'e a crack anither time. Eh, Macgreegor?"

"I – I'll bide if ye like, Granpaw," Macgregor murmured, casting a longing glance at his new treasure.

"Na, na," the old man returned, with a gratified smile at John and Lizzie. "I'm no' gaun awa' fur an 'oor yet, sae ye've time to try the barra and come back an' tell me if it rins weel."

"Ay, I'll dae that," said Macgregor, and, obviously relieved, he departed without delay.

At the close-mouth he encountered a little girl with whom, for some time, he had been familiar in rather a patronising fashion. On one occasion he had chased away a small dog which in a playful mood had caused her much alarm, and since then she had regarded him in the light of a hero, and had somewhat embarrassed him with her attentions, for Macgregor was sorely afraid of the chaff of his boy friends, who, with the exception of his chum Willie Thomson, were not slow to make jeering observations when they caught him in the company of his admirer. Therefore, as a rule, he passed her without speaking, or at most with a hurried and awkward reply to her shy but eager remark, made in the fond hope of interesting him.

But with his new wheelbarrow he was in a mightily pleasant humour, and grinned so kindly that the little girl was quite flurried with pride and delight.

"Ha'e!" she said modestly, presenting a tiny packet.

"Whit's that?" asked Macgregor, accepting and opening it. "Chokelet! Whaur did ye get?"

"I got it fur gaun a message."

"It's awfu' guid! Did ye get twa bits, Katie?"

"Na. Jist the yin. But – but I'm no' heedin' aboot chokelet."

Macgregor stopped eating. "Pit that in yer gab," he said, handing back half the dainty. "Whit wey did ye gi'e it a' to me?"

"Jist," said Katie.

"See ma new barra!" said Macgregor, at the end of a short silence.

"My!" she exclaimed admiringly.

"It's an awfu' fine barra!"

"Ay!"

"I got it frae Granpaw Purdie."

"Did ye?"

"Ay, did I! An' I'm gaun to gi'e folks hurls in it."

"My!"

Macgregor reflected for a moment; then remarked, "If ye wis a laddie I wud gi'e ye a hurl."

Katie's bright eyes clouded, and her fair head drooped. From a pinnacle of pride she fell into the depths of humiliation. She wanted to say, "I'm no' heedin' aboot hurls!" but her throat tightened and her lip trembled, and she remained speechless.

"Dae ye no' wish ye wis a laddie?" inquired Macgregor, bending over his grand possession and making the wheel revolve.

Katie made no response, and the boy rose and looked up and down the street preparatory to making the trial trip. Behind him, Katie raised the hem of her pinafore to her eyes.

Macgregor stepped out of the close and stood on the pavement, gripping the handles. There were few people walking in the street, and not one of his playmates was in sight.

Without turning his head, he said abruptly, "Come oot, Katie, an' I'll gi'e ye a hurl."

Katie took a step forward, and halted.

Macgregor repeated the invitation, with a glance in her direction.

Katie cast down her eyelashes and stood still.

"Are ye no' wantin' a hurl?" he inquired, a trifle impatiently.

"Ay," said Katie hastily, but without moving.

"Whit wey are ye greetin'?"

"I'm no greetin!"

"Ye are so! Ye're greetin' because ye're a lassie. Lassies is aye greetin'?"

"They're no' aye greetin'!" she exclaimed in a flash of indignation. But she was a gentle little soul, and she could not be cross with her hero. "I'll no' greet again," she said humbly. "An' I wud like a hurl in yer nice barra, if ye please." She was too young to know, and he was too young to see the beauty of her eyes at that moment, but they looked at each other, and their friendship became less one-sided than it had been so far.

"Sit doon in the barra, Katie," said Macgregor graciously.

"Ye'll no' coup me?" said she, with an inquiring yet confiding glance.

"Nae fears! I'll no' coup ye! Haud yer feet up."

She raised her feet obediently, and pulled her short skirts over the darns on her knees.

"I'll hurl ye to the corner an' back again," said Macgregor.

"Ay," assented Katie, who was holding on to the sides of the vehicle and looking just the least thing afraid.

They set off at a good pace, and when the corner was reached Katie was smiling fearlessly, and enjoying the envious stares of several little girls whom she chanced to know. The journey back was all too brief in its duration, and she rose from the barrow with undisguised reluctance. What a splendid thing it was to be "hurled" by her hero!

"Ye're an awfu' strong laddie," she observed admiringly.

"Ay, I'm gey strong," he returned, trying not to pant.

"It wis awfu' nice!" she murmured, with a little sigh.

Macgregor spat on his hands. "Wud ye like anither hurl?" he asked.

"Ay, wud I. Am I no' ower heavy?"

"Ye're no' heavy ava'. Get into the barra, an' I'll hurl ye to the ither corner. It's faurer."

Away they went again on a journey even more delightful than the first. Children scattered before them, and grown-up people hurriedly skipped against the wall or into the gutter, their varied remarks being unheard or unheeded.

"Ye're awfu' kind!" said Katie when they stood at the close-mouth once more.

"Och, it's naethin' ava'," returned Macgregor, hot and happy.

"Ah, but ye are awfu' kind. Ither laddies is no' as kind."

"Ay, but ye're rale kind yersel'. An' ye're no' as daft as ither lassies."

It was a rare compliment, and Katie appreciated it too deeply for words. At the end of half a minute she said softly, "I like ye unco weel … Dae ye like me?"

"Ay," admitted Macgregor.

"Dae ye like me unco weel?"

"Ay. Wull I gi'e ye anither hurl?"

Katie nodded and beamed upon him. She took her place in the barrow, and Macgregor was just about to start off when a heavy paw was laid upon his shoulder, and a disagreeable voice said, "Len's yer barra, an' I'll gi'e the lassie a hurl."

The voice was that of a great, lumpy boy, the terror of the youngsters in the vicinity of Macgregor's abode, a coarse creature, who never herded with fellows of his own size, but prowled about teasing and bullying the little ones, and even annexing their playthings when it pleased him to do so.

Little Katie looked up in terror.

"I'm no' wantin' him to hurl me," she cried to Macgregor, who was white and angry.

"She's no' wantin' ye to hurl her," he said to the bully, who had already grabbed one of the handles.

"I'll gi'e her a faur quicker hurl nor you," said the bully, with an ugly laugh. "Louse yer haun'!"

"I'll no'!"

"I'll shin gar ye louse it."

"I'm no' wantin' to len' ye ma barra," said Macgregor.

Katie rose to her feet. "Dinna len' him it," she said, making a face at the tormentor.

"Gi'e's nane o' yer lip," said the latter. "Get in yersel', Macgreegor," he added, with an attempt at pleasantness, "an' I'll gi'e ye a graun' hurl."

"I'm no' wantin' a hurl frae you," said Macgregor, retreating into the close.

The bully vented some language which need not be repeated, and tried to jerk the barrow from its owner's grasp. But Macgregor held on gamely, and a desperate struggle occupied about two minutes, during which Katie looked at her hero in fear and trembling, and longed for the appearance of Willie Thomson or another of his friends.

Suddenly there was a nasty cracking sound, and Macgregor was left with one leg of his barrow in his hands, while the bully laughed loudly as he found himself in possession of the remainder.

"Ye've broke ma barra," screamed the youngster, tears of rage and grief starting to his eyes, and he made an onslaught with the sundered leg upon the villain, who at first grinned scornfully, but soon found it necessary to defend himself. Macgregor caught him a nice thwack over the knuckles, causing him to drop the barrow; but a moment later the valiant one was in the other's clutches and being cruelly cuffed.

Katie could bear no more. With a cry of childish wrath, she fell upon the bully from behind, and put in some really effective work with her hands and feet. Still, the battle might have been to the strong had not Willie Thomson appeared on the scene. Willie was not muscular, but he had an idea. Signing to Katie to keep clear, he suddenly grabbed the bully's right leg, and brought him to the ground with Macgregor on top. The latter shook himself free, and stood up a sorry picture.

The bully rose with a roar, and made for Willie Thomson, who dashed off, and did not reach his own door a second too soon. There he had the good fortune to meet his elder brother, who administered to the bully a trouncing which would have been longer but for the arrival of a policeman, but which could not have been stronger while it lasted.

And, left to themselves, Katie and Macgregor dissolved in tears. She was the first to see clearly, and lo! Macgregor, with his broken barrow, his bruised, tear-stained countenance, and his gusty sobs of pain and wrath – Macgregor was still her hero!

"Dinna greet ... Never heed," she said over and over again in her anxiety to comfort him.

"Ma barra's broke," he groaned.

"Ay, but it's easy mendit. Wull ye no' gang hame to yer maw, noo?"

He shook his head and grieved afresh, though he hated to weep in anybody's, especially in a girl's presence.

Katie choked, and recovered herself. "Come," she said gently. "I'll help ye up the stair wi' yer barra, an' I'll tell yer maw how thon muckle sumph set on ye, an' hoo ye lickit him."

"But – but I – I didna lick him."

"Aweel, ye vera near did it. Ye wisna feart, onywey. I ken ye wisna feart."

Her words were balm to his sore spirit. But he was feeling weak and shaky, and it was a while ere the tears ceased.

"Wipe yer e'en on ma pinny," said Katie at last; and somehow he bowed and obeyed her.

Then together they slowly climbed the stairs, bearing the damaged barrow; and, waiting for the door to open, Katie spoke softly and encouragingly, while Macgregor sniffed violently to keep the tears from flowing afresh. She would fain have kissed her hero, but something forbade her.

Wee Macgreegor Again

An Invitation

"IT'S frae Mistress Purdie," said Lizzie, handing the letter which she had just perused to her husband, who was reading his paper and smoking his pipe in the fulness of contentment in front of the kitchen fire.

"Dod," exclaimed John, grinning as he examined the envelope, "but yer guid-sister's gettin' up in the warl' wi' her fancy paper an' mauve ink. Whit's she writin' ye aboot?"

"Luk at the inside, an' ye'll see. I wis expectin' the letter, fur I seen her yesterday, an' she tell't me it wis comin'.'."

"Ye never tell't me ye seen her, Lizzie."

"Aw, weel, I wantit to let ye get a bit surprise," said Lizzie with a faint smile.

John extracted a gilt-edged card from the envelope. "Whit's a' this, whit's a' this?" he cried, staring at the card upon which was written in bright purple the following:

Mr. and Mrs. Robert Purdie
requests the pleasure of
MR. and MRS. ROBINSON'S
company for dinner on Thursday
evening, 25th December, at 7 o'clock P.M.

John read it through aloud, and then gaped at his wife.

"Weel?" said Lizzie interrogatively.

"At seeven o'clock!" muttered John feebly.

"Tits, man!" said his wife. "Can ye no' see we're askit to a Christmas dinner?"

"Oh, that's it, is't?" And John burst into a great guffaw.

"I dinna see muckle to lauch aboot," his wife said a little impatiently.

"It's a serious maitter, nae doot," returned John, continuing his laughter. "You an' me, wumman, askit to a Christmas dinner! Haw, haw, haw! An' yer guid-sister wis tellin' ye a' aboot it, wis she?"

"Ay," said Lizzie shortly.

"Weel, tell us whit she said. Dod, but her an' her man are the gentry noo! No' but whit it wisna unco kind o' them to ask us to their pairty. But I doot we'll no' be able to eat muckle sae shin efter wur tea."

"Aw, we'll jist miss wur tea that nicht, John," said Lizzie, recovering her good humour. "Fur Mistress Purdie tell't me she wis gaun to gi'e us a graun' dinner – soup, an' a turkey wi' sassingers roon' aboot, an' plum puddin', an' pies, an' frit furbye."

"I'm thinkin' ye wud be as weel to get a botle o' yer ile ready fur me, Lizzie, for this day week," he observed jocularly. "But whit wey is yer guid-sister no' ha'ein' her pairty at Ne'erday?"

"Aweel, John, she thinks it's mair genteel-like to haud Christmas. As ye ken, I'm no' jist in love wi' ma guid-sister, but Rubbert has aye been a rale kind brither, an' I wudna like to refuse to gang to the pairty. An' I'm rale gled ye're pleased aboot it."

"I didna say I wis pleased aboot it, wumman, fur I'm no' up to gentry weys," said John seriously. Then he suddenly brightened as his son entered the kitchen. "Here he comes wi' as mony feet 's a hen!" he cried merrily. "Come awa', Macgreegor, an' gi'e's yer crack. Hoo's Wullie the nicht?"

"Fine," returned Macgregor. "Wullie's Maw bakit tawtie scones fur wur tea."

"Did she that? Aweel, ye'll be gettin' mair nor scones this time next week, ma mannie! Ye'll be gettin' turkeys, an' pies, an' sassingers, an' terts, an' orangers, an' – "

"Whisht, man, whisht!" cried Lizzie in dire dismay.

"Och, it's nae hairm tellin' Macgreegor aboot the guid things he'll be gettin' at his Aunt – "

"Is't a pairty, Paw?" asked Macgregor delightedly.

"Deed, ay! Yer Aunt Purdie's gaun to dae the thing in style! It's to be a rale high-class Christmas dinner! Whit think ye o' that?"

Lizzie groaned helplessly.

"I like ma Uncle Purdie awfu' weel," observed Macgregor, "an' I like sassingers an' terts furbye."

"John, John!" broke out the unhappy Lizzie. "Ye've dune it noo!"

"Whit ha'e I dune, dearie?" her husband asked in amazement.

"I'll tell ye efter. But, fur mercy's sake, dinna cheep anither word aboot the pairty the noo."

"Vera weel, wumman," said John, in a state of complete bewilderment.

"Is turkeys guid fur eatin', Paw?" inquired Macgregor, whose vision of future delicacies prevented him noting the disturbed condition of his parents.

"Aw, it's no' bad. I tastit a turkey yinst, an' I liket it weel enough. But we'll no' heed aboot turkey the noo. Yer Maw's feart ye'll dream aboot bubbly-jocks an' sassingers till ye think ye've ett dizzens, an' then she'll be fur gi'ein' ye ile." John patted his son's head, and tried to laugh, but failed.

"I'm awfu' gled we're gaun to the pairty," said Macgregor.

"Ay, ay," said his father. "But keep quate fur a wee, an' I'll tell ye a story."

The story was of sufficient interest to keep the youngster from the tabooed subject till bed-time, but when his mother was tucking him in he murmured sleepily:

"I – I'll behave masel' awfu' weel at Aunt Purdie's pairty, Maw."

"Aw, wee Macgreegor!" whispered Lizzie, checking a sigh, as she clapped and kissed him.

With a lump in her throat she returned to her husband, and regarded him reproachfully.

"John, John," she said at last. "Wull ye never be discreet? Ye kent fine Macgreegor canna gang to the pairty."

"No' gang to the pairty?" He sat up, staring at her. "Whit fur no'?"

"Jist because he wisna askit."

"But – but Macgreegor likes pairties!"

"Ay; that's a' richt. But I tell ye, Macgreegor wisna askit."

John's countenance turned very red. "An' whit wey wis he no' askit?" he demanded, almost fiercely.

"Oh, man, man, it's no' the thing fur a wean ava'. An' supposin' Macgreegor had been askit, I wud be gey sweirt

to let him gang. But noo I dinna ken whit to dae. Ye've tell't
the wean he's to gang, an' – an' he canna gang."

"Ach, he can gang fine, Lizzie. He'll no' eat that muckle,
an' shairly yer guid-sister can mak' room fur a wee yin. Ye
can easy tell her we're bringin' Macgreegor."

"Wud ye ha'e me affrontit, John?" cried Lizzie.

"Toots, havers! She kens fine, onywey, we wudna gang
wantin' Macgreegor. Deed, ay!" he added, struck by a
happy thought, "that'll be the reason she didna fash to write
his name on the caird. She jist kent we wud bring him. Ye
needna be disturbin' yersel', dearie."

Lizzie shook her head mournfully.

"They tell me ye're unco smairt at yer wark, John, an'
maybe that's enough for a man; but – but aweel, I daursay
ye dae yer best." She heaved a great sigh and took up her
knitting.

A minute passed ere John said slowly, "Did yer guid-sister
say we *wisna* to bring Macgreegor?"

After some hesitation Lizzie replied, "She jist said she
supposed we wudna be feart to leave him in the hoose that
nicht, an' I tell't her I had nae doot I wud get Mistress
M'Faurlan to bide wi' him an' wee Jeannie till we got hame."

"Aw, I see... I see," said John thoughtfully. "She supposed we wudna be feart to leave him in the hoose, did she
suppose?" And suddenly his wrath got the better of him. "I
tell ye whit it is, wumman," he cried, "she didna want
Macgreegor!"

"Tits! Ye needna flee up like that, John," said his wife.
"Ye're fair rideec'lous aboot Macgreegor. Whit wud ye say
if I wis to tak' the huff because wee Jeannie wisna askit?"

"Wee Jeannie's no' heedin' aboot pairties. There's time
enough fur her... There's time enough fur you to tak' the
huff, as ye ca' it, wife, when she likes pairties an' disna get
askit... Ye needna say anither word, Lizzie... I'll no' pit a
fit inside yer guid-sister's door fur a' the turkeys, an'
sassingers, an' snashters in creation! I'm jist tellin' ye!" And
John rose abruptly, caught up his cap, and stalked from the
kitchen and out of the house.

When he returned half an hour later he was calm, but absolutely firm in his determination not to be present at the Purdies' Christmas dinner.

"Them as disna want Macgreegor disna get me," he said, in reply to Lizzie's pleadings.

"My! but ye're a dour yin!" she said at last. "Hoo dae ye ken Mistress Purdie disna want Macgreegor?"

"She aye had a spite at the wean; an' fine ye ken it!" he retorted.

Lizzie wavered. She knew the aunt and nephew had never got on comfortably, yet she was anxious to keep on friendly terms with the former for her brother's sake. "I wudna ha'e let Macgreegor gang even if he had been askit," she said, after a pause. "He's ower young, an' he needs haudin' doon instead o' bein' pit furrit afore his elders. But – but I'm vexed – oh, John, I'm vexed fur the wean, fur he'll be that disappintit. Oh, I wisht ye hadna said onythin' aboot the pairty."

"'Deed, Lizzie, I wisht I hadna, tae," admitted John despondently. "But, ye see, I thocht the wean – "

"Ye'll jist ha'e to tell him we're no' gaun to the pairty efter a'," said Lizzie.

"Wud ye no' gang yersel', dearie?"

"John!"

"Weel, I thocht ye wis set on the pairty."

"Ach, John, ye ken fine I thocht you wud like it... Sins, the day! it's an unco peety... But I'm rale gled I didna tell Mrs. Purdie we wud gang fur certain."

"Ye're a wice wumman!" said her husband admiringly.

"I'll jist ha'e to tell her we canna gang. But whit aboot Macgreegor? Wull *you* tell him, John?"

"Na, na! Never let bug to Macgreegor there's to be nae pairty till I can mak' up some ither treat fur him," said John, beginning to recover his spirits.

"Whit kin' o' a treat?"

"Och, I'll tell ye when I get it a' arranged."

"Ah, but, John, ye're no' to gang an' be wasterfu'," said Lizzie warningly. "Wud it no' be best jist to tell him he'll get his treat at Ne'erday?"

"I'll see, I'll see," replied her husband. "But never let bug aboot the pairty till I tell ye. Promise, dearie."

Lizzie promised reluctantly, and John lit his pipe, which had been cold for some time, and smoked steadily for the next ten minutes without speaking a word.

"But whit am I to write to Mistress Purdie?" inquired Lizzie ere she slept that night.

"Oh," said her husband with a chuckle, "jist say we're vexed we canna gang to her pairty, because Macgreegor's ha'ein' a pairty o' his ain that nicht."

"Ma word, John!" said Lizzie, and proceeded to ask questions to which she got no answers

The next day, Friday, John was exceedingly thoughtful.

On Saturday he was grave; on Sunday he was unusually glum.

On Monday he was distinctly irritable and nervous; and on Tuesday he was wrapped in gloom.

But on Wednesday he came home to his dinner in a state of repressed excitement, and his wife made many inquiries, without receiving any satisfaction. At tea he burst out into frequent guffaws without apparent reason.

"Macgreegor's talkin' aboot naethin' but his Aunt Purdie's pairty the morn's nicht," said Lizzie, in an undertone, as she started to clear away the dishes.

"Dod, he'll get his pairty," he returned.

"Man, man," she whispered, full of curiosity, "whit's his treat to be? Tell me noo, John."

But he laughed, and rose from the table, and put on his cap.

"Here, Macgreegor, come on ootbye fur a dauner," he cried.

Father and son returned about eight o'clock.

Macgregor came first up the stair, panting and puffing with excitement and exhaustion; John followed, chuckling.

They took breath before John softly turned his key in the door. Then they crept into the little house like a pair of burglars.

Lizzie was sitting by the kitchen fire when the door flew open and her son tottered in, screaming with laughter, tripped, and fell with a squelch on something soft. He rose at once, still screaming with laughter, and the something soft was seen to be a medium-sized turkey. Macgregor picked it up and dumped it into his astounded mother's lap. Then John entered – somewhat shame-faced, to be sure – bearing sundry parcels.

But, on recovering herself, Lizzie did not look gratified.

"John," she cried, "ye've been at the savin's bank the day! Oh, John, John!"

But John laid his parcels on the dresser, and went close to his wife. "Haud the turkey, Macgreegor," he said, and then began to whisper to her.

"Ye're jist jokin'!" cried Lizzie after a minute's whispering.

"As shair's daith!" said John.

She gave a short sob. "They've really made ye foresman at the works, John!"

"Jist that."

"But ye – ye micht ha'e tell't me shinner, dearie."

"I didna like. Ye see, it wis last Thursday… But I never thocht o' speirin' aboot the place till last Thursday… But somewey I – I thocht then I wud like mair cash fur yersel', an' wee Jeannie, an' – an' fur Macgreegor. An' I says to masel' – 'Naethin' bates a trial.' … An' I tried, wumman… An' I – I got the place… I'm foresman efter the holidays… Dod, but ye're no' to greet, dearie… Ye'll no' be angry if I tell ye it wis the thocht o' Macgreegor's pairty that gi'ed me the neck to try fur the place… But the pairty's fur wursel's, an' nae-body else, fur I'm no' haudin' wi' Christmas – as a rule… Are ye pleased, Lizzie?"

Lizzie nodded, speechless.

"Paw," said Macgregor, "come on an' ha'e a scud at wur turkey. It's fine fun skelpin' t!"

The Sunday School Soiree

"IT'S an awfu' peety ye canna get in to the surree," remarked Willie Thomson to his chum, who was accompanying him to the church hall wherein an entertainment to the Sunday School children was about to be held.

Macgregor made no response, but looked exceedingly gloomy.

"If ye hadna plunkit sae mony times, ye wud ha'e gotten a ticket; but ye wis absent ower often," continued Willie, without meaning to be offensive.

"Ye wud ha'e plunkit yersel' whiles, if ye hadna been feart," retorted Macgregor.

"I wudna!"

"Ay, wud ye! An' it's jist as bad as plunkin' to spend yer bawbee on sweeties an' let on ye've pit it in the heathen mishnary boax."

"When did I dae that?" Willie loudly demanded, without, however, meeting the other's eye.

"Fine ye ken when ye done it."

"Weel, if I ever done it, I aye gi'ed ye hauf the sweeties."

"So ye did, Wullie," said Macgregor more kindly. "But ye needna think ye deserve to get in to the surree ony mair nor me. D'ye hear?"

"Ay, I hear," Willie replied with some irritation in his voice. "But ye sudna ha'e plunkit sae often, fur ye micht ha'e kent ye wudna get a ticket –"

"If ye say that again, I'll – I'll –"

"I'll no' say it again."

"We'll that's a' richt. But it wisna fair to ha'e the surree sae early this year. It's faur earlier nor last year. If I had kent it wis to be sae early I wudna ha'e plunkit till efter the surree wis ower."

"But this is an extra surree. It's the new meenister, that's peyin fur't."

"Weel, it's no' fair coontin' merks fur an extra surree. An' I dinna think it'll be a vera nice yin. Ye'll get naethin' efter the tea but twa-three hymns an' a lang lectur."

"We're to get a magic lantern an' a con*joo*rer," said Willie elatedly.

"Are ye?" said Macgregor, taken aback. "He maun be a nice meenister. But it wisna fair coontin' merks fur an extra surree… I wisht I hadna plunkit sae often."

"I wisht ye hadna," the other sympathetically returned.

The twain walked a score of yards in silence.

"D'ye think I can jink the man at the door?" enquired Macgregor suddenly.

"It's aye the beadle that tak's the tickets at the surrees," his friend replied.

"Aw! He's ower fly," said Macgregor, dolefully. "I doot I canna jink him. If it wis yin o' the teachers, I wud try it."

"Ye best no' try it wi' the beadle. I – I doot ye canna get in, Macgreegor," said Willie hopelessly.

Macgregor considered. "Can ye no' tak' a fit on the doorstep?" he asked at last. "I yinst seen a lot o' folk gettin' inside a show fur naethin' when a wife tuk a fit jist at the door."

Willie shook his head. "I dinna ken hoo to tak' a fit; an' if I wis takin' yin, they maybe wudna let me in to the surree."

"I didna think o' that, Wullie… Wud it no' dae to say I had lost ma ticket?"

"Naw! They wud speir yer name an' then luk up the book to see if ye had the richt merks. They're awfu' fly at oor Sawbath schule. Ye sudna ha'e plunkit sae mony –"

"If ye say that again, I'll –"

"I didna mean to say it, Macgreegor."

"Weel, dinna say it! … I wudna strike ye onywey. Ye're ower peely-wally."

"I'm no'!"

"Ay, are ye! … But ha'e *you* got the richt merks in the book?" enquired Macgregor abruptly.

"Ay," returned Willie, proudly.

"But I bet ye a thoosan' pound ye wudna get in if ye had lost yer ticket."

"I wud get in fine," said the virtuous William.

"Weel, ye can jist dae't! Gi'e's yer ticket!" cried Macgregor.

His friend regarded him blankly.

"Come on! Gi'e's yer ticket," Macgregor repeated pleasantly. "I'll gi'e ye ma next Setturday penny, if ye'll promise to gi'e us hauf whit ye buy wi' 't."

Still the other looked woefully undecided. They had now almost reached the door of the hall.

"Ma next Setturday penny," said Macgregor again. "Come on, Wullie."

Willie, who got no regular Saturday penny, and who usually depended on his chum's bounty for his weekly treat of sweets, was certainly tempted by the proposal; but after a brief period of consideration he said, "Naw," and quickened his steps.

Whereupon Macgregor exclaimed, "I'm no' in wi' ye ony mair," and turned away.

This was too much for Willie. He turned also and hastened after Macgregor, crying, "I'll gi'e ye the ticket, I'll gi'e ye the ticket!"

"Wull ye?" said his friend, halting.

"Ay. But – but I'll no' try to get in to the surree."

"Whit?"

"I'll let ye gang in instead o' me."

"Nae fears! I wudna dae that, Wullie. No' likely!"

"Wud ye no' gang in wi'oot me?"

"Awa' an' bile yer heid! As if I wud gang in wi'oot ye! Jist you gi'e me the ticket an' come to the door efter me, an' I'll shin get ye in. An' if they'll no' let ye in, I'll gi'e ye back yer ticket, an' I'll gang awa' hame."

The ticket being transferred, they approached the entrance to the hall of happiness.

"Wullie," said Macgregor in a whisper, "can ye no' greet?"

"Whit wey?"

"To mak' the beadle vexed fur ye because ye've lost yer ticket. Ye see? ... Try an' greet, Wullie."

"I canna," said Willie, despairingly. "I'm ower big to greet."

"Weel, try an' luk awfu' meeserable."

Through sheer nervousness Willie succeeded in doing so, and they climbed the few steps to the doorway, where the church officer had taken his stand.

Macgregor held out the ticket, and carelessly pointing to his friend, who looked like running away, remarked:

"This yin's lost his ticket."

"Eh?" said the beadle.

"I'm sayin' he's lost his ticket."

"Whaur did he loss it?"

"Ootbye."

"Mphm. He's no' the first yin that's lost his ticket the nicht," the beadle observed severely. "Whit's yer name?" he demanded of Willie.

"Wullie Thomson."

"Wha's yer teacher?"

"Maister M'Culloch."

The beadle passed in several children who presented their tickets, and then, opening the swing-doors, bawled across the hall, "Maister M'Culloch, ye're wantit, please."

"I'll wait fur ye inside, Wullie," hurriedly whispered Macgregor, afraid of meeting the young man who was his teacher as well as Willie's.

"But – but if he winna let me in," said Willie.

"If he winna let ye in, I'll come oot again. Ye needna be feart, Wullie." And Macgregor disappeared through the swing-doors.

Two minutes later he was joined by his chum.

"I kent ye wud get in," said Macgregor.

"Ay," said Willie, adding, "but *you're* nickit, Macgreegor."

"Did he see me?"

"Ay; he seen ye!"

"Is he gaun to pit me oot?"

"I dinna ken. He jist askit me whit wey ye didna wait ootside fur me. But he wis rale nice. He wisna angry at me fur gi'ein' – I mean, fur lossin' – ma ticket."

"Wis he no'? Come awa' this wey, Wullie. I'm no' wantin' him to catch me."

"Maybe he wudna pit ye oot," said Willie, following his friend. "He's rale kind. D'ye mind when ye fell in the glaur an' he cleaned yer face wi' his guid hanky?"

"Ay. But I'm no' wantin' him to speak to me the nicht. We'll get a sate at the back thonder."

"But we'll no' see the magic lantern an' the conjoorer as weel there," the other objected.

"We'll gang furrit when they screw doon the lichts fur the lantern. Come on! There a man gi'ein' oot the pokes, an' thonder anither comin' wi' the tea."

"Haud yer tongue," said a little girl beside them; "the meenister's gaun to ask a blessin'."

"Aw, *you*'re here, Maggie, are ye?" retorted Macgregor as jauntily as possible, recognising a dweller in his own street who usually saluted him by putting out her tongue.

"Ay, it's jist me. Hoo did ye get in, Macgreegor?" she enquired with an unpleasant grin, immediately the brief grace was finished.

"Through the door," replied Macgregor smartly.

"An' ye'll gang oot through the door gey shin," Maggie exclaimed unkindly. "I ken fine ye had nae ticket. Ye're jist a cheat! An' cheatery'll choke ye!"

Fortunately most of the youngsters were already being served with tea and bags of buns, otherwise more heads would have turned in Macgregor's direction.

"If ye wisna a lassie, I wud knock the face aff ye!" the boy muttered wildly. "I'm no' a cheat!"

"I ken ye're no' a cheat, Macgreegor," said the small voice of another little girl.

"Ye dinna ken him, Katie," said Maggie sharply.

"Ay; I ken him. He wudna be a cheat," returned Katie gently, with a shy glance at her hero.

But Willie was dragging his friend away to another part of the hall, and the latter took no notice of his girl champion. Perhaps he was feeling ashamed.

Twenty minutes later Willie genially observed: "I've ett mair nor you, Macgreegor."

"Ye've a bigger mooth," returned Macgregor sulkily. He

felt that nearly everyone was watching him, and Maggie's words rankled.

After tea the minister delivered a very brief address on Honesty and Truth, and the youngster, though he assumed his most unrepentant expression, trembled inwardly, and was glad when the speaker finished. Then came the conjurer, but it was not until the lights were lowered for the magic lantern item of the entertainment that Macgregor began to feel free to take his pleasure with the other children.

"We'll gang furrit noo," he whispered to Willie, and in the dim light the twain crept forward and crushed themselves into a seat well in front, much to the indignation of its occupants. Indeed, a disturbance seemed inevitable, when happily the operator uncapped the lantern and the first picture shone upon the screen.

"If ye kick me again," said Macgregor, hoarsely, to the boy next him, "I'll gi'e ye a shot on the nose!"

"Keep quiet, Macgregor," said a voice from the bench behind, and the voice was that of Mr. M'Cullloch, his teacher.

Macgregor kept *very* quiet throughout the lantern exhibition.

As the children departed from the hall, each received a bag of sweets and shook hands with the minister and also with his or her teacher.

For a moment Macgregor was tempted to make a bolt for freedom, but his courage prevailed, and, after receiving his sweets, he kept his place in the line of boys and girls that filed slowly towards the door. And – strange thing! – he received as kindly a look and handshake from the minister as did any of the other scholars. So surprised was he that he dropped the sweets, and lost his place in the line, having to stand aside till all had passed. And then he found himself shaking hands with the minister a second time.

A nasty choky feeling came in his throat as he approached his teacher. Where was the latter's severe and vengeful look?

"Well, Macgregor," said Mr. M'Culloch ever so kindly, laying a light hand on the boy's shoulder.

Macgregor gave a queer, gulping sound. "I'm no' wantin' the sweeties!" he cried, and, shoving the bag into the teacher's hand, he rushed from the hall.

Willie was waiting for him in the street. "Did ye catch it frae Maister M'Culloch?" he enquired.

"Naw," said Macgregor sharply.

They walked some distance in silence, Willie observing that his chum was in trouble, but knowing from experience that the latter was not always grateful for unsolicited sympathy.

But at last Willie said in a shamed manner, "I – I think I'll no' buy sweeties again wi' ma heathen mishnary boax bawbee."

The other made no remark, and there was another long silence, broken again by Willie.

"Are ye gaun to the schule next Sawbath?" he asked timidly.

"I'll see."

This was not encouraging, so Willie changed the subject, by starting a rather one-sided discussion on the conjurer and the magic lantern, which was kept up till they came to the parting of their homeward ways.

"They're awfu' guid sweeties we got the nicht," remarked Willie, conveying a couple from his pocket to his mouth.

"Ay," assented Macgregor dismally, and turned abruptly away.

He walked slowly home, and when he reached the house his father was waiting for him at the door.

"Ye furgot yer sweeties at the surree, Macgreegor."

"Eh?" cried the boy, taken aback.

"Yer teacher wis here the noo an' left thur fur ye. He didna want ye to be disappintit. Ye're the lucky yin!" said his father, laughing and bringing *two* bags from behind his back.

His son smiled broadly, it might even be virtuously.

Granpaw Comes To Tea

"IT wud be gey cauld on the boat," said Mrs. Robinson to her father, who had just arrived from Rothesay.

"It wis a' that," returned Mr. Purdie. "But ye're fine an' cosy here, Lizzie. Ye ken hoo to mak' a fire," he added approvingly, stretching his hands to the blaze.

"I'm aye thenkfu' fur plenty meat an' plenty coals. I hope ye'll get as guid a fire at Rubbert's hoose. Mistress Purdie thinks mair o' her graun' freens' firesides nor her ain, I doot." Lizzie could not resist a hit at her sister-in-law now and then.

"Och, wumman," said Mr. Purdie pleasantly, "ye're no' to be ower severe on yer brither's guidwife. Ye sud try to mind she hasna got a Macgreegor an' a wee Jeannie; an' maybe that's the reason she's kin' o' daft aboot comp'ny an' pairties."

"Weel, maybe ye're richt, fayther," admitted Mrs. Robinson, somewhat unwillingly. "A' the same, I'm rale gled ye cam' here fur yer tea afore ye gaed to stop wi' Mistress Purdie an' Rubbert. But wud ye no' be the better o' a taste o' speerits?"

"I thocht ye didna keep onythin' in the hoose, Lizzie," said the old man.

"John said I wis to be shair an' ha'e a dram in the hoose in case ye needit it," said Lizzie, producing a small bottle from the dresser drawer.

"Deed, it wis rale kind o' John to mind an auld man. It's a guid sign when the young minds the auld Lizzie."

"Hoots! ye're no' to talk like as if ye wis Methusalah! John didna want ye to feel ye cudna get a taste if ye wantit it. I daursay John wud like a dram hissel' whiles, an' I wudna be interferin'; we've never even spoke aboot it; but I jist ken, since the day Macgreegor wis born, John's been teetotal, except fur maybe a gless at the New Year, an' the Fair, an maybe a mairriage. Ay, John's a rale – "

"Ye've got a rale proper man, ma lass," observed Mr.

Purdie gently, as he helped himself to a moderate supply of whisky.

"Och, John's weel enough," said Lizzie, afraid of having been sentimental.

"He's shairly late the nicht," said her father, consulting his fat silver watch.

"Aweel, ye see, fayther, he's foresman noo, an' he disna aye get awa' prompt to the meenit. Macgreegor's awa' oot to meet him. He gangs near every nicht, an' they come hame thegither, chatterin' an' lauchin' like a pair o' weans. Whiles they tell me their bit joke, but I canna say I see muckle to lauch at. Hooever, if they're pleased, I suppose that's a' aboot it."

"An' ye canna help bein' pleased yersel', if they're pleased – eh?" said the old man, chuckling. "Weel, weel, ye wudna be yersel', ma dochter, if ye let on ye wis as pleased as ye kent ye wis. Ye never wis the yin to mak' a hullabaloo aboot things that pleased or hurtit ye – no' even when ye wis a bit lassie … Weel, here's ma love to you an' yer man an' yer weans! Ye'll be a prood wumman aboot John bein' appintit foresman. Dod, ye needna be pretendin' ye're no'! I'm thinkin' ye'll be removin' to a bigger hoose some fine day afore lang."

"Na!" she replied soberly. "We'll no' move fur twa year onywey."

"Is that John's wey o' thinkin'?"

Lizzie smiled slightly. "John wis fur movin' at the term, but I tell't him he wisna to gang an' get peery heidit ower his bit rise. Ye maun creep afore ye rin, as Solyman says."

"I hope ye didna vex yer man," said Mr. Purdie seriously.

"Vex him? 'Deed no! But if it wisna fur me haudin' him doon, John wudna be lang afore he wis spendin' a' he got. He's that kind-hertit an' free, ye ken," she said with a touch of warmth; "but as lang as I'm spared he's no gaun to get wastin' his siller… Whit's that ye're sayin', Duckie?" she asked wee Jeannie, who was playing about the floor. "D'ye hear yer Paw comin'?"

"Paw and Greegy tummin'," replied wee Jeannie; "tummin' wi' gundy," she added.

"Na, na, dearie; this isna the gundy nicht," said her mother gently.

"I wudna be ower shair o' that," remarked Mr. Purdie. "Come to yer granpaw, daurlin', an' ripe his pooches."

"Aw, fayther," cried Lizzie. "But wee Jeannie mauna get ony till she's had her tea... Here John an' Macgreegor noo."

There was a sound of mingled laughter, and a moment later father and son entered to exchange hearty greetings with Mr. Purdie.

"An' hoo's ma auld freen, Macgreegor?" enquired the old gentleman genially of his grandson, while John was enjoying a wash, and Lizzie, having laid the tea-table, was hastily giving her daughter a tidy-up.

"I'm fine," returned Macgregor, adding "thenk ye," as he caught a look from his mother. "Wis ye dry, Granpaw?" he asked, noticing the glass in Mr. Purdie's hand.

"Haud yer tongue, an' dinna ask impiddent questions," exclaimed Lizzie, while John guffawed into the towel with which he was polishing his face.

Mr. Purdie chuckled good humouredly. "Weel, I wisna jist whit ye wud ca' dry, Macgreegor, but yer Maw thocht I wis needin' a wee drap meddicine," he replied, emptying the glass.

"It wisna ile?" began the boy. "Naw, I ken it wisna ile, fur ye wud ha'e got ile in a spune. Wis ye badly on the boat?" he enquired sympathetically. "Wis ye throwin'?"

Fortunately Lizzie did not hear, and Mr. Purdie chuckled again, and explained that he had not had a rough passage, but only a very cold one.

"Wis the boat no' whumlin'?" asked the boy, obviously disappointed. "I like when the boat's whumlin' aboot. I'm no' feart. Whit kin' o' meddicine did Maw gi'e ye? Wis it unco ill to tak'?"

"Deed, I've swallowed waur, Macgreegor."

"Did ye no' get ony carvies to pit awa' the taste? Carvies is awfu' guid efter ile."

"Na; yer Maw didna think I needit carvies. An' hoo are ye gettin' on at the schule?"

"Fine! I gi'ed Geordie M'Culloch a bashin' the day," whispered Macgregor, so that his mother should not hear.

"Ah, but ye sudna fecht," said Mr. Purdie, choking back a chuckle, and looking solemn. "Ye ken the pome – 'Let dugs delight to bark an' bite' – "

"It's a daft pome! Geordie M'Culloch needit a bashin'."

"Whit wis he daein' to ye?"

"Naethin'. He's feart fur me."

"Ah, but ye sudna strike a laddie less nor yersel'."

"He's faur bigger nor me, an' he wis stealin' pincils frae the wee yins, an' I tell't him to gi'e back the pincils, an' he said he wudna, an' I bashed him, an' he gi'ed back the pincils, an gaed awa' bummin'."

"Weel, weel... An' whit aboot yer spellin'? Ye'll be able to spell lang words noo."

"I'm no heedin' aboot spellin'."

"But ye maun pey attention to yer lessons, Macgreegor. Ye'll no' be dux, I doot, frae the wey ye speak aboot spellin'."

"Naw, I'm no' dux."

"Whaur are ye?"

"Second fit," said Macgregor, after a little hesitation.

"Ye'll no' like that?"

"Ay; I like it fine. Wullie Thomson's fit, an' him an' me likes sittin' thegither."

"But that'll never dae," said Mr. Purdie; and he was about to give some kindly advice when Lizzie summoned them all to the tea-table.

"Noo, wait till yer Granpaw asks the blessin'," said Lizzie to Macgregor, who was reaching out for a slice of hot toast – the "outside" bit – which lay on the top, and which he particularly desired.

Old Mr. Purdie bowed his head and murmured a simple grace, at the end of which Macgregor's eager hand went forth again.

"Pass the toast to yer Granpaw," commanded his mother.

Macgregor obeyed, but, his mother being busy with the teapot, he took the opportunity of whispering to his grandfather – "Dae ye no' like the inside best?"

"I'm no' heedin', ma mannie. Maybe the ootside's a wee thing cheuch fur ma auld grinders."

"Ay; it's awfu' cheuch," said Macgregor. "But I'll tak' it if ye like, Granpaw." Which he did, much to the amusement of John, who had pretended not to notice anything.

"Maw! am I no' to get an egg?" said Macgregor in a hoarse undertone to his mother, as his father and grandfather chipped the tops of their eggs.

"Hoots! laddie, ye're no' needin' an egg," replied Lizzie, as she stirred a hot mess of bread and milk for her daughter.

"Gi'e him an egg, Lizzie," said John.

"Tits! John," she returned.

"Whit wey can I no' get an egg, Maw?" enquired the son.

"Jist because ye're no' needin' an egg; an' there's no' anither in the hoose, onywey."

"Ha'e, Macgreegor," said his father, a few seconds later, "here the tap aff mines." (It was really half the egg.)

"An' here the tap aff mines," said Mr. Purdie.

With a brief acknowledgment Macgregor fell to.

"Ye jist spile the wean," said Lizzie, frowning.

"I like fried eggs better nor biled," observed the boy when he had cleaned the shells.

Lizzie, with a great effort, restrained herself.

After tea Mr. Purdie produced his offerings of sweets, and while the young folks enjoyed them the elders had an opportunity for a short "crack." When the old man said he must go, John rose to accompany him. So did Macgregor, donning his woollen muffler and bonnet in the twinkling of an eye.

"Whit are ye efter noo, Macgregor?" enquired his mother.

"I'm gaun ootbye wi' Paw and Granpaw, Maw."

"Ye're no' gaun ower the door the nicht," said Lizzie, decidedly.

John was silent, looking uncomfortable; Mr. Purdie
appeared to be trying to pretend he did not notice anything.

"Whit wey, Maw?" said Macgregor.

"Jist because I say ye're no' to gang," said Lizzie.

"Paw said I wud get, Maw."

"Eh? When did yer Paw say that?"

"When we wis comin' hame the nicht."

"Ay, Lizzie," put in John, "I tell't the wean he wud get
oot wi' his Granpaw. An' whit fur no'?"

Lizzie ignored the appeal. "Ha'e ye learned yer spellin'
fur the morn?" she demanded of her son.

"Ay."

"When did ye learn it? No' in the hoose, I'm shair."

"Comin' hame frae the schule."

"Hoo cud you learn it comin' hame frae the schule,
laddie ?"

"Me an' Wullie Thomson gaed up a close, an' he heard
me, an' I heard him."

"H'm!" muttered Lizzie, dubiously.

"Bring yer book to me an' I'll hear ye."

It was without much alacrity that Macgregor brought his
book and showed his mother the place.

"Can ye spell 'people'?" she asked.

"Ay."

"Aweel, let me hear ye spell it."

"P – E –" began the boy.

"John," said Lizzie to her husband, "it ill becomes ye to
mak' faces. Awa' oot to the stairheid an smoke yer pipe."
And poor John, who had been trying to signal "O" to his
son by lip language, reluctantly obeyed.

"Rest ye a meenit," said Lizzie to Mr. Purdie, who also
made to depart. Then she resumed the lesson. "Come awa',
dearie. Spell 'People.' "

"P – E – O – P –"

"Ay; but that's no' it a'."

" – L – E," said Macgregor at last.

"Richt!" said Lizzie. "Spell 'Money.' "

He spelled it, and the next half-dozen words correctly, though with some hesitation.

"Ye're a wee thing slow, but ye're better at the spellin' nor I thocht. 'Deed, it's the first nicht ye've been kin' o' shair o' the words. Weel, jist yin mair; an' if ye spell it richt, ye'll gang wi' yer Granpaw. Spell 'Receive.' "

"R – E – C –"

"Weel, whit mair?"

(At this point Mr. Purdie nearly put his finger in his left eye.)

"Come awa'," said Lizzie, encouragingly. She was really quite proud of her son.

"R – E – C – IEVE," said Macgregor in a burst of triumph.

"Ye're wrang," said Lizzie sadly.

Grandfather Purdie smote his breast.

"Aw! Did I tell ye wrang, ma wee man?" he cried. "I aye had a deeficulty wi' thae – " He stopped in confusion.

The most valuable variety of humour is that which enables people to laugh when they find they have been deceived – to laugh away the natural anger.

Lizzie laughed eventually, and Macgregor had his own way. But she rose half-an-hour earlier the next morning – which was pretty early – roused up her son, and drummed the spelling into him. If it hadn't been for Willie Thomson he *might* have reached the top of the class.

At The Circus

MRS. ROBINSON wrung her hands. "Oh, laddie, laddie," she cried, "whit wey did ye gang an' file yer nice collar?"

"It wisna me, Maw," returned her son. "It wis wee Jeannie. She wis wantin' me to taste her jeely piece, an' I wisna wantin' to taste it, an' she tried fur to pit it in ma mooth, an' I tell't her no' to dae't, but she played dab at me wi' her piece, an' jaupit ma collar wi' the jeely."

"Whit wey did ye dae that, Jeannie?" asked Mrs. Robinson of her daughter, who, having absorbed her "piece," was sitting on the floor, her countenance bright with smiles and jelly.

"Gi'e Greegy jeely piecey," said wee Jeannie pleasantly. She was just beginning to pronounce her "r's" properly, and "Greegy" was, as nearly as can be described on paper, the name she gave to her brother.

"Aw, ma wee duckie-doo!" exclaimed the mother, with a gush of affection, picking up her daughter and cuddling her, "ye wis fur gi'ein' a taste o' yer piece to Macgreegor, wis ye? Ye daurlin'! But ye sudna ha'e pit jeely on his braw clean collar. Macgreegor's gaun to the circus wi' his Granpaw Purdie, ye ken, an' he canna gang wi' a jeely collar. Eh, ma lamb?"

Wee Jeannie smiled complacently as her mother set her on the kitchen bed, and began to play contentedly, if somewhat noisily, with a metal dish-cover and a porridge spurtle.

"Here, Macgreegor," said Lizzie, "an' I'll get ye anither collar... Mercy me! ye've got jeely doon yer neck."

"Ay; an' in ma lug furbye."

"Tits! Ye sudna ha'e let her jaup ye wi' her piece," sighed his mother, as she set to work with the wet corner of a towel.

"If I hadna let her jaup me," returned Macgregor, "she wud ha'e grat. She aye greets when she disna get daein' whit she likes."

"Aweel, dearie, ye see she's but a wean," observed Lizzie

soothingly, polishing her son's neck till it glowed.

"Ach, ay. But a' lassies greets when they dinna get whit they like... Dicht the inside o' ma lug, Maw. It's that sticky."

"Puir laddie. Never heed," said his mother sympathetically. "Ye maun aye be kind to wee Jeannie, an' when wee Jeannie grows big she'll pey ye back. Wull ye no', ma wee pet lamb?" she enquired, turning to her daughter, who was battering away industriously on the dish-cover with the spurtle. "Ye'll be rale kind to yer brither when ye're a big lassie, wull ye no'?"

"Gi'e Greegy jeely piecey," replied wee Jeannie promptly.

"I'm no' wantin' ony mair jeely pieces," said her brother. "Ma face isna needin' to be washed, Maw."

"Hoots! Ye canna be ower clean, ma mannie," said Mrs. Robinson. "Keep yer een shut, an' dinna let the sape in... There, noo! Ye're a fine caller laddie to gang to the circus wi' yer Granpaw Purdie. See! Tak' the towel, an' dry the corners yersel'... An' here a braw clean collar... Dinna waggle yer heid till I sort yer tie... Mphm! Ay! Ye're a' richt noo... There's somebody at the door. Rin, an' see if it's yer Granpaw."

They took their seats some little time before the commencement of the morning performance, and for five minutes or so Macgregor, who had never before been in a circus, sat dumb and stared about him, heedless of his grandfather's remarks. When he did speak, he said:

"Whit wey ha'e thon sates ower thonder got wee tidies?"

"Oh, thon sates is the best sates," replied Mr. Purdie.

"We've faur brawer tidies nor thon. We've a mauve tidy wi' a yella paurrit on it, an' a green yin wi' bew spotes a' ower it, an' – "

"Ay, ay," said Mr. Purdie. "Are ye fur a sweety, Macgreegor?"

"Thenk ye, Granpaw. I like peppermints awfu' weel. I like pittin' yin in ma gab an' fuffin' wi' ma breith. Dae *you* like fuffin' wi' yer breith, Granpaw? Phoo-oo! Phoo-oo! That wey, ye ken."

"Aweel, Macgreegor, I aye jist sook it slow," Mr. Purdie replied, smiling as he placed a peppermint on his tongue.

"Aw, but ye sud try fuffin'. Ye blaw oot, an' then ye draw in. Phoo-oo! Phoo-oo! Ye see? It's rale nice an' cauld an' nippy. Oh there the baun!"

The orchestra struck up the usual martial air, and people began to occupy the higher-priced seats.

"If I wis playin' the drum I wud hit it faur harder," Macgregor observed presently. Then he turned his attention to the stalls. "Granpaw, see thon fat wife sittin' on the sate wi' the tidy — her that's gi'ein' chokelets to the wee lassie wi' the rid heid."

"Weel, whit aboot the fat wife?" asked Mr. Purdie, adjusting his specs and suppressing a chuckle.

"Is she gentry, Granpaw?"

"Ay, I wud say she wis gentry, Macgreegor."

"I wudna like if ma Maw wis like her. I wudna like ma Maw to be that fat. Thon wife's fatter nor Mistress Dumphy that bides ablow us."

"But if yer Maw wis takin' ye to sates wi' tidies, an' gi'ein' ye as mony chokelets as ye cud haud, ye wudna care if she wis fat or lean," said Mr. Purdie, trying to look solemn.

"Ay, wud I! I wudna like ma Maw to be as fat as — Oh, oh! the horses! the horses! Granpaw, see the horses!"

For some minutes Macgregor was silent, gazing at the beautiful, highly-trained creatures as they careered round the ring. At last he said:

"If I had horses like thur, I wudna whup them."

"But the man's no' whuppin' them," said Mr. Purdie. "He's jist crackin' his whup to gar them rin."

"He's no' a nice man... Whit's the folk lauchin' at, Granpaw?"

"They're lauchin' at thon man wi' the white face an' the rid neb," said Mr. Purdie, chuckling, and indicating a clown who had just entered with the searching query, "How's your mother-in-law?"

"Whit wey are they lauchin'?"

"Thon yin's the comic," explained Mr. Purdie.

"Whit wey dis he no' – My! he's tum'lin' the wulket! ...
Again! again! again! Granpaw, thon man tummilt the wulket
fower times! Whit wey dis he no' get watter on the heid?
Maw tell't me if I tummilt the wulket often I wud – Aw, I
ken the wey he disna get watter on the heid. He tummles
back furbye tum'lin' furrit!"

"Ah, but ye're no' to try tum'lin' the wulket like thon
man," whispered Mr. Purdie. "Ye micht hurt yesel'!"

"Nae fears! Me an' Wullie Thomson tried wha cud staun'
on wur heids the langest, and Wullie Thomson got bew an'
I wis jist a wee bit rid. An' staunin' on yer heid's faur waur
nor tum'lin' the wulket... Oh, my! see the faces thon man's
makin'! ... See, Granpaw, hoo the horses is fleein' roon'!
Whit wey dae they no' get dizzy? ... Granpaw! Whit's thon
man daein?"

"He's jooglin', Macgreegor."

"Aw! jooglin'? But he hisna got a joog. He's jist playin'
hissel' wi a wheen plates... Whit's he wastin' the cairds fur –
teerin' them a' in twa? ... Oh, see the knifes! Three – fower
– five! If he drappit yin on his fit, it wud cut aff his taes –
wud it no', Granpaw?"

"'Deed, wud it! But he kens better nor to drap a knife on
his taes."

"But d'ye no' think he'll maybe drap a knife, Granpaw?"

"See thon man playin' a tune on a teapot, Granpaw!"

"Ay. It's wunnerfu', is't no', Macgreegor?"

"We've a brawer teapot nor thon yin. Maw got it frae Mrs.
M'Ostrich because she broke the stroop aff wur guid yin
when she had the len' o' 't. Wur new teapot's bew, wi' white
staurs a' ower it... Whit wey dis thon man play on the
teapot? Whit wey dis he no' play on a whustle? ... I wish I
had a rid neb like the ither man."

"It's no' a real rid neb," said Mr. Purdie.

"I ken it's no' a real rid neb. It's jist pentit. But I wud like
to pent ma neb rid, an' gi'e folk frichts. Your neb's ridder
nor mine, Granpaw."

"Here the acrobats comin', Macgreegor!"

"Ay. They're a' daein' wee bit dances to theirsel's. Whit wey dae they dae wee dances, Granpaw?"

"Oh, jist fur a stairt, laddie. They're pretendin' they're shy, an' a' that, ye ken."

"They dinna luk vera shy… Oh, there yin whurlin' roon' the pole! He maun hurt his hauns gey sair… There anither sclimmin' up his freen's neck an' haudin' anither yin under his oxter; an' the yin under his oxter's stairtin' fur to sclim' up to – Oh! Granpaw, see them! … If thon yin on the top wis to fa', he wud get awfu' bashed, an' – "

"Aw, luk at the lassie wi' the rid legs!"

"Thae's no' her legs, Macgreegor; thae's her stokins."

"Whit wey is she wagglin' her feet?"

"Aw, she's dancin' jist to show the folk she's no' feart to staun' on the horse's back. She's a braw bit lassie, Macgreegor, is she no'?"

"Naw! Whit wey dis she no' ride the horse the richt wey?"

"Granpaw, thon fat wife in the sate wi' the tidy's gi'ein' the wee lassie wi' the rid heid mair chokelets."

"Are ye fur anither peppermint, Macgreegor?"

"Ay, thenk ye, Granpaw… Phoo-oo! Phoo-oo!"

"Are ye likin' the circus, Macgreegor?"

"Ay. Fine!"

"It's no' near ower yet."

"Is't no'?"

"No' hauf ower yet. Ye're no' gettin' wearit, are ye, laddie?" enquired Mr. Purdie anxiously.

"Nae fears! I like it fine!" Macgregor replied. "It's faur better nor the Sawbath schule surree… Thae peppermints is awfu' guid. Phoo-oo! … See, Granpaw! thon fat wife in the sate wi' the tidy's gi'ein' the wee lassie wi' the rid heid mair chokelets… Whit wey is the folk lauchin', Granpaw? …"

"Arms And The Boy"

"BUT it wis rale kind o' Mistress Purdie to mind Macgreegor's birthday," said Mrs. Robinson to her husband, who was critically examining a rather gaudily covered little book, entitled *Patient Peter, or The Drunkard's Son*.

"Ay; it wis rale kind o' her," replied John, slowly and without much enthusiasm.

"Efter a'," she continued, endeavouring to do justice to her sister-in-law, whom she really disliked, "it's no' the present itsel' we've got to think o', but the speerit –"

"Dod, but ye're richt there, wumman! There's nae want o' speerit aboot this book," he interrupted with a dry laugh. "*Patient Peter, or The Drunkard's Son*! That's a bonny like book to gi'e til a wean!"

"Whisht, man!" said Lizzie, checking a smile. "Ye ken fine whit I meant. An' ye're no' to let on to Macgreegor ye dinna like it. Him an' wee Jeannie'll be in the noo."

"Dis Macgreegor like it hissel'?"

"Weel, I daursay he wud ha'e liket somethin' else, John. He wantit to gi'e it til wee Joseph, the puir laddie that's been lyin' badly sic a lang while; but, of coorse, I wudna let him."

"Wee Joseph wudna be muckle the better o' this book, I'm thinkin'. But it wis unco nice o' Macgreegor to think o' his puir wee freen. I'll ha'e to gi'e him an extra bawbee fur that."

"Na, na, John!" cried Lizzie.

"Whit fur no', dearie? I tell ye, I like when the wean thinks o' ither weans. Ay; an' fine ye like it yersel'!"

"Ah, but ye see –"

"Aw, I ken ye think he sudna be rewardit fur bein' kind. But I'm shair he wudna expec' ony reward."

"Maybe no'. But –"

"But, a' the same, I like to encourage him."

"Ay; that's a' richt, but –"

Lizzie's remonstrance was here interrupted by the return of her son and daughter.

"Did ma doo like bein' ootbye wi' her big brither?" she cried affectionately.

"Ay, Maw, she likes it," replied Macgregor, who, occasionally, was good enough to oblige his mother by taking the toddling Jeannie for a short walk up and down the street. "But she gangs awfu' slow," he added, as he relinquished the small fingers, "an' she's aye tum'lin'."

"She'll shin be rinnin' races wi' ye, Macgreegor," said his father pleasantly.

"Deed, ay!" said his mother. "Ye'll shin be rinnin' races wi' Greegy – eh, ma daurlin'?"

"Lassies canna rin fast," returned the boy. "Their legs is ower wake."

"I hope ye didna let yer sister fa'," his mother interposed, as she brushed a little dust from the child's lower garment.

"I canna help her coupin' whiles, Maw," said Macgregor easily. "But I aye keep a grup o' her haun, an' I never let her fa' furrit – jist backwards; an' she jist sits doon an' disna hurt hersel' ava'."

"No' hurtit," observed the mite gravely.

"There, ye see!" said her brother triumphantly.

"I'm shair he aye tak's guid care o' wee Jeannie," put in John, appealing to his wife.

"I'm shair I never said he didna," rejoined Lizzie, patting her boy's shoulder.

John's face assumed an expression of complete satisfaction. "Here, Macgregor! come ower here till I speak to ye," he cried in a pleased voice.

Macgregor obeyed willingly, while his father fumbled in a pocket.

"John," whispered Lizzie warningly.

But John smiled merrily back to her, and then turned to his son. "I wis gaun to gi'e ye a bawbee, Macgreegor, but I hivna yin, so here a penny instead."

"Oh, John!" murmured his wife.

"Thenk ye, Paw," said Macgregor, grinning.

"D'ye ken whit it's fur, ma mannie?"

"Naw," replied Macgregor, who had already received a

bright shilling as a birthday offering from his parent. (The bright shilling, however, had been promptly taken by his mother, much to his own disgust, to the Savings Bank, along with a half-crown received from Grandfather Purdie.)

"Aweel, it's fur thinkin' o' gi'ein' yer book to puir wee Joseph," said John, stroking the back of the boy's head.

"I wud like fine to gi'e it to Joseph, Paw. Maw said I wisna," said Macgregor, with a glance at his mother, whose attention was apparently entirely taken up by her daughter.

"Yer Maw thinks it's no' jist the thing to gi'e awa' a present," John explained; adding, "an' I daursay she's richt."

"Whit wey, Paw?"

"Weel, ye see, whit wud ye dae if yer Aunt Purdie cam' to the hoose an' speirt if ye liket the book, an' if ye wis keepin' it nice an' clean? Yer Maw'll ha'e to pit a cover on it fur ye. Eh, Lizzie?"

"Ay, I'll dae that," his wife answered pleasantly. She felt that, on the whole, her man was behaving really discreetly.

"But I'm no' heedin' aboot the book, Paw, an' wee Joseph likes readin'," said Macgregor. "An' it's a daft story onywey."

"Hoo can ye say that, Macgreegor, when ye've never read it?" his mother enquired.

"I've read some o' it. There's naebody gets kilt in it. I like stories about folk gettin' their heids cut aff or stabbit through an' through wi' swords an' spears. An' there's nae wild beasts. I like stories about black men gettin' ett up, an' white men killin' lions, an' teagurs, an' bears, an, –"

"Whisht, whisht, laddie," cried Lizzie.

"Aw, the wean's fine," said John smiling. "Dod, I doot I like thur kin' o' stories best masel'."

"But I'm no' heedin' aboot this book," Macgregor went on, regarding the volume with great contempt. "It's jist aboot a laddie ca'ed Peter, an' his Maw's deid, an' his Paw's an awfu' bad man, an' he's aye strikin' Peter an' gi'ein' him crusts to eat, an' Peter jist eats the crusts an' asks a blessin' furbye, an' in the end he gangs ootbye when it's snawin' to

luk fur his Paw, an' gets drookit, an' gets the cauld in his
kist, an' dees, an' his Paw gets rin over wi' a lorrie, an' dees
tae; but Peter gets tooken up to the guid place, an' his Paw
gets tooken doon to the –"

"Whisht, Macgreegor!" cried his mother again. "Ye're no'
to –"

"It's in the book, Maw."

"Weel, weel, dearie. It's a sad story that. But ye wud be
gey sair vexed fur puir Peter deein'?"

"Naw, I wisna."

"Aw, Macgreegor!" said Lizzie reproachfully, while her
husband barely checked a guffaw.

"Weel, it's no' a true story, Maw."

"Hoo dae ye ken that?"

"I ken it fine."

"But mony a laddie's got nae Maw – puir thing! – an' a
bad Paw, an' has to eat crusts."

"Ay; but they dinna ask a blessin' fur the crusts."

John jumped up and went to the window, where he stood
with his hand to his mouth and his shoulders heaving.

"I'm vexed to hear ye speakin' like that, Macgreegor,"
said his mother sternly.

"Whit wey, Maw?"

"Because ye sudna mak' a mock o' sic things. An' maybe
the laddie in the book wis gled to get the crusts."

"But it's a' lees aboot him! I dinna believe a word!"

"Haud yer tongue, Macgreegor! That's no' the wey to
speak aboot the present yer Aunt Purdie sent ye."

"But I wud rayther ha'e gotten a pistol fur firin' peas."

"Mercy me! I'm thenkfu' ye didna get *that*! Ye wud shin
ha'e us a' blin'."

"I wudna fire it at ony o' you yins," he graciously returned,
with a glance at his relatives.

"Na, na," said Lizzie not unkindly. "That's no' the kin'
o' toy fur a laddie. An' onywey there's nae use wishin' fur
whit ye canna get, dearie. Yer Paw wudna like ye to ha'e ony
kin' o firearms aboot ye. Wud ye, John?"

John pretended not to hear.

"He micht pit oot wee Jeannie's een in mistak'," she continued. "Every day ye read i' the papers o' –"

"I *wudna!*" exclaimed Macgregor indignantly. "Wud I, Jeannie?" he cried, appealing to his little sister.

"Ay," cheerfully assented the cherub, who had been too busy playing with some blocks of wood on the floor to pay any attention to the conversation of her elders.

"Ach! She disna ken whit she's sayin'!" exclaimed the boy in disgust.

"There's mony a true word spoken in eegnorance, as Solyman says," observed Lizzie sagely.

"I wisht I had a pistol," he muttered, as if he had not heard her.

"Weel, laddie, I've tell't ye ye canna get a pistol. Whaur wud ye get the money to buy it. Eh?"

"It wud jist cost thruppence, an' I can get the money oot the bank."

"Na, na. The money maun bide in the bank, Macgreegor."

"I dinna like ma money bidin' in the bank, Maw."

"Ye'll like it some day... John, come ower here an' tell Macgreegor a story."

John left the window, but his son put on his bonnet and moved to the door.

"Whaur are ye gaun, Macgreegor?" enquired Lizzie.

"Ootbye."

"Ay; but I want to ken whaur ye're gaun."

"To see wee Joseph."

"Aw. That's a guid laddie!" said Lizzie, and John beamed approval. "But ye're no' to bide lang. An' when ye come back I'm gaun to write to yer Aunt Purdie to tell her ye like yer book."

"But I dinna like it, Maw."

Lizzie was going to speak, but John, with a laugh he could not restrain, interposed, saying: "Weel, weel, we'll see aboot the letter when Macgreegor comes back."

Macgregor returned to the table and picked up *Patient Peter*.

"Can I gi'e wee Joseph the *len'* o' ma book?"

"Dod, ay!" said John, delighted.

"'Deed, ay!" said Lizzie, also pleased. "But bide a wee, an' I'll pit a cover on it." She opened a drawer in the dresser wherein she methodically placed odds and ends, and drew forth a sheet of tough brown paper, in which she encased the covers of *Patient Peter*.

"That'll keep it clean," she said. "Tell wee Joseph to pit a bit paper at the place, an' no' to turn doon the pages."

"Ay, Maw," said Macgregor, and departed.

When he had been gone a couple of minutes John turned to his wife, and said diffidently: "It's a peety the wean's disappintit wi' the book."

"It is that," said Lizzie. "But it wudna dae to let him get everythin' he wants."

"But it's his birthday, wumman... I – I wud like fine to gi'e him a pistol."

"Weel, I never!"

"The pistol he wants isna dangerous, Lizzie."

"I'm no' sae shair o' that!"

"It's jist like a pop-gun, ye ken."

"Is't?"

"Ay. It wudna hurt a flee."

"Flees is no' that easy *hit*."

John laughed heartily. "Dod, but ye had me there! ... But wud ye no' let me buy the wean a pistol? I'll see he disna dae ony hairm... 'Deed, I mind fine when I wis a wean, I aye wantit a gun or a pistol."

"I dinna think it wud be wice to gi'e yin to Macgreegor. Ye never ken whit he'll dae."

"Hoots, toots! Say the word, an' I'll rin an' buy him yin, Lizzie. Thon book wisna the thing to gi'e a wean ava'."

"Ye sudna say that, John... But, a' the same, I dinna think it wis a vera nice book. Nae doot Mistress Purdie meant weel," she added grudgingly... "Weel, John, if ye'll promise no' to let him be reckless, I'll say nae mair aboot it... Awa' an' buy the pistol!"

And John went without delay.

As he ascended the stairs on his return in the dusk, John heard a click and something stung his cheek. This was followed by a badly stifled cackle of laughter, which he recognised.

"Macgreegor!" he exclaimed.

For a moment there was dead silence; then someone descended the flight of stairs above him.

"I thocht ye wis a brigand, Paw," said his son. "I didna hit ye, did I?"

"Ay, ye hut me!"

"Aw, Paw!" The regret in the boy's voice was intense. "Whaur did I hit ye?"

John put a finger to his cheek.

"I wis aimin' at yer hert," said Macgregor. "I'm gled I missed."

John wondered what *he* should say.

"I – I – I didna mean to hurt ye, Paw," murmured his son. "I – I didna mean it."

"But whit did ye hit me wi'? My! it wis gey nippy!"

"It wis a pea, Paw."

"Ha'e ye gotten a pistol?"

"Ay. It's wee Joseph's. He wis gaun to gi'e me it fur the book, but noo I jist got the len' o' 't. I'm vexed I hurtit ye."

"Weel, weel, we'll say nae mair aboot that, Macgreegor, but ye mauna fire at folk like thon again. Mind that, or ye'll maybe get the nick."

"I'll never dae't again, Paw."

"A' richt, ma mannie. But ye best rin ower to wee Joseph an' gi'e him back his pistol."

"But he'll no' ha'e read the book yet," objected Macgregor.

"Never heed. Let him keep the book till he's read it; but gi'e him back his pistol."

John spoke firmly, and Macgregor felt that he must obey.

"I'll gang up to the hoose," said his father, who had great difficulty in keeping his secret.

Ten minutes later Macgregor, having dutifully accomplished his errand, reached home to find his father firing peas at a mustard tin on the mantelpiece, and his mother applauding or commiserating the sportsman.

John immediately placed the weapon in the boy's hands. "There, ma mannie," he said, "there a pistol fur ye!"

Macgregor looked at his mother.

She nodded: "Be awfu' carefu' noo, dearie," she said.

Somehow the youngster was touched. "I'm no' heedin' aboot it, Maw! I'm no' awfu' heedin' aboot it!" he cried, and ran to her arms.

Later on he pointed out that it wasn't quite such a good one as wee Joseph's.

"For Granpaw Purdie"

"D'YE ken, John, that fayther an' mither'll ha'e been mairrit fifty year on the seeventh o' Mairch?" said Mrs. Robinson one January evening as, having put her little daughter to bed, she joined her husband at the kitchen fire and prepared to do some sewing.

"Is that a fac'?" exclaimed Mr. Robinson, laying aside his evening paper. "I didna think they wis that auld."

"They're no' that auld, man! Ma fayther wis jist twinty-wan, and ma mither wis nineteen when they got mairrit."

"It's you bein' the youngest that confuses me, wumman. But it's a great thing to be mairrit fifty year. Dod, is it! I suppose they'll be haudin' a dimond jubilee."

"A golden waddin' ye mean, John. I've nae doot they wull. An' I wis thinkin' it wud be nice if we gi'ed them a bit present."

"'Deed, an!" her husband agreed heartily.

"Paw," exclaimed Macgregor, looking up from his reading and spelling book which he was supposed to be studying diligently, "is Granpaw Purdie gaun to get mairrit again?"

"Na, na. He an' yer Granmaw's gaun to haud their golden waddin' – jist like haudin' Ne'erday, ye ken – because they've been mairrit fur fifty year."

"I wudna like to be mairrit fur fifty year, Paw. Wull there be a pairty?"

"Haud yer tongue, laddie," interposed his mother. "Attend to yer lessons."

"I ken them, Maw."

"Are ye shair? Whit aboot yer spellin'?"

"I ken it."

"An' the meanin's o' a' the big words? Are ye shair ye ken them a'?"

"Ay, Maw."

"Aweel, let's see the book, an' I'll hear ye twa-three meanin's … H'm! Whit's the meanin' o' the word *corporation*?"

"That's no' in the lesson."

"But it's markit."

"Ay, but that wis yesterday's. The morn's lesson's on the ither page."

"But ye sud ken the meanin' of *corporation* if it wis in yer lesson yesterday."

"I kent it, but – I furget."

Lizzie shook her head. "I doot, I doot ye're vera careless."

"I dinna see the use o' big words like thur," said the boy rebelliously.

"They're jist daft!"

"Haud yer tongue, an' tell me the meanin' o' the word *temperate*."

"It means angry – ragin'."

"Na, na. Whit's the meanin' o' the word *current*?"

"It's a kin' o' frit, Maw," he replied hopefully.

"If ye had lukit at yer lesson, ye wudna ha'e said that, Macgreegor. Can ye tell me the meanin' o' the word *halibut*?"

"It's a thing fur playin' tunes on."

"Tits, laddie! It's a fish."

"It's no' a fish in the Bible, fur we had it in wur Bible lesson on Monday, an' it wis a thing fur playin' on."

"Ach, ye mean *sackbut* – whitever that means," said Mrs. Robinson. "Na, na. I doot ye dinna ken yer meanin's. But I'll gi'e ye yin mair. Whit's the meanin' o' the word *contemplate*?"

"It means to be ashamed," replied Macgregor after considerable reflection.

"It disna! But ye micht weel be ashamed o' yersel', Macgreegor! Tak' yer book, an' dinna lift yer een frae it fur hauf-an-'oor, an' then I'll hear ye yer meanin's again, an' yer spellin' furbye."

Taking the book from his mother, Macgregor returned unwillingly to his seat, while his father, who was glad when the little examination was over, jocularly observed –

"Never heed, ma mannie. Ye'll dae a' richt next time! There's some o' yer words wud puzzle me. Eh, Lizzie?"

"Ye needna confess yer eegnorance to the wean, onywey," muttered Lizzie, with a touch of sharpness. "That's no' the wey to gar him strive wi' his lessons."

John accepted the reproof in silence, and presently changed the subject by enquiring –

"Whit wis ye thinkin' o' daein' aboot the golden jubilee – I mean the waddin', Lizzie?"

"Paw, is a julibee the same as a pairty?" asked Macgregor.

"Macgreegor," said his mother, "I tell't ye to learn yer meanin's."

"But I want to ken the meanin' o' *jubilee*, Maw."

"Weel, I'll maybe tell ye the meanin o' the word *jubilee* – no *julibee* – when ye can say yer lesson fur the morn." Mrs. Robinson turned once more to her husband. "I wis thinkin', John," she said softly, "it wud be a rale nice thing to gi'e mither a wee gold brooch – that's if ye think we can afford it. I've nae doot we wud get yin aboot–"

"Oh, I think we'll manage that, wumman. I suppose yer brither Rubbert an' his guidwife'll be gi'ein' somethin' vera graun'."

"Vera likely. Mistress Purdie wis sayin' it wis an occasion when somethin' gorgeous wis the correc' thing. But you an' me, John, cánna keep up wi' her an' Rubbert."

"An' we're no' gaun to try it. We'll jist dae wur best, Lizzie, an' gi'e yer mither as guid a present as–"

"Paw, I want to gi'e Granpaw Purdie a present," cried Macgregor, and dropped his book with a smack on the floor.

"Is that no' nice o' the wean!" John exclaimed, gazing at his wife in admiration.

"'Deed, ay," she assented, trying not to look as gratified as she felt. "But pick up yer book an' gang on wi' yer lesson, dearie, an' then we'll think aboot yer present fur yer Granpaw."

"Is the julibee shin, Maw?" he enquired as he secured his book.

"No' fur sax weeks. But gang on wi' yer lesson, like a guid laddie."

"But wull I be there, Maw?"

"We'll see, we'll see."

"'Deed, ye'll be there, Macgreegor," cried his father, "but dae as yer Maw bids ye the noo," he added, catching a look from Lizzie.

"But whit'll I gi'e to Granpaw fur his julibee?"

His mother repressed her impatience and said quietly: "Weel, dearie, yer Paw an' me'll see aboot that; an' ye better begin to save yer pennies, an' we'll add them to wur ain, an' buy somethin' fine fur yer Granpaw. Ye see? Noo try an' learn yer—"

"But I want to gi'e him a present masel'," the youngster objected.

"I doot ye'll no' ha'e enough pennies in time, Macgreegor."

"Ay, I wull."

"Let him try, Lizzie," interposed John.

"Wull ye promise no' to gi'e him mair nor his usual Setturday penny, John?" she asked quickly.

"A'richt, wumman," he stammered, reddening.

"Aweel," said his wife, with the faintest suspicion of a smile, "Macgreegor can try. Ye've sax weeks, Macgreegor, to save up fur yer Granpaw's present, so ye maun be carefu' wi' yer pennies an' no' be spendin' them as shin's ye get them on trash."

"I'll be awfu' carefu', Maw," said her son in the first flush of a generous impulse. "But I wunner whit I'll buy fur Granpaw. I wud like to buy a—"

"Noo that'll dae," his mother interrupted firmly. "It's near time fur yer bed, an' if ye canna say yer lesson when the time's up, ye'll ha'e to rise early the morn's mornin', fur I'm no' gaun to ha'e ye sittin' at the fit o' the cless a' the year roon'."

"I wudna ha'e been fit the day, if Wullie Thomson hadna been absent. It wis his turn to be fit. If he disna be fit the morn, I'll bash him!"

"If ye say anither word, Macgreegor, I'll sen' ye to bed this vera meenit, an' I'll mak' ye rise at sax. You an' Wullie micht think shame o' yersel's! I'm thinkin' Wullie's maybe no' the richt companion fur ye, an' if ye dinna dae better shin I'll no' let ye gang wi' him. Mind that!"

"Wullie's faur nicer nor ony o' the ither laddies, an'–"

"SH!"

The interjection warned Macgregor that further conversation on his part would not be tolerated, and after a glance at his father who, however, appeared to be deeply immersed in the contents of the evening paper, he bent over his lesson book and endeavoured to master, for the time being at least, the spellings and meanings of two short columns of more or less long words.

His parents refrained from discussing the Golden Wedding further in the meantime.

The weeks slipped away, and so, alas! did Macgregor's pennies. Perhaps it was more habit than actual selfishness that proved too strong for boy. The coin he received immediately after dinner each Saturday he at first mentally dedicated to the purchase of a gift for Grandfather Purdie, but somehow before the afternoon was over it lay in the till of Mrs. Juby's sweet-shop, while Macgregor and his chum Willie Thomson consumed the proceeds. It had, indeed, occurred to the careful Lizzie to offer herself as banker for the time being, but her husband had said, "Let him try whit he can save hissel'," and she had agreed, though not too hopefully.

So it came to pass that a couple of days before the old folks' "Julibee," as he persisted in terming it, Macgregor's total assets were a bankrupt pocket, a worrying conscience and a still earnest desire to show his affection for "Granpaw" with something tangible.

But love will find a way.

And on the evening before the happy anniversary he entered the home kitchen with his desire, if not his conscience, abundantly satisfied.

His parents were engaged in examining and admiring the brooch which Lizzie had chosen for her mother and the pipe John had selected for his father-in-law, and both were secretly wondering if aught had come of their son's generous resolve.

"Here, Macgreegor!" cried John, "come awa' an' tell us whit ye think o' thur."

"Canny noo, dearie, an' dinna drap the pipe," said Lizzie warningly.

"It's awfu' like the yin Granpaw broke at Rothesay last year," observed Macgregor . "I gi'ed him yin that whustled like a birdie, but I never heard him playin' on it. I wis aye to learn him. Maybe he hadna enough breith fur to play on it."

"It micht gar him hoast, ye ken," said Lizzie, "an' ye wudna like that." She and John were highly gratified to think that the new pipe might replace Mr. Purdie's old and frequently mourned favourite.

"An' hoo dae ye like the brooch, ma mannie?" John enquired, laying an arm about the boy's shoulders.

"It's gey wee," Macgregor replied after a brief inspection.

"Ay, but ye see it's gold – real gold," his mother informed him. "Gold's awfu' dear, ye ken."

"Ay, it's gey dear. I bocht a – a – gaird fur Granpaw," he blurted out suddenly.

"A whit?" exclaimed Lizzie.

"A watch-gaird," said her son, very red and fumbling in his breast pocket. "It's a rale fine yin."

"Dod, but the wean's got a present fur his Granpaw!" cried John, delighted.

Macgregor at last produced a crumpled packet, and with trembling fingers unfolded it, laying bare a glittering and fairly massive watch-chain.

"Mercy on us!" Lizzie ejaculated, as her husband took it in his hands.

"It's gold, Paw!" said the youngster in a hoarse whisper, his excitement getting the better of his conscience.

"Ay, nae doot it's gold, Macgreegor," said his father, with a discreet wink to Mrs. Robinson.

"Whit did ye pey fur this, laddie?" she asked, taking it from her husband's hand.

"Thruppence."

"'Deed, ye've dune weel, ma mannie!" said John proudly.

Whereupon the young conscience gave a nasty twinge.

"Ay, ye've dune rale weel, dearie," added his mother, pretending to feast her eyes on the clumsy imitation. "Ye've dune rale weel," she repeated softly.

Macgregor tried to speak, but could not. His readiness and jauntiness deserted him.

One of John's hands stole to the pocket where he kept his purse. "Lizzie?" he muttered enquiringly.

She frowned for a moment; then she nodded. "I'm ower weel pleased to try to prevent ye, John," she whispered.

"Macgreegor," said his father. "Yer Maw an' me's rale pleased wi' ye fur savin' yer money to buy yer Granpaw a present. I cudna ha'e dune it masel' when I wis a laddie like you. An' here a saxpence fur ye."

The boy took the gift, but the words "Thenk ye, Paw," would not pass his lips.

And all of a sudden the sixpence fell from his fingers, and rolled across the floor, and Macgregor dropped on his father's breast sobbing very bitterly.

It was some time ere the incoherent confession conveyed any meaning to the alarmed parents.

"But," said his mother at last, "if ye spent a' yer Setturday pennies, whaur got ye the money to buy the watch-gaird? Come awa', Macgreegor. Jist tell yer Paw an' me a' aboot it."

"P – Peter, Maw," mumbled the penitent.

"Wha?" asked John gently.

"P – patient Peter; or the Drunkard's Son. Oh! Oh!"

"Whit dis he mean?" the parents cried together. Then the truth dawned on Lizzie.

"Is't the nice book ye got frae yer Aunt Purdie on yer birthday?" she enquired in a shocked voice.

"Ay … But it wisna a nice book."

"But hoo did ye get the money?" asked John, signing to his wife to keep silent. "Did ye sell the book?"

"N – na. I gi'ed it til wee Joseph, an' – an' he gi'ed me his p – pistol."

"But ye've a pistol o' yer ain, Macgreegor."

"Ay. But I gi'ed wee Joseph's pistol til Wullie Thomson, an' he gi'ed me a – a – a knife an' a big bew pincil; an' I gi'ed the knife til Geordie Scott fur tippence an' the pincil til Jimsie M'Faurlan fur a penny, an' then I – I bocht the gaird, an' – an' it wisna a nice book onywey." And here Macgregor broke down.

"Lizzie," whispered John awkwardly, "wull ye no' tak' him aside ye? Aw, Lizzie!"

"Come ower aside me, laddie," she said after a brief hesitation... . "Whit am I to say to ye?" she asked, wiping his eyes. "Ye ken it wisna the richt thing to dae... . dearie. Wis it, noo?"

"N – naw. But – but I – I cudna help it, Maw."

"Weel, this is whit ye've got to dae. I'll get anither book fur wee Joseph, an' ye'll get yer ain yin back, an' ye'll gi'e me a ha'penny every Setturday till the new yin's peyed fur. Wull ye dae that?"

"Ay, Maw. But – but – "

"He's wantin' ye to say ye furgi'e him, Lizzie," said John. "Is that no' it, Macgreegor?"

The youngster nodded and hid his face on his sleeve.

His mother took him in her arms.

When he had gone to bed comforted, she picked up the sixpence that had lain neglected on the floor, remarking to her husband, "I'm gaun to keep it, John."

"D'ye think it's a vera lucky yin, wife?" he asked anxiously.

"I'm thinkin' it is," said Lizzie, who as a rule was not given to sentiment.

In Trouble

"WHAUR'S Macgreegor?" inquired John, as he hung his jacket and cap behind the kitchen door.

"I sent him a message; he'll be back the noo," replied Lizzie, who was bustling about, setting the tea-things on the table.

"Is the tea no' near ready?" he asked, picking Jeannie from the floor, and seating himself, with her on his knee, before the fire.

"Man, John, I'm rale vexed ye've got to wait the nicht," said his wife, "but I've been that thrang the day."

"Och, never heed. I'm no' in a hurry," the starving John returned. "I can thole a wee onywey," he added, producing his silver watch for his daughter's amusement.

"I'm shair it's the first time yer tea wisna ready when ye cam' hame," said Lizzie, who hated making the smallest apology.

"Dod, ay!" he answered pleasantly "An' I'm no' complainin'. Whit wis ye thrang wi' the day?"

"Gettin' ready Macgreegor's claes an' yer ain fur the nicht."

"Ach, but wha's gaun to luk at wur claes at the pantymine?"

"Oh, wis there ever sic a man?" she cried. "Am *I* no' gaun to the pantymine wi' ye?"

"Deed, are ye. But ye canna see folk's claes in the pit. Gi'e's a clean face an' a clean collar, an' that's a' I'm wantin'."

"Havers, John! Folk sees mair nor ye think. Onywey, ye've jist got to pit on yer guid claes an' – "

"No' the masher collar!" exclaimed John in alarm.

"Aw, John! An' I erned it that nice."

"But I canna lauch wi' thon thing aboot ma neck, dearie."

"Weel, weel, please yersel' aboot the collar," said Lizzie, giving in for once. "It's a mercy I got Macgreegor dressed in guid time. Whit a job I had gettin' the greese aff his guid jayket! I wis tellin' him he wud ha'e to get a daidley if he cudna tak' his meat wi'oot splutterin' hissel'."

"I doot I gi'ed him ower plenty gravy on his plate," said John, referring to the previous Sunday dinner. "But the wean's that fond o' gravy."

"If ye had to rub at greese spotes fur twa-three 'oors, ye maybe wudna be as free wi' the gravy," Lizzie retorted, a trifle sharply. "But I'll no' say ony mair aboot it," she continued, more gently. "The spotes cam' oot in the end, and the claes luk as weel as new."

"Ye're a wunnerfu' wumman!" he exclaimed admiringly... "I think I'll tak' a tate breid till the tea's ready," he said presently.

"Bide a wee, John, till Macgreegor comes wi' the eggs. I canna think whit's keepin' him," she said, glancing at the clock. "Mercy me! he's been awa' mair nor hauf an 'oor, an' I tell't him he wisna to speak to ony o' the laddies... But he canna be lang noo... Jist thole a wee, an' ye'll get a nice egg to yer tea. I'm rale vexed ye've got to – "

"A' richt, wumman, a' richt. Dinna fash yersel'. I'll enjye ma tea a' the better. An' Macgreegor likes an egg to his tea."

"Eggs is awfu' dear the noo," remarked Lizzie, as she set the teapot on the hob to warm, preparatory to charging it. "But they're rale strengthenin' an' guid fur folk this cauld weather. Is't freezin' again the nicht, John?"

"Freezin'? Dod, ay! It wud nip the neb aff a brass monkey! ... I think I hear Macgreegor at the door."

"It's high time! Dinna rise, John. He's got the check."

"Chape snuff!" said John jocularly to wee Jeannie, who had just sneezed. Then, hurriedly, to his wife, "Dinna be angry wi' Macgreegor, Lizzie, fur keepin' us waitin'. He wud jist be furgettin' the time."

"He sudna furget the time. We'll be ower late fur the pantymine, as shair's I'm here... Is that you, Macgreegor?" she called, as she filled the egg-pan with water.

"Ay," said a voice, after a pause.

"Weel, come ben wi' the eggs this meenit. Ye're Paw's

wantin' his tea, an' we'll a' be ower late fur the pantymine... Haste ye, laddie!"

A cloud of anxiety fell suddenly on John's countenance, and he opened his mouth, but remained speechless.

The kitchen door opened slowly, and on the threshold stood Macgregor, a pitiable object. In his hand he bore a crushed paper bag, from which oozed and dripped a yellow semi-liquid. His hands and clothing were liberally bedaubed with the same substance, which appeared to have been rubbed well into the latter.

Lizzie, crossing the floor, stopped short, stared, and laid the pan on the dresser. Then her hands shot up in horror and dismay.

"Macgreegor!" she exclaimed at last, in a voice that was almost terrible.

"Greegy, Greegy," chirruped wee Jeannie, holding out her arms.

John said nothing at all. He looked like a man detected in a crime.

The boy remained in the doorway; and as a fat blob fell from the bag with a pap on the floor, two big tears escaped his winking eyelids and rolled down his cheeks.

Wee Jeannie again called her brother affectionately, but he paid no heed; and a moment later he was leaning against the doorpost, his face hidden, his shoulders heaving. He always felt his mother's angry silence more than her words.

"Whit kep' ye, Macgreegor?" Lizzie broke the painful silence. "Whit wey wis ye sae lang on the road?"

"I fell," said Macgregor, without removing his face from his arm.

"Ye fell? An' whit gar'd ye fa'?" Lizzie was trying to control herself, but her voice was stern. "Whit gar'd ye fa'?" she repeated.

"Maybe – maybe the wean's hurt hissel'," put in the unhappy John, longing to excuse his son. "Did ye hurt yersel', Macgreegor?" he asked softly.

For a moment the youngster hesitated, tempted, no

doubt, to accept the way of escape offered him... "Naw," he muttered.

His mother's face lost the tenderness which had dawned at her husband's question.

"Whit gar'd ye fa', Macgreegor?" she demanded once more.

"I slippit," murmured the penitent.

"Whaur did ye slip?"

"On a slide."

"An' whit wis ye daein' on a slide the nicht? Did I no' bid ye come stracht hame?"

Again John interposed. "Maybe he didna see the slide, Lizzie. I near fell masel' comin' hame the nicht... Ye didna see the slide, did ye, ma wee man?"

A pause. Then – "Ay, I seen it," said Macgregor with a gulp.

"Wis ye slidin', meanin' fur to slide?" asked his mother.

"Ay."

"Wi' Wullie Thomson?"

"Ay."

"Did ye no' tell Wullie ye wis to come hame direc'ly ye got the eggs?"

"Ay."

"An' whit wey did ye no' come hame?"

"He said – he said – he – "

"Weel! whit did he say?"

"He – he said he – he cud dae coorie-doons better nor me; an' – an' when we cam' to a slide, he said I wis feart to – to try... I wisna feart fur him... I done a coorie-doon, but he cam' ower quick efter me, an' – an' tummilt me... An' the eggs wis a' broke – oh, Maw!"

"An' whit wey did ye no' come hame then?"

"Wullie said he wud clean ma claes, but – but he made them waur. I'll bash him the morn!"

"Come furrit, an' let's see whit's to be dune," said Lizzie wearily.

Very unwillingly Macgregor came forward. At the sight of him in the full light of the kitchen, his mother leant against the dresser and groaned.

"Sic a mess, sic a mess! Yer guid claes! – yer braw stockin's! – yer buits! – yer bunnet! Hoo did ye file yer bunnet? Shairly ye didna try to dicht aff the eggs wi' yer bunnet."

"I – I furgot it wis ma guid yin… I didna think eggs wis sae – sae sticky."

"Oh, dearie me!" cried Lizzie while wee Jeannie, whom John had vainly endeavoured to keep quiet, burst out wailing.

"Tak' aff yer jayket, Macgreegor," continued Lizzie… "Oh, dearie me! Yer guid new Sawbath claes! An' me rubbin' an' rubbin' a' the efternune to get the greese oot… Whit am I to dae wi' him, John?" she demanded of her husband.

"Gi'e him his tea, wumman," returned John, whom worry and hunger had made unexpectedly bold. "We best a' tak' wur tea noo, or we'll be ower late fur the pantymine."

"Pantymine! 'Deed, ye're no' blate, John! There'll be nae pantymine the nicht, I can tell ye."

"Whit fur no'?"

"Luk at the jayket," she cried, holding the garment up for inspection, while her son wept with shame, remorse and disappointment. "Luk at it! Mercy me! He's rubbit the egg till it's through to the vera linin'!"

"Wullie rubbit it," said Macgregor desperately. He *did* want to go to the pantomime.

"Let him gang in his auld claes," said his father gently. "An' – an' I'll pit on the masher collar to attrac' folk's attention frae him, as it were. Noo, Lizzie."

"Macgreegor's gaun to nae pantymine the nicht," she returned firmly. "It's nae mair nor a just punishment fur his disobedience… Louse yer buits, an wash yer hauns, Macgreegor… We maun ha'e wur tea onywey… Drap the poke in the baikie," she commanded her son, who was still clinging to the ruin.

Macgregor obeyed the various commands as one who realises that all is lost – all lost through his own fault. His sobs ceased, but every now and then he emitted a sniff which went to his father's heart. John tried to busy himself in cheering his daughter, who soon smiled again and invited "Greegy's" attention.

"Greegy bad?" queried the little one of her father.

And, Lizzie being engaged in the cupboard, John shook his head and whispered, "Na, na, dearie. He'll maybe play wi' ye in a whiley."

"John," said his wife a minute later. "Ye maun ha'e somethin' to yer tea."

"Aw, I'm no heedin', Lizzie."

"Ay, but ye need it. Ha'e!"– she gave him a piece of silver from her store – "ye micht rin doon the stair an' get three eggs – mind an' get the best fresh – frae Mistress M'Corkindale i' the dairy – the best fresh, mind!"

"I'm no' heedin' aboot an egg, but I'll gang to please ye," said John, seating wee Jeannie on the floor, and rising. He looked behind him. His son was industriously washing his hands, and as John looked the boy's shoulders went up, and an involuntary sniff escaped him.

John sighed as he turned to Lizzie. Her face was severe. He sighed again.

"John, be as quick's ye can," she said, taking a slice of bread to toast.

"A – a – Lizzie," he whispered.

"Whit is't?"

"Whit wud ye say if I fell an' broke the eggs?" A faint twinkle danced in his eyes.

"I wud say ye tried it," said Lizzie, coolly.

The twinkle went out. "Wife," he said, still in a whisper, "dae ye no' think he's had enough? He's but a wean."

Lizzie hesitated. "But, John, John, hoo dae ye think he'll grow up if he isna punished? It wis a' through his ain disobedience, ye ken as week as I dae."

"Ay; but a' weans is disobedient, an' they dinna' a' tell the truth like oor laddie. He micht easy ha'e made up a story aboot fa'in', an' ye wudna ha'e wantit to punish him fur an accident. Wud ye?"

Lizzie stared at the slice of bread. John eyed her anxiously.

"Macgreegor's no' realy a bad laddie," he murmured.

"Weel, weel, whit am I to dae?" she said at last.

"Let him gang to the pantymine in his auld claes. It's no' ower late yet, if we hurry."

Lizzie looked at her man, and her lip trembled. "Ha'e it yer ain wey, dearie," she said with sudden tenderness.

"Aw, Lizzie, ye're that guid til us a'!" said John. Then he recovered himself, and crossed the kitchen for his jacket and cap.

"Here, John," said his wife, and he returned to her.

"Ay, dearie?"

"Tell Macgreegor to gang fur the eggs hissel'," she said in a strained whisper, and set about toasting the bread.

"Weel," muttered John, when the full meaning of the words illuminated his being, "I – I thocht I cud mak' the wean pleased, but the guidwife kens a better wey."

"Tell him to gang the noo," said Lizzie without looking up.

John cleared his throat. "Macgreegor," he cried, "yer Maw wants ye to gang doon to the dairy fur three eggs. Here the money... An' – an' – ye're aye to dae whit yer Maw bids ye... An' be as quick's ye can, fur yer Maw says we're to get to the pantymine."

And so mourning gave place to rejoicing in the Robinson family.

Katie

KATIE the patient had waited at the close-mouth for over an hour ere she heard a door above open and slam. Then she put one hand behind her back, and tried to look as if she had not been waiting a minute. The boy came clattering down the stair, and almost ran past her, but pulled up somewhat unwillingly on catching sight of her.

"Haw, Katie!" he exclaimed, not so pleasantly as usual, for he was late for an appointment with Willie Thomson, his mother having kept him in the house after the Saturday dinner to look after wee Jeannie while she and her husband did a bit of early spring cleaning. Consequently Macgregor's condition was one of impatience.

"I've brocht ye somethin'," said Katie shyly.

"Ha'e ye?" said Macgregor, a little more genially.

"Ye mind I tell't ye I wis gaun to gi'e ye somethin' when – when it wis ready."

"Ay, I mind. Wis yer Maw makin' gundy the day?" Katie's mother had a reputation for gundy, most of which was exposed for sale every Saturday afternoon in the window of a tiny shop kept by an old woman whose chief business was in "penny things" of an extremely varied nature.

"But it's no' onythin' fur eatin'," said Katie, uneasily.

"Is't no'? I thocht it wud be gundy. Whit is't?"

"I'm feart ye winna like it, Macgreegor."

Macgregor did not know what to say, so he looked away and said nothing.

"Whit dae ye think it is?" she asked with an effort.

"I dinna ken. I thocht it wud be fur eatin'."

"I'll get ye a bit gundy next Setturday."

"Wull ye?"

"Ay."

"Whit wey wull ye no' let's see whit ye've brocht the day, Katie?" he inquired after a pause, his curiosity prompting him.

"I – I'm feart ye winna like it when it's no' fur eatin'," she replied without the merest suggestion of reproach.

"Och, ye needna be feart. Come on, Katie, let's see whit ye've brocht?"

Katie slowly brought her hand from behind her back.

"It – it's jist a floo'er," she said in a shamed whisper. Only five minutes earlier she had been such a proud little soul, for somehow she had made up her mind that her Knight would be gratified to receive the first bloom that had sprung from the pot which a beautiful young lady had given her when she lay sick a month ago. She had never told her Knight of the beautiful young lady's gift, for she had wanted to surprise and delight him with her own.

Macgregor was certainly surprised, but it cannot be said that he was delighted.

"Is that whit ye wis aye tellin' me ye wis gaun to gi'e us when it wis ready?" he demanded.

"Ay," she answered huskily.

He looked for a moment at the feeble little yellow crocus which Katie had almost killed with kindness, and which, in her disappointment, she no longer held out for his acceptance.

"Aw, I'm no' wantin' yer floo'er," he said, not by any means roughly. "I'm no' heedin' aboot floo'ers, Katie. Jist keep it to yersel'. I can get plenty floo'ers if I want them. Granpaw brings big bunches to Maw frae Rothesay whiles, but they jist dee. An' I'm no' heedin' aboot them... Here, Katie! Whaur are ye gaun? ... Whit wey – "

But Katie had bolted past him, and was running homewards as fast as her sorry heart could force her.

Macgregor looked puzzled for a few seconds, and then left the close, whistling, in search of Willie Thomson. He found him half an hour later, but not at the appointed place, for Willie, having grown tired of waiting on his chum, had strolled into a neighbouring street, where a monkey with an organ and organist was performing in a pathetic fashion before a curious but mostly impecunious little crowd. It was while watching the monkey that Willie caught sight of the weeping Katie – but of that, more anon.

He greeted Macgregor cheerfully, and Macgregor was just going to explain his late arrival when he caught sight of something unusual about his friend, and, pointing to the latter's head, exclaimed–

"Whaur got ye the floo'er?"

Both boys wore Glengarry bonnets, the difference between their headgear being that Macgregor's, thanks to his mother, always had the customary two ribbons, while Willie's had none. But to-day, in Macgregor's eyes at least, Willie's bonnet was a much finer affair than his own, for in the shabby bow at the side was jauntily stuck a single yellow crocus.

"Whaur got ye the floo'er?" repeated Macgregor.

Willie grinned half proudly, half sheepishly. "Och, I jist got it frae Katie the noo," he said, trying to squint up at the adornment.

"She didna gi'e it to ye," said Macgregor.

"Ay, did she. She wis greetin', tae."

"Whit did ye gar her greet fur? Eh?" cried Macgregor threateningly. "Whit did ye gar her greet fur? Come on; tell us, or I'll bash ye!"

"I didna gar the lassie greet," returned Willie, drawing back in amazement and dread at the sudden unfriendly attitude shown him.

"Ay, but ye did!"

"I didna!"

"Whit wud she be greetin' fur?"

"I didna ken. I speired at her, but she wudna tell me."

"Weel, ye sudna ha'e tooken her floo'er."

"I didna tak' it. She gi'ed it to me."

"Fine ham!"

"It's no' a fine ham! I jist tell't her no' to greet, an' she askit me if I wis fur a floo'er. An' I said I wis, an' she gi'ed it to me. An' I pit it in ma bunnet, an' she tell't me I wis rale like her big kizzen, him that's a sojer."

"Ye're liker a loony nor a sojer," said Macgregor unkindly.

"I'm no'!" cried Willie indignantly, clenching his fists.

"Gaun! hit me!" said Macgregor mockingly.

Months ago the twain had had a fight in which Macgregor proved himself much the better "man," and now Willie, though irritated, refrained from delivering the first blow. He wasn't a coward, and he wasn't a fool, and he was pretty certain that Macgregor would not strike until himself had been struck. So he sulkily muttered:

"Ye needna flee up aboot naethin', Macgreegor."

"I'm no' fleein' up! But – but the floo'er's mines!" burst out Macgregor.

"Whit?"

"It – it's mines!"

"Ach, awa' to Fintry! I ken fine ye didna gi'e it to Katie, an' she didna steal it frae ye, fur she tell't me she gar'd it growe hersel'! She got a pot frae a leddy fu' o' dirt an' things like wee ingins, an' the floo'er cam' oot efter she pit watter on the dirt an' ingins. I ken fine, fur she tell't me. Sae ye needna try to let on the floo'er's yer ain." And Willie took off his bonnet for a moment, and straightened the crocus, making his headgear look smarter than ever.

For a brief period Macgregor was speechless. Then he said, "Katie gi'ed the floo'er to me first. She – "

"Whit wey did ye no' keep it?"

"I – I didna get time to tak' it. See, gi'e's the floo'er!"

"Nae fears! I'm thinkin' it wis *you* gar'd the lassie greet."

"If ye say that again I'll ca' the face aff ye! Whit fur wud I gar her greet?"

"Maybe ye wantit the floo'er an' she wudna gi'e it to ye," was the disagreeable reply.

"I wisna heedin' aboot the floo'er."

"Weel, whit are ye wantin' it fur noo?" inquired the logical William.

For an instant Macgregor was checked, but not for longer. "Ye think ye're gey fly," he said, "but I'm jist tellin' ye the floo'er's mines, an' I'm gaun to ha'e it." And he made a threatening movement.

Willie promptly snatched the blossom of discord from his bonnet and stuffed it into his jacket pocket. (Alas poor crocus!) "Ye'll ha'e to ripe ma pooch fur't," he said, "an' then ye'll be a dirty thief."

Macgregor paused. In his anger he might have helped himself to the flower from Willie's bonnet, but the latter's "pooch" was sacred. He wheeled about, and moved away with the curt remark, "I'm no' in wi' ye ony mair."

Willie was paralysed. What would he do without Macgregor? He wasn't a sturdy youngster, and who would stand up beside him now and see that he got fairplay in the playground and the street? He ran after Macgregor.

"I – I'll len' ye the floo'er if ye like," he said eagerly.

Macgregor paid no attention.

And just then Katie came up, having been sent by her mother upon an errand. She would have passed them, but Willie caught her by the arm.

"Macgreegor says ye gi'ed him the floo'er," he said, producing it.

Katie said nothing.

"Macgreegor wants it, an' he says he's no' in wi' me because I wudna gi'e it to him."

"Is Macgreegor wantin' a floo'er?" she asked.

"Ay. But – "

Katie, however, had left him to run after Macgregor, who had walked on. Overtaking him, she enquired gently: "Wis ye wantin' a – a floo'er, Macgreegor?"

"Och; I'm no' heedin'."

"But – but there's a bew yin – it's faur bonnier nor the yella yin Wullie's got – an' it'll be ready gey shin – an' – an' I'll gi'e it to ye fur yer bunnet, if ye like."

"Wull ye?" exclaimed Macgregor, quite unable to resist the "bew yin."

"Ay; I'll gi'e it to ye as shin's it's ready."

"When'll it be ready? The morn?"

"Na. But maybe Wensday. I'm gled ye didna tak' the yella yin, fur bew's faur finer nor yella. Is't no'?"

"Ay... Whit gar'd ye greet the day, Katie?"

"Aw, naethin'."

"It wisna Wullie Thomson?"

"Na, na! Oh, na, na!"

"If it had been Wullie Thomson I wud ca' the face aff him!"

"Are ye no' in wi' Wullie Thomson?"

"Naw. Come on Katie, an' I'll – "

"Whit wey?"

"Aw, jist because I'm no' in wi' him. Come on, an' I'll buy sweeties," said Macgregor, chinking his two Saturday "bawbees."

"Wull ye? Oh, ye're awfu' kind, Macgregor!"

They walked together a few paces, and then Katie said softly:

"Wull ye no' tell Wullie to come wi' us?"

"Naw!"

"But Wullie's vexed at ye no' bein' in wi' him. Wullie thinks ye're a rale fine, strong laddie. Dinna be angry at him ony mair. I'll gi'e ye a white floo'er furbye the bew yin when it's ready."

"Ach, I'm no' wantin' to tak' a' yer floo'ers, Katie."

"Ah, but I like to gi'e ye ma floo'ers, Macgregor… Wull ye no' tell Wullie to come wi' us? He's staunin' at the corner yet," she added glancing swiftly behind her and walking slower.

It took some time to persuade Macgregor, but at last Katie won, and he turned round, and waved his hand and bawled:

"Haw, Wullie! Here!"

The Museum

"PAW, I want to gang inside the Mu-e-sum," said Macgregor, as the family party strolled through the Park one Saturday afternoon.

"An' ye'll gang inside the Museum, ma mannie," returned his father agreeably. "Here, Lizzie," he called to his wife, who, with the toddling wee Jeannie, was a few paces in front. "Here, Lizzie; Macgreegor's fur gaun inside the Museum."

"Mu-e-sum," corrected Macgregor, who frequently altered the order of a big word's syllables in autocratic fashion.

"Macgreegor's no' gaun inside ony museum the day," said Lizzie, with a glance behind her.

"Whit wey, Maw?"

"Because it's ower fine a day. My! there hasna been as braw a day as the day fur mony a lang week. I'm shair it's faur nicer here nor in ony museum. Is't no', John?"

"Ay; it's rale nice, Lizzie," replied her husband, "an' I'm enjyin' masel' jist first-class; but, ye see, the wean wants – "

"It's no' whit the wean wants; it's whit the wean needs," she said, interrupting him. "An' whit Macgreegor needs is fresh air. He's been lukin' gey peely-wally the last twa-three days... Come on, dearie," she said kindly, halting and turning to her son, "come on, an' see the foontain. Maybe it'll be playin' the day."

"I'm no' wantin' to see the foontain. I want to gang inside the Mu-e-sum, an' see the skeletins an' the serpents in the botles, an' – "

"Aw, haud yer tongue, Macgregor! I wunner whaur ye get thae nesty notions... John, tak' him awa' to see the jucks an' the ither birds in the pond."

"I like skeletins better nor jucks, an' I wisht I had a serpent in a – "

"Be quate this meenit, or I'll sort ye! ... John! ye micht think shame o' yersel', lauchin' awa' there," she said in an undertone to her husband. Then she turned for consolation and support to wee Jeannie, who was amusing herself by flinging handfuls of gravel over a carefully tended flower-plot. "I'm shair ma wee doo wudna like to see the nesty things in the Museum. Eh, ma daurlin'?"

"She wud like it fine," said Macgregor sulkily. "The skeletins an' serpents canna hurt folk. They're a' deid," he added in a tone of pitying superiority.

"John!" exclaimed Lizzie warningly, and walked on with her daughter.

John, with an effort, came to the scratch. "Ma mannie, ye're no' to speak ony mair aboot sic things. Yer Maw disna like it. Come awa', an' we'll ha'e a keek at the jucks. I thocht ye liket seein' them soomin'."

"Naw. Ye canna get flingin' stanes. If ye fling stanes at the jucks, ye get the nick," remarked Macgregor in an aggrieved voice.

"I doot ye canna get flingin' stanes," said his father sympathetically. "Weel, if ye dinna want to see the jucks, whit wud ye like?"

"I wud like to gang inside the Mu-e-sum. See! – thonder it is!"

"Ay; I see it, Macgreegor. But I doot we canna gang the day. Ye see – "

"John," said Lizzie, looking back, "wee Jeannie an' me's gaun to ha'e a sate here fur a wee. You an' Macgreegor can gang an' see the jucks, an' we'll wait till ye come back."

"A'richt, dearie," said John. "We'll no' be lang. Ha'e ye got wee Jeannie's baurley sugar?"

"Ay; I've got it here. Ye can gi'e Macgreegor a taste o' the taiblet, John, but jist a taste, fur he's no' to spile his tea."

The father and son strolled off in the direction of the duck-pond, and the father produced the poke of "taiblet." "Noo, jist a taste, Macgregor," he said, looking away, and allowing the boy to help himself.

"Can I get takin' this bit, Paw?" inquired the latter, holding up a three-inch slab. With all his faults, Macgregor was honest.

"Weel, it's a guid big taste, ma mannie. I think I best tak' a bite aff it masel'."

John stooped, and the boy held the tablet to his lips. John pretended to bite off a couple of inches, but really removed only a few grains from the end, whereupon Macgregor grinned and proceeded to enjoy himself.

But the tablet was soon finished, and as they neared the duck-pond they also neared the Museum. In fact, according to the path they had taken, to reach the former they would be compelled to pass the very door of the latter.

Presently Macgregor, whose hand was in his father's, began to lag, "sclifterin' " his feet over the gravel in a languid fashion, and paying little or no heed to his parent's remarks, though they were obviously made with the intention of entertaining him. At that minute there was not a more irritating youngster in Glasgow.

"D'ye see the jucks ower thonder?" said John, pointing a little to the right.

"Naw," replied Macgregor, who was staring gloomily at the Museum a little to the left.

John tried not to feel snubbed. "We're gettin' a graun' day," he observed pleasantly. "It's fine an' warm, is't no', Macgreegor?"

"I'm cauld," muttered his son.

"Are ye? Aweel, we'll gang quicker," said John cheerfully.

"I'm wearit," said Macgregor, and lagged more than ever.

"Dod, Macgreegor," said John, not quite so cheerfully, "I dinna ken whit I'm to dae wi' ye. Ye'll neither dance nor haud the caun'le. If ye're cauld, I canna mak' ye tak' a sate; an' if ye're wearit, I canna bid ye gang quicker. Whit dae ye want?"

"I – I want to gang inside the Mu-e-sum."

His father drew a longer breath than usual before he replied. "But ye ken yer Maw disna want ye to gang inside the Museum the day."

"Whit wey?"

"She wants ye to get the fresh air ootbye."

"I'm no' heedin' aboot fresh air. It's faur warmer in the Mu-e-sum."

"Weel, ye'll get inside the Museum anither day. See! We're jist comin' to the jucks noo. I'm shair thon big yin's no' an or'nar' juck. I'm thinkin' it's whit they ca' a peelican. Luk at its lang neb, Macgreegor."

But Macgregor refused to be interested. He had never before found his father so hard to influence.

John made several further observations more or less jocular, but looked in vain for any signs of animation in the boy's countenance. At last he gave up in despair, and, keeping his patience with an effort, suggested that they should return to Lizzie and once more ask her permission to enter the temple of Macgregor's heart's desire.

Macgregor graciously assented to the proposal, and they retraced their steps to where they had left Lizzie.

She rose on catching sight of them, and came forward to meet them. "If I hadna been feart I micht miss ye, I wud ha'e come efter ye," she said. "Jist efter ye gaed awa' an auld man cam' by and speirt if I wisna gaun up the hill to see the sojers."

"Whit sojers?" asked John.

"He didna say, but he tell't me it wis a big regiment hame frae furrin pairts, and they wis to mairch through the pairk – up thonder on the high road – in a wee whiley. I like seein' the sojers, John, an' sae dis wee Jeannie, an' – "

"Oh, ye maun see the sojers, Lizzie. But Macgreegor's set his hert on the Museum – ha'e ye no', Macgreegor?"

"Ay," said Macgregor, but with less eagerness than might have been expected.

"Aw, weel," returned Lizzie kindly, "the laddie maun ha'e his ain wey... But keep him awa' frae the nesty things, John," she added in a whisper. Then, aloud, "Wee Jeannie an' me'll meet ye here in aboot hauf-an-'oor. Wull that dae?"

"Ay, that'll dae fine," replied John, who was longing to see the soldiers. "Wull it no', Macgreegor?"

"Ay," said Macgregor, who could not bear to confess himself beaten.

Lizzie, who had a cousin in the army, was quite excited, and departed forthwith up the slope, while father and son went back the way they had come.

"Noo, ye see, it's faur nicer daein' a thing when yer Maw says ye can dae't, is't no'?" John cheerily inquired.

"Ay," admitted the boy after some hesitation. "Wull there be a baun' wi' the sojers?" he asked as they proceeded.

"Dod, ay. Maybe twa baun's."

There was silence for a little.

"I like baun's," observed Macgregor thoughtfully.

"Ay; baun's is fine," said John.

There was another short silence, during which they came to the door of the Museum.

"I hear the baun', Paw," said the boy, halting.

"Ay; the sojers is comin'. See – thonder!" And John turned and pointed to the summit of the park slope.

It was on Macgregor's tongue to say, "Come on, Paw, we'll rin!" But alas! he realised it was too late.

Inside the Museum the skeletons looked rather blurred, and the bottles containing the snakes had a misty appearance, while neither were quite so entertaining as Macgregor had anticipated. But he braved the situation – with the assistance of an extra large bit of "taiblet," which fortunately did not lie as heavily on his stomach as it did on his parent's conscience.

A Lesson In Kindness

GRANDFATHER Purdie seated himself on a rock, wiped his wrinkled brows with a large red handkerchief, and produced his pipe.

"Noo, dinna gang faur, Macgreegor," he said, "an' dinna get yer feet wat."

"Nae fears, Granpaw," returned the boy, who had announced his intention of proceeding a little farther along the shore.

"I'm rale vexed I canna come wi' ye, but I'm no' as soople as I wis, an' the stanes is ower slippy fur me. If I wis fa'in' I wud be dune fur. But I'm no' wantin' to keep ye frae enj'yin' yersel', so aff ye gang, ma mannie; but dinna gang faur, an' dinna bide ower lang. Dinna gang whaur I canna see ye."

"I'll no' gang faur," said Macgregor agreeably; "an' ye needna be feart," he added, somewhat patronizingly. "I'm gey soople."

He walked off, and half a minute later sat down abruptly with a squelching sound on a weed-covered boulder.

"Guidsake, laddie! are ye hurt?" exclaimed Mr. Purdie, rising in alarm.

"Naw!" came the ungracious reply, as the youngster rose, undamaged save in dignity.

"I'm gled ye're no' hurt, Macgreegor," said the old man, much relieved. Then, anxiously, "Ha'e ye gotten yer breeks wat?"

"Naw. I'm fine. I'll no' gang faur." And Macgregor went off, leaving the old man saying to himself, "I wisht I wis shair he hasna got hissel wat."

The boy had not gone very far when, in a rocky cove, he came upon a little girl of about his own age searching among the pebbles and small boulders, and emitting frequent half-stifled sobs.

He stood and stared awhile, then went forward. "Whit wey are ye greetin'?" he demanded.

The little girl went on searching, but made no response.

"Gaun! Tell us!" said Macgregor. "Whit are ye lukin' fur?" he enquired, with more curiosity and less authority in his voice.

"I – I've lost ma penny," said she, gulping and weeping afresh.

"Hoo cam' ye to loss yer penny?"

"I wis flingin' it up an'–an' keppin' it."

"That wis a daftlike thing to dae wi' a penny."

"It wasna!" cried the little girl, indignantly.

"It wis! But a' lassies is daft," retorted Macgregor, with the air of an experienced man. "Whaur did ye loss it?" he asked, without giving her time to reply to his rude assertion.

"It wis jist aboot here, I think," she replied, pointing rather vaguely. "But I'm no' daft."

He ignored the latter statement. "I'll help ye to luk fur yer penny," he said, after a glance round to make sure that no boys were about.

She gave him a quick, searching look, as if to fathom his purpose, and his expression seemed to satisfy her. She was a white-faced, poorly dressed little creature, and though she and the boy might have lived in the same street in town, her appearance lacked what was patent in his – the touches of a careful mother.

"Whit's yer name?" enquired Macgregor, abruptly, as he poked and peered among the stones at his feet.

"Jessie Cameron," she told him, and asked shyly, "Whit's yours?"

"Macgreegor Robison. I dinna think Jessie's a vera nice name."

Her tears, which had ceased, threatened to start again, and she gave a sniff.

"If ye greet, I'll no' help ye to luk fur yer penny. But I think Jessie's nicer nor Bella."

The concession was better than nothing, and Jessie took heart and wrought eagerly among the stones.

"Dae ye bide at Rothesay?" the boy asked presently.

"Na. I bide in Glesca."

"I bide in Glesca tae, but I'm bidin' at Rothesay the noo. I'm bidin' fur mair nor a week."

"I cam' to Rothesay this mornin', an' I'm gaun hame the nicht."

"I wudna like to be gaun hame the nicht," remarked the boy. "D'ye no' wish ye wis stoppin' as lang as me?"

"Ay," she said longingly. "But fayther canna stope."

"Whaur's yer paw the noo?"

"He gaed awa' an' said he wud be back in a wee while. He gi'ed me a penny, an'–an' I've lost it."

"Aw, ye'll maybe fin' it yet," said Macgregor, encouragingly. "Whaur's yer maw?"

"Ma mither's deid," she replied.

"I wudna like if mines wis deid... I – I'm vexed fur ye... Dae ye like wulks?" he asked, holding up a small specimen, perhaps with the idea of distracting her thoughts from sadness.

She shook her head, and gave her eyes a hurried wipe.

"I didna mean to vex ye," he said, uncomfortably, dropping the whelk, and once more setting himself to search for the missing penny.

Jessie kept silence, but she glanced at him as she stooped, and her expression was tender.

But it's tiresome work searching for a penny which isn't one's own, and Macgregor at last grew impatient.

"Are ye shair ye drappit it here?" he asked, standing up and stretching himself.

"Ay; I'm shair... I wisht I had it."

"Wull yer paw no' gi'e ye anither penny?"

Jessie did not reply, but she looked doubtful.

"Whit wis ye fur buyin' wi' the penny?" was his next query.

"I dinna ken. I didna ha'e the penny lang enough – to think whit I wud buy."

"Sweeties?"

"Maybe. I dinna ken."

"If ye had the penny, I'd tell ye whaur to buy sweeties in Rothesay. I ken a shope whaur ye get an awfu' big poke fur a penny! Dae ye like taiblet?"

"Ay."

"Weel, ye dinna get muckle taiblet fur a penny, but ye get a big poke o' mixed ba's or broken mixturs. Dae ye like mixed ba's an' broken mixturs?"

"Ay, fine!"

"It's a peety ye lost yer penny."

"Maybe I'll fin' it yet," said Jessie, searching more fever-ishly than ever.

"I dinna think ye'll fin' it noo," said Macgregor without any intention of being unkind.

"If I fin' ma penny I'll buy sweeties, an' I'll gi'e ye hauf."

"Wull ye?"

"As shair's I'm here!" she said solemnly.

Whereupon Macgregor renewed his efforts, but without success.

"I'm gaun awa' noo," he said, at the end of five minutes.

"Are ye?"

"Ay! I'm thinkin' yer penny's no' here ava'... My granpaw'll be wantin' me. He's got plenty siller."

Jessie said nothing, and continued grubbing away desper-ately.

Macgregor watched her in silence for another minute, and then strolled back to Mr. Purdie.

"Whit lassie wis thon ye wis speakin' to?" enquired the old man, as his grandson drew near.

"Jessie Cameron. That's whit she said her name wis."

"Is she getherin' wulks?"

"Naw. She's lukin' fur a penny."

"A penny?"

"Ay. She tell't me she lost her penny, but it's no there."

"Puir lassie!" murmured Mr. Purdie, putting on his spec-tacles and gazing at the little bent figure. "Wis ye helpin' her to luk fur her penny?"

"Ay, Granpaw."

"That wis a guid laddie. Whaur dis the lassie come frae?"

Macgregor supplied the details, concluding with—"It wis a daftlike thing to be playin' at keppers wi' a penny on the shore."

Mr. Purdie at first made no remark, but after he had taken off his spectacles and returned them, in their case, to his pocket, he said, quietly:

"If I wis gi'ein' ye a penny the noo, Macgregor, whit wud ye dae wi' 't?"

"I wud spend it."

"Ay; but hoo wud ye spend it?" asked Mr. Purdie anxiously.

"I wud buy mixed ba's an' broken mixturs. They're awfu' guid at Rothesay, an' I ken whaur ye get awfu' big pokes."

Mr. Purdie was suddenly depressed. He had hoped for better things of his grandson. "But ye dinna need to buy sweeties, Macgreegor," he said, gently, "when yer bidin' wi' yer granny an' me. I'm thinkin' thon lassie thonder disna get mony sweeties."

"She sudna ha'e lost her penny."

"Aw, puir lassie!" said Mr. Purdie. "If I wis gi'ein' ye a penny the noo, wud ye no' like to gi'e it to her to mak' up fur the yin she lost? Eh, ma mannie?"

"Naw; I wudna," promptly replied Macgregor.

The old man sighed. "I'm thinkin' it wud be a rale kind thing if ye gi'ed her the penny. An' I'm shair she wud think ye wis a rale kind laddie." He paused, watching the boy's face.

"I'll gi'e her the penny if ye like, Granpaw," said the youngster at last.

"Ah, but wud ye no' like gi'ein' it frae yersel'?"

"Och, ay; I wud like it fine," Macgregor replied, carelessly. "But—"

"That's a guid laddie!" exclaimed Mr. Purdie, beaming with satisfaction, and producing the coin. "Awa' an' tell her ye're vexed fur her, an' gi'e her the penny."

Obedient for once in a while, Macgregor went off immediately.

"Ha'e ye no' got yer penny yet?" he enquired as he approached Jessie.

"Na," she replied, despondently.

"Here anither yin fur ye," he said, presenting her with the copper.

"Oh my!" she cried, hesitatingly. Then she accepted the gift, saying, "Ye're that kind; ye're jist *awfu'* kind!"

Macgregor, without further remark, went back to his grandfather.

"Did ye gi'e her the penny?" the latter enquired.

"Ay."

Mr. Purdie patted the youngster's shoulder. "Ye'll be feelin' gey prood," he said, delightedly.

"Ay," said Macgregor, doubtfully.

"Whit did the lassie say, Macgreegor?"

"I dinna mind. Is't near time fur wur tea, Granpaw?"

Mr. Purdie consulted his fat silver watch. "Deed, so it is! It's time we wis hame. Gi'e's yer haun', ma mannie."

They started homewards, but they had not proceeded far when Jessie overtook them, panting. "Here yer penny! I fun' ma ain," she gasped.

Macgregor held out his hand, but his grandfather gently pushed away Jessie's fingers. "Ah, ma dearie, ye're a guid lassie, so ye are! Keep the penny, and buy somethin' to taste yer gab wi' 't."

Jessie looked from grandfather to grandson.

"Macgreegor wudna tak' back the penny," said Mr. Purdie. "Wud ye, Macgreegor?"

"N – naw," said Macgregor, sulkily.

"Ma fayther's waitin' fur me. Thenk ye kindly," said Jessie, looking at the boy.

"Weel, weel, ye maun gang to yer fayther, ma lassie," said Mr. Purdie genially. "Dinna loss yer penny again." And, with a chuckle, he nodded to her and went with Macgregor, who was pulling impatiently at his hand.

They walked perhaps a hundred yards in silence, and then the old man said, quietly, "Ye're no' sorry ye gi'ed yer penny to the puir lassie, are ye, Macgreegor?"

Macgregor kicked at the turf bordering the road, and made no reply.

"I doot thon lassie disna get mony pennies to hersel'... Ye're no' sorry, are ye, ma mannie?"

"Naw," said Macgregor, bravely. After all, to give grudgingly and feel ashamed is better than to give freely and feel virtuous.

After tea they went down to the pier to see the last boat leaving for Glasgow – a spectacle which Macgregor insisted on witnessing every fine evening.

The bell had been rung, and the steam was roaring from the escape-pipe, while the tail of the crowd of passengers wagged from the gangway.

"Granpaw, whit wey–"

Macgregor's question was interrupted by a small husky voice that said, "Ha'e!" and a small hand that crushed a small paper parcel into his own.

"Come on, Jessie!" cried a weakly-looking man from the tail of the crowd; "come on, or we'll lose the boat."

Jessie smiled wistfully at Macgregor, and ran after her father.

Old Mr. Purdie's eyes had tears in them as he turned to his grandson after they had waved to the little girl in the steerage of the departing steamer.

"Ye see, ma mannie, hoo yin guid turn deserves anither...Puir wee lassie! An' she gi'ed ye her sweeties! Eh! but it wis rale nice o' the lassie!"Macgregor had opened the "poke," and was regarding the sweets with a critical air.

"Aw, Macgreegor, aye be kind to folk that's no' as weel aff as yersel'," continued Mr. Purdie. "An' – an' here a penny fur ye, ma laddie. Na! here a thrup'ny-bit."

"Thenk ye, Granpaw."

"An' it wis unco kind o' the lassie to gi'e ye her sweeties, wis't no', Macgreegor?"

"They're no' vera nice yins," remarked Macgregor, putting one in his mouth, and eyeing the rest with disfavour.

Fishing

"GRANPAW," cried Macgregor from the doorstep, "are ye no' comin' oot to the fishin' wi' me an' Paw an' Maw?"

"Na, na," Mr. Purdie replied, stepping out of the parlour, where he had just settled down to his after-tea pipe. "I'm gettin' ower auld fur gaun oot in wee boats."

"Are ye feart?"

"Ay, I'm feart a big fish gets the haud o' me," said the old man good-naturedly. "Ye wudna like to see a whale soomin' awa' wi' yer puir auld granpaw – wud ye, Macgreegor?"

"N – naw," the youngster replied with the slightest hesitation, tempted perhaps for a moment by the exciting vision suggested by Mr. Purdie's words. "Naw, I wudna like that, Granpaw. But ye tell't me afore there wis nae whales at Rothesay."

"'Deed, ye're the yin fur mindin' things, laddie! But I wis jist jokin' aboot the whale. It's the cauld I'm feart fur, an' the wat. It gets intil ma auld banes, ye see. So yer Granmaw an' me'll jist bide in the hoose an' tak' guid care o' Jeannie till ye come back wi' yer fish... Here yer Paw an' Maw comin'. Are ye ready fur the road?"

"Ay, I'm ready."

John and Lizzie appeared from the kitchen, where the former had been playing with his daughter while the latter helped her mother to wash up.

Lizzie regarded her son for an instant, and said sharply: "Did I no' tell ye to pit on yer auld troosers, Macgreegor?"

"I dinna like ma auld yins, Maw."

"Weel, ye're no' gaun oot to the fishin' in yer guid yins. I'm no' gaun to ha'e yer nice new navy-bew yins spiled afore ye've had them a week. The saut watter'll jist ruin them. Awa' an' pit on yer auld yins this meenit."

"Sailors aye wear navy-bew claes, Maw, an' ma auld yins is faur ower ticht," said her son appealingly.

"I'm no' heedin' whit sailors wears. Weans maun wear whit they're tell't."

"But ma auld yins is faur ower – "

"Macgreegor canna help growin', Lizzie," interposed John.

His wife took no notice of the observation, and Macgregor, realising that his case was hopeless, retired to do as he was bidden. In about five minutes he returned wearing his old clothes and an exaggerated look of martyrdom.

"Are ye no' wantin' to gang oot to the fishin'?" his mother enquired. "Ye needna come unless ye like."

"I want to gang oot to the fishin', Maw," he returned in a subdued tone.

"Weel, ye'll need to pit on yer topcoat, dearie," said Lizzie, losing her severity.

"It's no' cauld. I'm no' needin' ma topcoat."

"Pit on yer topcoat when I tell ye!" she said firmly.

Macgregor donned the garment in question.

"See an' catch a nice haddie fur ma breakfast, Macgreegor," said Mr. Purdie cheerfully, with the kindly idea of closing up the little rift.

"An' a wee whitin' fur mines," cried Mrs. Purdie, appearing on the scene.

"Dod, ay!" laughed John, taking his son's hand and gently gripping his wife's arm. "Macgreegor'll attend to yer orders jist as if he wis a fishmonger. Wull ye no', Macgreegor?"

"Dod, ay!" said Macgregor, suddenly recovering his spirits under his father's genial influence.

"Macgreegor! I'm shair I've tell't ye a thoosan' times ye're no' to say – " Lizzie began.

"Come awa', come awa'!" cried John, "or we'll no' get a boat the nicht!"

Lizzie waved an adieu to her daughter in Mrs. Purdie's arms, and the trio set out for the shore.

"Can I get oarin', Paw?" the youngster enquired when the boat-hirer had given the craft a farewell push, which sent it some five yards from the shore.

"Na, na," said Lizzie. "Yer Paw'll tak' us to the fishin' place hissel'... John, fur ony favour, dinna get in front o' thon steamer!"

"It's twa-three mile awa', Lizzie."

"Weel, keep close to the shore onywey."

"But it's a guid bit oot to the fishin' place," said John.

"I'm no' heedin'. Ye've got to keep close to the shore till the steamboat's by," said the nervous Lizzie.

It was Macgregor's turn. He sniggered rudely and remarked: "The steamboat's by lang syne. It's sailin' awa' frae us!"

"Dod, but the wean's richt!" cried his father with a laugh.

"Aweel," said Lizzie impatiently, "awa' to the fishin' place as quick's ye like, an' if we're a' droondit I'll ha'e an easy conscience onywey."

"Hooch, ay! We'll a' ha'e easy consciences!" exclaimed her husband jocularly.

"Ye micht ken better nor to mak' fun o' solemn subjects, John." Mrs. Robinson spoke reprovingly and possibly offendedly.

John did the best thing that could be done under the circumstances. He kept silence and rowed his hardest till they reached the fishing ground, where a small cluster of boats had already anchored.

"Paw! Thonder a man got a fish!" said Macgregor excitedly, half-rising.

"Keep yer sate, dearie," said his mother, smiling with recovered good-nature, as she laid a restraining hand on his shoulder.

"Paw, can I get flingin' in the anchor?"

For once in his life John said "No!"

"Whit wey, Paw? I wud mak' a graun' splash!"

"Na, na, Macgreegor," put in Lizzie. "The anchor's a dangerous thing. There wis yinst twa laddies oot in a boat, an' yin o' them wis castin' the anchor, an' he gaed ower wi' 't, an' wis cairrit doon to the bottom o' the sea, an' droondit. Ay!"

"Whit wey did the ither laddie no' pu' him up?"

"He – he wis ower heavy."

"Whit wey did he no' sclim' up the rape hissel'?"

"His claes had got fankled in the anchor."

Macgregor considered for a few seconds. "Is that a true story, Maw?" he demanded.

"Mercy!" exclaimed Lizzie, as John flung the anchor overboard and the rope ran out.

"I wud ha'e made a bigger splash," remarked the boy... "Maw, wis thon a true story?"

"Ye better be gettin' the lines ready," said John, unconsciously coming to his wife's rescue. "Macgreegor, dae ye ken hoo to pit on yer baits?"

"Ay, fine! ... The baits is awfu' slippy, Paw."

"See an' no' let the hooks catch yer fingers."

"Nae fears, Paw!" sung out Macgregor, who had already baited one hook with a mussel and the other with one of the knees of his knickerbockers.

"John!" sighed Lizzie, "I dinna like tichin' thae slithery beasts. Are they leevin'?"

"Na, na, wumman; they're no' leevin'. Jist bide a wee, an' I'll come an' bait yer line fur ye," returned John cheerily. He made the anchor rope fast and came cautiously to the stern. "Whit's ado, Macgreegor?" he asked of his son, who was struggling with the hook in his nether garments.

"It's a mercy I made him change his guid troosers," Mrs. Robinson observed when her husband with his knife had, not unskilfully, extracted the errant hook.

"If I had had on ma guid troosers, I wudna ha'e let the hook catch them," said Macgregor.

"Mphm!" murmured Lizzie.

"Thae auld yins is that oosie, they wud catch onythin'."

"Haud yer tongue, Macgreegor," said Lizzie, "an' see if ye canna catch a fish."

His father having put the baits in order, Macgregor dropped the sinker and hooks over the side, and gradually unwound the line.

"Paw, it'll no' gang doon ony furder," he said, after a short silence.

"Ye'll be at the bottom, ma mannie," John explained.

"But I dinna feel ony fish."

"Patience! patience! Pu' up a wee bit, an' keep yer line

hingin', an', when ye feel onythin' at it, gi'e it a chugg."

John illustrated what he meant, and proceeded with bait-
ing his wife's line.

"Paw, I think I feel somethin'!"

"Weel, gi'e a chugg."

Macgregor jerked with such goodwill that he fell off his
narrow seat, upset the bait dish over his mother's feet, and
caused her to cry:

"Oh, John, John! I kent we wis in fur a wattery grave!"

John smiled reassuringly as he assisted his son back to his
seat and set about gathering up the mess of homeless
shell-fish. "Dinna fash yersel', Lizzie," he said, when he had
baited her line. "Macgreegor's fine, an' he'll no' tum'le
again. Noo fur the fish!"

But the fish were not so enthusiastic, and at the end of
about twenty minutes of silence and expectation Macgregor
observed:

"Paw, I dinna feel onythin' yet."

"Aw, ye've got to gi'e the fish time," his father replied
hopefully. "I expec' they'll be smellin' aboot the baits the
noo an' gettin' up their appetites, as it were."

"I wisht I cud see richt doon to the bottom, Paw. If I seen
a fish, I wud jist nick it wi' ma hooks."

"Wud ye?"

"Ay, wud I."

"Macgreegor," said Lizzie, who was beginning to feel at
home in the boat and to enjoy the calm sea and mild air, "ye
sudna boast aboot whit ye ken ye cudna dae. Sud he, John?"

"Och, whit's the odds as lang's ye're happy? Are ye feelin'
the cauld, Lizzie?" said her husband.

"No' a bit! I'm enjyin' masel' rale weel, John," she returned.

"That's guid!" he exclaimed in a tone of supreme satisfaction. "I'm shair the fish'll shin be comin'! ... Macgreegor,
pu' up yer line, an' see if yer baits is a' richt."

The youngster hauled in, to find that the baits were intact,
showing no signs of having been touched, however gently.

"Never heed," said John. "Let doon yer line again... Ha'e
ye had ony nibbles, Lizzie?"

"No' yet, John," replied his wife, whose interest was absorbed by a young couple in a neighbouring boat. "I wud like to see Macgreegor gettin' yin," she added in an undertone.

"Dod, ay! I wud like him to get the first fish."

"Ay; it wud be nice if he got the first fish... Macgreegor, ye're no' to lean ower the side o' the boat like that."

"Whit wey, Maw?"

"Because ye'll maybe fa' in an' get droondit."

"Nae fears, Maw. I wis jist lukin' at a jeely-fish. Whit wey dae they ca' them jeely-fish, Paw?"

"Because they're like jeely, Macgreegor."

"Ach, they're no' a bit like jeely. They wudna mak' a nice jeely piece, Paw. Wud they?"

"Maybe no'," said John, jerking at his line. "Na; I doot they wudna mak' a vera nice jeely piece, Macgreegor," he continued with another jerk. "'Deed, no! Fur there a big difference atween a jeely fish an' a jeely piece – is there no', Lizzie?"

"Ay," said Mrs. Robinson, as though she had just been awakened from a dream. "Thon lad an' lass is gaun to get marrit, I'm thinkin'," she added, indicating the couple she had been watching.

John jerked his line once more. "Ye're the yin to notice!" he said to his wife. Then to his son: "Macgreegor, ye micht tak' ma line till I see if yer baits is a' richt. Change places wi' me. Canny noo, an' dinna frichten yer Maw... That's a clever laddie! ... Haud on to ma line, an' maybe ye'll bring us luck."

Macgregor changed places with his father, and the latter, with a wink at Mrs. Robinson, who seemed to be somewhat suspicious, began to pull in the line.

But ere he had drawn up three fathoms there was an excited yell from Macgregor.

"Paw! There a fish on ma line! It's chuggin' like mad! Whit'll I dae, Paw?"

"Pu' it up, ma mannie," said John, trying to conceal his delight.

Macgregor, gurgling with excitement, hauled in the line, and soon, with his father's assistance, a fine fish – quite an unusually big fish for Rothesay Bay – was flopping in the bottom of the boat.

"Is't a haddie, Paw?" cried the youngster, while John extracted the hook. "Is't a whitenin'?"

"A whitin'? Na! It's a code, Macgreegor."

"Can I get bashin' it, Paw?"

"Macgreegor," exclaimed his mother, "ye mauna be savage."

"I dinna like codes," cried Macgregor. "They mak' code ile! I want to bash its face!"

"Whisht, man!" said John. "It's a bonny fish, an' ye're no' to spile it. It'll dae fine fur wur breakfast. My! ye sud be prood at catchin' sic a graun' fish!"

The boy *looked* proud and refrained from his brutal intentions. "Did ye ever catch as big a fish, Paw?" he enquired.

"Never," said his father. "But you're the lucky yin, Macgreegor!"

"John," put in Lizzie, "the win's gettin' up."

She was quite right. The smooth sea was quickly rippled, and within five minutes the ripples turned into little breakers.

"I want to catch anither yin, Paw," said Macgregor.

"I want to get hame," said Lizzie.

John obliged his wife. He pulled up the lines, then the anchor, and got out the oars.

"We'll gang oot to the fishin' anither nicht," he said to his son. "It's gaun to be stormy."

"Ach!" ejaculated Macgregor disgustedly.

"John," whispered Lizzie, when they were safely ashore, "it wis rale nice o' ye to let the laddie think he had catched the fish."

"Tits, wumman!" said John smiling.

"Paw," said Macgregor a little later, "I'm vexed ye didna catch a fish the nicht."

"Aw, ye're ower smairt fur maist folk, ma mannie."

"Ay; I'm gey smairt, Paw."

Ships That Pass

THE small boy in the trim sailor suit, broad-brimmed straw hat with "H.M.S. Valiant" in gold letters on the dark-blue ribbon, spotless white collar with gold anchors at the corners, and fine shoes and stockings, stood helplessly on the sunlit shore and with misty eyes gazed hopelessly at his toy yacht drifting out to sea.

"Whit wey dae ye no' wade in efter yer boat?" demanded Macgregor, who for half an hour had been envying the owner his pretty craft from a little distance and who now approached the disconsolate youngster.

"Gaun! Tak' aff yer shoes an' stockin's quick, or ye'll loss yer boat," said Macgregor excitedly. "Gaun! Wade!" he repeated. "Are ye feart?"

"Mamma said I wasn't to wade," said the alleged member of the crew of "H.M.S. Valiant."

"Whit wey?"

"She said it was too cold." He gave a sniff of despair as his eyes turned to his toy.

"Ach! it's no' that cauld. I'll wade fur yer boat."

"Oh!" It was all he could say, but he looked with gratitude at Macgregor, who was already unlacing one of his stout boots.

A minute later Macgregor had rolled up his breeches, and, checking an exclamation at the first contact with the water, was wading gingerly after the model yacht.

"It's awfu' warm," he declared with a shiver.

"Don't get your trousers wet," said the other.

"Nae fears!" returned Macgregor, stepping into a small depression and soaking several inches of his nether garments. "I'm no' heedin' onywey," he said bravely.

"You can't get it. It's too deep," cried the anxious one on the shore. "Oh, my!"

The exclamation was caused by Macgregor taking a plunge forward, soaking his clothes still further, but grabbing successfully at the boat. Then he turned and waded cautiously to the shore and presented the owner with his almost lost property, remarking: "There yer boat. Whit wey did ye no' keep a grup o' the string?"

The other clasped his treasure and gazed with speechless thankfulness at the deliverer.

"It's a daft-like thing to be sailin' a boat if ye dinna wade," observed Macgregor, sitting down on a rock and proceeding to dry his feet and legs with his bonnet. Suddenly he desisted from the operation, as if struck by an idea, and getting up again said easily: "I'll help ye to sail yer boat, if ye like."

The other looked doubtful for a moment, for Macgregor's previous remark had offended him somewhat.

"Come on," said Macgregor with increasing eagerness. "You can be the captain an' I'll be the sailor."

Evidently overcome by the flattering proposal, the owner of the yacht nodded and allowed the proposer to take the craft from his hands.

"My! It's an unco fine boat!" Macgregor observed admiringly. "Whaur got ye it?"

"Uncle William gave me it," replied the other, beginning to find his tongue, "and it's called the 'Britannia.' "

"It's no' an awfu' nice name, but it's a fine boat. I wisht I had as fine a boat... Whit's yer name?" he enquired, wading into the water. "Mines is Macgreegor Robison."

"Charlie Fortune."

"That's a queer-like name. Whaur d'ye come frae?"

Charlie looked puzzled.

"D'ye come frae Glesca? Eh?"

"Yes."

"I never seen ye afore. Whaur d'ye bide in Glesca?"

"Kelvinside. Royal Gardens, Kelvinside."

"Aw, ye'll be gentry," said Macgregor scornfully.

"I don't know," said Charlie. "Are you – gentry?"

"Nae fears! I wudna be gentry fur onythin'!"

Charlie did not quite understand. Presently he asked shyly: "Has your mamma got a house at Rothesay?"

"Naw. But Granpaw Purdie's got a hoose an' I'm bidin' wi' him. Hoo lang are ye bidin' in Rothesay?"

"Three months."

"My! I wisht I wis you! I'm gaun hame next week... But I'll be back again shin. Granpaw Purdie likes when I'm bidin' wi' him. Thon's him ower thonder." And Macgregor indicated the distant figure of the old man who sat on a boulder reading a morning paper.

Mr. Purdie reminded Charlie of an old gardener occasionally employed by his wealthy father, but he offered no remark, and Macgregor placed the boat in the water, crying out with delight as her sails caught a mild breeze.

"Gang ower to thon rock," Macgregor commanded, forgetting in his excitement that, being the sailor, it was not his place to give orders, "an' I'll gar the boat sail to ye."

Charlie obediently made for a spur of rock that entered the water a few yards and waited there patiently while his new acquaintance managed the yacht, not perhaps very skilfully, but entirely to his own satisfaction.

"I'm daein' fine, am I no'?" exclaimed Macgregor as he approached the captain, who had soaked his nice brown shoes in a shallow pool and was now crouching on a slippery rock, fearful lest his mother should come down to the shore and catch him.

"I'm daein' fine, am I no'?" repeated Macgregor.

"Yes," returned Charlie rather dejectedly.

"Weel, I'll tak' the boat ower thonder an' sail it back to ye again."

"I wish I could sail the boat too," said Charlie.

"But ye canna sail it if ye canna get takin' yer bare feet. But never heed. Captains never tak' their bare feet," said Macgregor wading off with the yacht.

He enjoyed himself tremendously for nearly an hour, at the end of which period Charlie announced, timidly, that it was time for him to go home.

"Wull ye be here in the efternune?" enquired Macgregor, leaving the water on bluish feet and relinquishing the "Britannia" with obvious regret.

"No, I'm going to take a drive with mamma."

"Are ye gaun in the 'bus? Granpaw whiles tak's me fur a ride to –"

"Mamma has a carriage," said Charlie.

"I thocht ye wis gentry," said Macgregor, with a pitying gaze at Charlie. There was a pause, and then his eyes turned again to the yacht. "Wull ye be here the morn?"

"I don't know," said Charlie, who wasn't sure that he liked Macgregor's manner of speech, but who still felt grateful to him and was also impressed by his sturdiness.

"Ye micht try an' come. An' tell yer maw ye want to tak' yer bare feet, an' we'll baith be sailors. Eh?"

"I'll try. Thank you for – for saving my boat."

"Aw, never heed that. Jist try an' come the morn, an' I'll come early an' build a pier for the boat."

"I'll try," said Charlie once more; and with a smile on his small, delicate face he hurried up the beach.

Macgregor warmed his legs on the sunny shingle and got into his boots and stockings; then rejoined his grandfather, hoping the old man would not notice the damp condition of his breeches.

Mr. Purdie laid down his paper and smilingly looked at his grandson over his spectacles.

"I see ye've been makin' a new freen', Macgreegor. Whit laddie wis thon?"

"Chairlie – I furget his ither name. He lost his boat an' I tuk ma bare feet an' gaed in an' got it fur him."

Mr. Purdie beamed with pride and patted the boy's shoulder. "'Deed, that wis rale kind o' ye, ma mannie. He wud be gled to get back his boat an' he wud be unco obleeged to yersel' fur gettin' it. I'm thinkin' ye deserve a penny," and out came the old man's purse.

"Thenk ye, Granpaw... An' then I sailed his boat fur him. He canna sail it hissel', fur his maw winna let him tak' his bare feet. She maun be an auld daftie!"

"Whisht, whisht!" said Mr. Purdie reprovingly. "But whit like is Chairlie?"

"Och, he's gey peely-wally, an' I think he's gentry, but his boat's an awfu' fine yin."

"Whit gars ye think he's gentry?"

"He bides in Kelvinside, an' his maw rides in a cairriage,

an' he speaks like Aunt Purdie when she's ha'ein' a pairty."

At the last reason Mr. Purdie gave a half-suppressed chuckle. "Weel, weel, Macgreegor, ye're gettin' on. Ye're the yin to notice things."

"Ay; I'm gey fly, Granpaw," said Macgregor.

"But mind an' no' lead Chairlie intil ony mischief," Mr. Purdie went on. "An' yer no' to temp' him to tak' his bare feet if his mither disna want him to dae it. Noo it's time we wis gaun hame to wur dinner. Gi'e's yer haun', ma mannie."

Next day, when Macgregor had almost given up hope, and stood disconsolately eyeing the pier he had constructed as promised, Charlie arrived, panting, with the "Britannia" in his arms.

"I thocht ye wisna comin'," said Macgregor.

"Mamma didn't want me to play on the shore to-day."

"Did ye rin awa' frae her the noo?"

"No. But Uncle William came in and he asked her for me, and then she said I could go for half an hour. But I'm not to go wading."

"Are ye no'? I wudna like to be you," said Macgregor, dabbling his bare feet in the water. "Weel, ye can be the man on the pier. Some o' the stanes is a wee thing shoogly, but ye'll jist ha'e to luk whaur ye pit yer feet, Chairlie."

Charlie, after a little hesitation, walked gingerly down the narrow passage of loose stones which terminated with a large flat one, where he found a fairly sure foothold.

"That's it!" cried Macgregor, wading out from shore till the water was within half an inch of his clothing. "Ye're jist like a pier-man."

Charlie was so gratified that he nearly fell off his perch. Very cautiously he placed his model afloat and the wind carried it out to sea, Macgregor moving along so as to intercept it.

Macgregor wanted to have the "Britannia" sail back to its owner, but the mystery of navigation was too much for him, so he carried it to Charlie, who set it off again.

After all, it wasn't such bad fun, being a pier-man, and in about ten minutes the youngsters were as friendly as could be. And they spent a glorious hour and a quarter.

"Wull ye be here the morn?" asked Macgregor when his new chum said, rather fearfully, that he must depart.

"Yes." There was a flush on Charlie's face that ought to have done his mother good to see. "Yes," he repeated eagerly. "And I'll bring my other boat."

"My! Ha'e ye anither boat, Chairlie?"

Charlie nodded. "Not as big as the 'Britannia,' " he said... He smiled shyly at his friend. "I – I'm going to give it to you, Macgreegor," he stammered, pronouncing the name as he had heard it from its owner.

"Ach, ye're just sayin' that!" cried Macgregor, overcome with astonishment.

"Really and truly," said Charlie.

"Ye – ye're faur ower kind," whispered Macgregor, fairly at a loss for once in his little life. He did not know that Charlie had never had a real boy companion, for Charlie, between his clever father, his would-be "fashionable" mother and his plaintive tutor, was being brought up to be a "gentleman" and nothing more.

Feeling and looking more awkward and awkward, Charlie took the liberty of touching Macgregor's arm between the wrist and the elbow.

"Please take the boat," he murmured.

Macgregor fumbled in his pocket. "I'll gi'e ye ma penny," he said, producing it.

But Charlie drew back, and somehow Macgregor understood he had done something stupid.

Charlie ran off, and Macgregor, gazing curiously after him, resumed his boots and stockings.

The day following was wet as it can be on the west coast of Scotland, and in spite of Macgregor's open yearning for his new toy, his grandparents would not allow him out-of-doors.

"Maybe Chairlie'll be there wi' ma boat," he pleaded.

But Grandfather Purdie gently said: "It's no' vera likely"; and Grandmother Purdie remarked: "Ye wud jist get yer daith o' cauld, ma dearie."

But the morning after broke brilliantly – too brilliantly, perhaps, to last.

At ten o'clock Mr. Purdie was sitting on his favourite rock, his pipe in his mouth, his specs on his nose, and his newspaper before him. "I wud like to come an' see yer freen' Chairlie," he had said, ere his grandson left him; "I like weans that's kind til either weans." And Macgregor had promised to wave a signal when Charlie came with the boats. Mr. Purdie had filled his pocket with sweets for the occasion.

Macgregor reached the appointed place, which seemed so familiar, although it was only his third visit, and, his friend not being in sight, proceeded to repair the pier, which several tides had disarranged.

He became so busy and so interested that he did not hear the sound of flying feet until they were close upon him. Then he rose from his stooping posture and beheld Charlie with a beautiful little boat in his arms.

"Here's your boat, Macgreegor," gasped Charlie.

"My!" cried Macgregor, taking it. "Oh Chairlie, ye're awfu' –"

"Mamma said I wasn't to play with you any more, but – but I ran away, and –"

"Whit wey?"

Charlie shook his head. "I like you," he panted. "I never had another boy to – to play with. I – I –"

"Charlie, come here at once! "

"Good-bye, Macgreegor," said Charlie, and turning, ran some fifty yards to the elegantly dressed lady who had called him.

"She's gentry," said Macgregor to himself, but he, of course, did not hear her say crossly to Charlie:

"What do you mean by speaking to that horrid boy after I told you never to speak to him again?"

Macgregor, after waiting in the hope that Charlie would return, hastened toward his grandfather to exhibit his prize, but as he proceeded his pace slackened.

"Ye've got yer boat, Macgreegor!" the old man exclaimed. "Dod, but it's a bonny boat! It wis unco kind o' Chairlie to gi'e ye that. But whit wey did ye no' wave on me? Eh? Is Chairlie waitin' ower thonder?" .

Macgregor laid his boat on the ground. "Chairlie ran awa'. He said his maw didna want him to play wi' me ony mair... Granpaw, whit wey –?"

"Whit's that ye're sayin', Macgreegor?"

"Chairlie said his maw didna want him to play wi' me ony mair... I think she's gentry – she's an auld footer... I like Chairlie."

"Ah!" exclaimed Mr. Purdie suddenly. Then he uttered several words, wildly.

Macgregor gaped. Never before had he heard his grandfather use such words.

Mrs. M'ostrich Gives a Party

"I'VE news fur ye the nicht, John," said Mrs. Robinson shortly after the family had gathered at the tea-table one evening towards the end of the year.

"Weel, I hope it's guid news, fur if it's bad I'll ha'e ma ham an' eggs first," returned her husband pleasantly.

"Oh, it's no' whit ye wud ca' bad news."

"*I* ken whit it is," exclaimed Macgregor, grinning. "It's aboot Mistress M'Ostrich. She's gaun to ha'e a pairty, an' I'm gaun!"

"Haud yer tongue, laddie," said his mother, slightly annoyed. "An' dinna speak wi' yer mooth fu' o' breid."

"It's no' breid, Maw; it's toast. I like Mistress M'Ostrich."

His father, checking a laugh, enquired the date of the party.

"The morn's nicht," replied Mrs. Robinson. "I wis gaun to tell ye, John, that – "

"It's to be a hot supper, Paw, because Mistress M'Ostrich's uncle's deid," Macgregor interrupted gleefully.

"Tits! Macgreegor! Can ye no' haud yer tongue when I tell ye? An' ye're jist as bad, John, to lauch like that at his stupit sayin's."

"Och, Lizzie, I canna help lauchin'. But gang on wi' yer story, an' Macgreegor'll keep quate," said John, shaking his head at his son in a mildly warning fashion.

"Weel," said Lizzie, somewhat mollified, "I'll jist tell ye a' aboot it. (Macgreegor, butter a piece breid fur yer wee sister.) Mistress M'Ostrich cam' to me the day to tell me – "

"She got the len' o' wur bew vazes, Paw, an' wur mauve tidy wi' the yella paurrit on it, an' wur–"

"Whisht, man!" whispered John. "Never heed him, Lizzie," he added to his wife. "Whit did Mistress M'Ostrich tell ye?"

"She tell't me she had gotten near a hunner pound left her by her uncle in Americy. She hasna seem him fur thirty year–"

"Her uncle's deid, Paw."

The parents wisely ignored the interruption, and Mrs. Robinson continued:

"An' she wis unco surprised at him mindin' her, fur he didna approve o' her mairryin' Maister M'Ostrich. (Whit wis it ye wis wantin',' Jeannie, ma doo? Did Macgreegor no' pit plenty butter on yer piece? Macgreegor, pit mair butter on yer wee sister's piece, an' dinna mak' sic a noise drinkin' yer tea!) But fur a' that, she wis gled to get the money."

"Dod, ay!" said John. "I cud dae wi' 't masel! But I thocht she micht be gettin' vazes an' tidies o' her ain wi' some of the siller."

"Ah, but ye see, John, she hasna gotten the money yet; an' furbye, she said she didna like to gang past her auld freen's that had obleeged her mony a time afore."

"Deed, that's yin wey o' lukin' at it," her husband remarked, smiling.

"Puir buddy, when I think o' her man, I canna grudge her onythin'. Fancy her man gaun aff to his bed i' the kitchen every nicht afore nine o'clock, an' her hearin' him snorin' a' the time she's ha'ein' a pairty in the paurlour."

"She sudna ha'e mairrit a baker. If Maister M'Ostrich has got to rise early, he maun gang to his bed early. But it's a peety he's sic a snorer. D'ye mind – ha! ha! – when Macgreegor thocht there wis a pig in Mistress M'Ostrich's kitchen?"

"I'm no' likely to furget that, John! I never wis mair affrontit in a' ma born days. I'm shair I hope Macgreegor'll behave hissel' the morn's nicht," sighed Lizzie. "An' I'm feart he'll be nane the better o' the hot supper."

"I'll no' affront ye, Maw," put in Macgregor.

"I'm shair he'll no' affront ye," said John, patting the boy's shoulder.

"Weel, weel, dearie," said Lizzie to her son, "I jist hope ye'll be carefu' whit ye say, an' carefu' whit yer eat, an' no' be impiddent to yer Aunt Purdie."

"Is ma Aunt Purdie to be at the pairty?" Macgregor enquired, his face clouding.

"Vera likely."

"I thocht Mistress M'Ostrich wudna be genteel enough fur Mistress Purdie," John observed.

"We'll see," returned his wife briefly, turning to replenish her little daughter's mug with milk.

"Paw," said Macgregor in a confidential whisper, "if Aunt Purdie's at the pairty, you an' me'll no' sit aside her."

Mrs. M'Ostrich's little parlour was decorated in so lavish and varied a fashion by the numerous ornaments borrowed from her guests that the dinginess of its walls and the shabbiness of its furniture were hardly noticeable. But whatever anyone might feel about her method of obtaining decorations, no one could deny that her hospitality was exceedingly generous. It was almost a craze of the elderly childless woman to give parties as frequently as she could scrape together sufficient cash for more or less light refreshments; and on this occasion, when money, or at anyrate the prospect of it, was assured, she rejoiced in loading her table with good things, turning a deaf ear to her husband's cry of "awfu' wastry." Moreover she had purchased a black silk dress – her dream of at least thirty years – which, besides accentuating the spareness of her figure, was likely to gain her the envy of not a few of her acquaintances. Yet with what conscious pride did she receive her guests, trying to forget that half-an-hour earlier Mr. M'Ostrich had retired to rest without a word of admiration or encouragement, and that he might begin to snore at any moment!

Mrs. Purdie was the last to arrive, as became one whose husband was a rising grocer, and she came more with a view to impressing the more humble guests with her importance than with any intention of making herself agreeable. It was quite a shock to her to find another silk dress in the parlour. She greeted the Robinsons in the patronising way which always irritated John and Lizzie into saying very plain things and behaving in their most unaffected manner.

"And how are you to-night, Macgregor?" she enquired, smiling sourly upon her nephew.

"Fine, thenk ye," he returned, trying to edge away.

"I didn't think a little boy like you would have been allowed to sich a late party," she observed so disagreeably, that John, overhearing her, clenched his fist involuntarily.

Macgregor, feeling the snub keenly, but unable to frame an effective retort, moved away to the chair where his father was seated, "Paw," he whispered, "Aunt Purdie's a – a – "

"Whisht, ma mannie. Come an' speak to Mistress Bowley, her that wis so kind to ye the last time we wis here."

Meanwhile Mrs. M'Ostrich, assisted by Lizzie, was laying the hot dishes on the otherwise prepared table, and doing her best to look cheerful, in spite of the fact that her husband had, on her last visit to the kitchen, grunted the following encouraging remark:

"You an' yer pairties! Humph! Awa' an' tell the folk that's come to eat ye oot the hoose that I canna get sleepin' fur their gabblin' tongues. You an' yer pairties!"

But soon the company was ranged round the table, and the hostess must have felt gratified by the appreciation bestowed upon her fare. Perhaps Mrs. Purdie's countenance wore a rather supercilious expression when big Mr. Pumpherston polished his forehead with a large red handkerchief and handed his cup for a third supply of cocoa; or when John put his knife in his mouth; or when Macgregor went nearly black in the face over half a baked potato; or when poor Mrs. M'Crae from round the corner, who didn't get a proper meal once a month, exclaimed in a gush of rapture, if not actual gratitude:

"Mistress M'Ostrich, may I drap deid in twa meenits if I ever tastit a finer white puddin'!"

As a matter of fact, it did not much matter to any of the elders how Mrs. Purdie looked or what she thought, and she was much disgusted to find that no one about her seemed particularly anxious to listen to her stories concerning her grand friends and their doings. So, having failed to impress the company, she set about depressing one of its members, to wit Macgregor, who, in spite of warning glances from his mother, had been enjoying himself very heartily. But with his aunt's gaze upon him he became uncomfortable.

"Paw," he whispered at last, "whit's she glowerin' at me fur?"

"Aw, never heed, ma mannie. Jist enjye yersel'," advised his father in a low voice.

"I canna, Paw," said the youngster dolefully.

Just then Mr. Pumpherston, possibly under the genial influence of the cocoa, offered to show the company how to swallow a whole apple and recover the same intact from one's elbow. While all eyes were turned on the conjurer, it occurred to Macgregor to perform a little trick on his own account, and he accordingly transferred the tartlet, which he had been unable to enjoy under his Aunt's cold eye, from his plate to his pocket for future consumption. The main difference between Mr. Pumpherston's sleight-of hand and Macgregor's was that everybody saw through the former and nobody noticed the latter, indeed, Macgregor himself audibly observed: "He had the aipple in his haun a' the time."

When the guests retired from the table, to allow of its being cleared by the hostess and Lizzie, Macgregor made himself comfortable in the only easy-chair in the room, and shortly afterwards discovered that the juice of the tartlet was leaking into the pocket of his best jacket. He therefore stealthily removed the dainty, laid it flat, to prevent further leakage, behind him on the chair, and prepared to accept any further entertainment which might be offered.

Mr. Pumpherston was the first to oblige. As soon as Mrs. M'Ostrich returned from depositing her last load of dishes in the kitchen – where she was saluted with the question, "Are thae gabblin' eediots no' awa' yet?" – Mr. Pumpherston, by general request, consented to sing the old song, "A guid New Year to yin an' a'."

He prefaced the song with a brief observation. "It's no' jist exac'ly the New Year yet, but it's gey near it. Some o' us here'll maybe no' leeve to see it, but we maun hope fur the best... Doh, me, soh, doh, soh, me, doh," he hummed. "Na, that's ower high. I'll ha'e to try anither key."

"He's a lang time catchin' his key the nicht," explained his wife, "but yinst he catches it he'll sing fur a year."

Mr. Pumpherston always had a difficulty in getting the key suited to his thin piping voice, and Mrs. Pumpherston always offered some little explanation.

At the conclusion of the song Macgregor remarked to his father, under cover of the general applause: "Thon man's a daft yin."

Then Mrs. M'Ostrich announced that Mr. Blaikie, who happened to be seated close to Macgregor, would oblige the company with a recitation, whereupon Macgregor beamed expectantly.

"The Uncle – a Mystery," began Mr. Blaikie, a youngish man who had not previously enjoyed Mrs. M'Ostrich's hospitality, but who was a distant relative from the country.

"I ken it fine," exclaimed Macgregor. "Granpaw Purdie whiles recites it."

"*Sh! sh!*" said several of the guests, and Mrs. Purdie took it upon herself to say, "Behave yersel'!" – much to the annoyance of Lizzie, who was puzzling as to how she could say the same thing without attracting too much notice to her impulsive boy.

"The Uncle – a Mystery," repeated Mr. Blaikie, smiling good humouredly on the youngster, and at once winning his respect." 'I had an uncle once, A man of – ' "

Here the reciter paused, listening.

Some of the guests listened also, others began to talk hurriedly about nothing in particular. Macgregor leaned from his chair, and in an audible whisper said to Mr. Blaikie:

"Never heed it. Dinna be feart. It's no' a real grumphy. It's jist Maister M'Ostrich – "

Several people could not refrain from sniggering, whereat Macgregor looked distressed. What had he said? What had he done? He grew miserably red.

"It's a' richt, dearie," said kindly Mrs. M'Ostrich at last. "Dinna fash yersel'. We're a' freen's here."

But Aunt Purdie rose from her seat beside Mrs. Robinson and strode across the room to her nephew. "Ye best gang an' sit aside yer mither," she said crossly and unkindly, forgetting her affected mode of speech, "an' no' affront us any mair."

Macgregor looked helplessly at his father. But the latter signed him to obey. The youngster saw that his mother was not regarding him so angrily as he expected she would – Lizzie could not bear her sister-in-law to interfere with her son – so he left the easy-chair, which his Aunt immediately occupied, and went over to his mother, with whom he sat quietly until the recitation was ended.

Then he whispered, "Maw, I want to gang hame noo."

"Hame?" said Lizzie, surprised.

"Ay, I – I'm wearit."

"But Maister Pumpherston's gaun to sing anither sang."

"I'm no' heedin'. I want to gang hame. Tak' me hame, Maw."

"I doot ye've ett ower mony guid things the nicht, dearie."

"Naw. I jist want to gang hame."

Lizzie beckoned her man to her and told him Macgregor's desire.

"Weel," said John. "If the wean wants to gang, he maun gang. But Mistress Purdie wis sayin', she had a cab comin' fur her, an' she wud gi'e us a hurl hame – no' that's I'm heedin' aboot it."

"Nor me either," said Lizzie promptly. "She can display her riches to ither folk, but I'm fur nane o' them."

"Maybe Macgreegor wud like a hurl."

"Naw. I want to gang hame noo, Paw," whispered the boy in alarm.

And presently they went, and Mrs. M'Ostrich, coming to the door with them, asked Macgregor for a kiss, and he put his arms round her neck and gave it heartily, for she had dealt gently with him.

On reaching home the neighbour who had been looking after wee Jeannie informed Lizzie that the child had been rather restless, and Lizzie hastened to her daughter to find, happily, nothing to alarm her.

"Whit gaed wrang wi' ye, Macgreegor?" enquired John, when the twain were alone together.

"Aw, naethin'."

"But are ye feelin' no' weel, ma mannie?"

"Naw, I'm fine, Paw. But I – I wis feart fur Aunt Purdie."

"Hoots, ye needna be feart fur her! Whit wey wis ye feart?"

"I – I left ma – ma tert on the chair, an' she sat on it, Paw."

"Yer tert? On the chair? I dinna see – "

Macgregor explained more fully. "An' I've lost ma tert," he ended.

"Aw, Macgreegor, Macgreegor, Macgreegor!" cried John, half-suffocated with suppressed laughter. "An' ye lost yer tert, did ye? Puir laddie! But get aff yer claes an gang quick to yer bed. I'm gaun ootbye fur a wee."

His wife was surprised to meet him hurrying from the house. "Whaur are ye gaun, John, at this time o' nicht?"

"Aw, I'm gaun oot to ha'e a – a – a – guid lauch. I'll tell ye a' aboot it when I come back in aboot five meenits. But dinna be severe on Macgreegor, dearie. Jist dinna say onythin' to him aboot the pairty till I come back. Dod, I maun gang, or I'll explode."

"I wunner whit that laddie o' mines has been tellin' John," said Lizzie to herself, as she went to hasten Macgregor to bed. "Maybe I best wait an' see. Onywey, I'm no' gaun to ha'e Mistress Purdie interferin' – "

"Maw," cried Macgregor as she entered the kitchen, "I'm wearit. Can I say ma prayers noo?"

New Year's Eve at Granpaw Purdie's

THE little parlour of the old people's modest abode at Rothesay was a picture of cosiness, and Grandfather Purdie and his spouse were hospitality and kindliness personified. The Robinson family had just arrived from Glasgow, and after a chilly, though not unpleasant journey, were enjoying the comforts of the tea table, Macgregor's appetite being, as usual, remarkably keen, especially for the luxuries.

"Macgreegor," said his careful mother in a whisper, "ye're no' to pit jeely on yer first piece."

The boy let the spoon slip back into the jelly dish, and, looking disappointed, applied himself to his bread and butter, while his father winked at Lizzie as much as to say that she might let the youngster have his own way, seeing that this was a special occasion.

Lizzie, however, ignored the signal, and proceeded to attend to her small daughter Jeannie, who was gulping her portion of milk and hot water rather too eagerly for safety. "Canny, ma dearie, or ye'll choke yersel'," she said, removing the mug gently, and giving the child a finger of bread and butter.

"Want jeely," said wee Jeannie.

"Ye'll get jeely in a wee whiley," returned the mother. "See, eat yer nice piece."

"Want jeely."

"Ah, but it's no' time fur jeely yet, ma daurlin'."

"Want jeely," repeated Jeannie, whose young mind was above arguments.

"Tits! Lizzie," interposed the grandfather, "gi'e the wean jeely if she wants it. Ye needna be that stric' on Hogmanay," he added smiling.

"Weel, weel," she returned, "maybe I needna, fayther."

"Here the jeely, Maw," said Macgregor, officiously passing the dish to her.

Mrs. Robinson took a spoonful, laid it on her plate, and

spread some of it on her daughter's bread and butter.

"Are ye no' fur ony yersel', ma mannie?" Mr. Purdie asked his grandson.

Macgregor glanced at his mother, and she, after a moment's hesitation, passed him the dish. " 'Deed, fayther," she said laughingly to the old man, "ye wud spile ony wean! But I mind fine when ye wudna let *me* tak' jeely on ma first piece."

"Dae ye, ma dochter? ... Weel, weel, ye needna gang an' veesit the sins o' yer parents on yer children," he retorted with a chuckle, "especially on the last nicht o' the auld year."

"'Deed, no!" exclaimed old Mrs. Purdie, from the other end of the table, where she smiled very happily and often, but seldom spoke.

So Macgregor tucked into the jelly and other good things till Mr. Purdie could not help saying:

"Mind an' leave room fur yer supper, laddie."

"Are we gaun to get supper furbye?" exclaimed the boy in gratified surprise.

"Na, na," said Lizzie. "Yer Granpaw's jist jokin.' Ye maun gang early to yer bed the nicht, an' ha'e a fine day oot-bye the morn – if it's no' ower cauld or wat."

"I dinna want to gang to ma bed early, Maw. I want to bring in the New Year."

"Oh, ye're ower wee to sit up that late, dearie."

"I'm no', Maw! Wullie Thomson's maw is gaun to let him sit up, an' he's faur wee-er nor me."

His mother shook her head. "I canna help whit Mistress Thomson lets Wullie dae. Maybe that's whit mak's him peely-wally – sittin' up late isna guid fur laddies."

"But Wullie aye gangs earlier to his bed nor me, Maw," Macgregor persisted.

Lizzie was at a loss, and her husband said boldly:

"Let Macgreegor bring in the New Year, wumman."

"An' let him ha'e his supper like the rest o' us," added Mr. Purdie.

"Jist that," said Mrs. Purdie, beaming across the table.

Mrs. Robinson laughed ruefully. "Ye're a' agin me, so I

suppose Macgreegor'll ha'e to get his ain wey. But I dinna believe in late suppers fur weans, an' I doot Macgreegor'll be needin' to get ile i' the mornin'.'"

"I'll tak' the ile, Maw," said Macgregor so eagerly that everybody laughed except his mother and sister, the latter being otherwise engaged with another long drink.

Lizzie was only human, and a sharp rejoinder was at her lips, when Mr. Purdie, who had taken off his spectacles for the purpose of wiping them, let them drop, in the most innocent manner imaginable, into his second cup of tea. The laugh was now against him, and he took it with the utmost good humour.

Macgregor was particularly delighted at the little mishap, and there is no saying how long he would have laughed had not a crumb of cake gone down the wrong way and changed his mirth to a fit of coughing so severe that his mother fell to thumping him on the back, while the others of the party sat aghast, Mr. Purdie inwardly reproaching himself for the trouble he felt he had caused.

"Ye sudna lauch wi' cake in yer mooth, dearie," said Lizzie when her son, much to her relief, was sitting panting with a very red countenance and tearful eyes, but "out of danger."

"I – I didna ken Granpaw wis gaun to drap his specs in his – his tea," said Macgregor, and his excuse was surely one of justification.

"'Deed, it wis a' ma fau't," said the old man regretfully. "I sudna ha'e tried to – I mean it wis a daft-like thing to dae."

And Mr. Purdie put on his spectacles, a proceeding which threw his grandson into a fresh fit of laughter, for, in his confusion he had omitted to dry them, and two brown tears ran down the ancient cheeks. He took them off, laughing as heartily as anyone, and Macgregor, recovering himself, fumbled in his breast pocket, and said:

"Ha'e, Granpaw. I'll len' ye ma hanky."

But Mr. Purdie was already wiping his face with a huge old-fashioned coloured handkerchief. "Thenk ye, thenk ye, ma mannie," he said, touched by his grandson's attention. "I'll no' spile yer braw white hanky."

"I wudna like to ha'e a rid yin like yours," agreeably remarked Macgregor, returning his white square to his pocket.

Fortunately his mother did not hear the remark, and presently the party rose from the table and gathered round the fire, where the elders sat chatting for an hour, at the end of which Mrs. Robinson decided to put the drowsy Jeannie to bed, and Mrs. Purdie set about clearing the tea things.

Mr. Purdie and his son-in-law set their pipes agoing, and Macgregor sat between them, feeling very manly indeed – and very uncomfortable too (though he would never have admitted that), for he sat just on the slippery edge of a horse-hair covered chair in order that his toes might touch the floor. It would have been so undignified to have dangled his legs!

"Wud ye no' like to sit on the hassock, ma mannie?" said his grandfather, kindly, producing from under his easy-chair a well worn carpet-covered footstool.

"Naw," the boy returned scornfully. "I'm fine here." With a view to showing how "fine" he was, he endeavoured to fling one leg over the other, as he noticed his father doing at the moment; but, as luck would have it, he slid from his perch and fell with a mild thud on the hearth-rug.

"Are ye hurt?" the twain exclaimed, the father rising hastily.

"Naw. I'm no' that easy hurt," muttered Macgregor with a ruddy countenance, and a tear of mortification in each eye, as he resumed his chair.

Grandfather Purdie was going to suggest the hassock a second time, but John, with a wink, whispered, "Jist let him tak' his ain wey. He disna like ye to think he's no' a big laddie, ye ken."

"'Deed, ay," said the old man, understanding at once. He and John conversed for perhaps ten minutes, and then they were interrupted by Macgregor, who, beginning to find it dull, started whistling in a peculiar hissing fashion, which would have been extremely irritating to anyone but his present companions.

"Are ye wearyin,' Macgreegor?" asked Mr. Purdie.

Macgregor replied: "Dae a recite, Granpaw."

"Haud yer tongue, Macgreegor," said John, most gently, wishing his wife could have heard him exercising the authority which he had promised her he would exercise over the youngster during the visit.

But Mr. Purdie genially replied: "An' whit wud ye like me to recite, ma mannie? Ye'll be wantin' somethin' new, I'm thinkin'. Eh? ... Aweel, here a bit I cut oot o' a paper, thinkin' ye micht like it. But I'll ha'e to read it, fur ma mem'ry's no' as guid as it used to be." As a matter of fact Mr. Purdie had been practising the reading assiduously for three weeks in view of his grandson's visit.

He adjusted his spectacles, cleared his throat, and began reading in his old-fashioned, impressive manner.

But the story did not appeal to Macgregor. He listened patiently enough during the first half, shuffled uneasily during the remainder, and at the conclusion remarked: "It's no' as nice as yer ither recites, Granpaw."

"I'm vexed ye didna like it," said the old man, trying to conceal his disappointment.

"I'm shair Macgreegor liket it fine," interposed John. "But, ye see, he kens the auld stories best."

"Ay," said the boy. "But dae yin aboot folk gettin' kilt. Dae thon yin aboot the man that drooned the ither man, an' then got nabbit by the ghost. Thon's an awfu' nice yin!" he added with a slight shudder.

"Na, na. That's no' a story fur Hogmanay, dearie."

"Aw, ay, Granpaw," said Macgregor, leaving his perch, and standing persuasively at Mr. Purdie's knee. "An' then dae the yin aboot the skeletin in the boax, an' the yin aboot the – "

Mr. Purdie smilingly shook his head, but was eventually persuaded to get out his old recitation book. He did not read all the extreme horrors requested, but he read many pieces familiar, and therefore acceptable, to Macgregor, until, hoarse as a raven, he laid the book aside.

"Dae anither, Granpaw," begged the youngster, to whom the hoarseness had been but extra enjoyment.

John, however, did his duty, and the old man was permitted a short season of rest.

And ere long Mrs. Purdie and Lizzie, who had both been very busy in the kitchen, appeared, and proceeded to lay the table for supper.

Macgregor kept silence awhile, but at last, Lizzie being alone, out burst the question: "Whit are we to get, Maw?"

His mother bit her lip and pretended not to hear him.

"Maw, whit's that nice smell?" he whispered.

"It'll be naethin' fur you, if ye dinna haud yer tongue," she replied in a severe undertone.

He held his peace for a couple of minutes. Then, in a tone of the tenderest enquiry: "Is't a pie, Maw?"

Lizzie replied with a look of solemn warning.

"Am I to get leemonade, Maw?"

"John!" she cried desperately. "Can ye no' gi'e Macgreegor somethin' to keep him quate?"

"He's no' makin' a noise, is he?" said John, who had dropped into a chat with his father-in-law. "Whit is't ye're wantin', ma laddie?"

"I wis jist speirin' whit we wis gaun to get to—"

Macgregor's reply was interrupted by his mother, exclaiming:

"Whisht! Anither word, an' ye'll gang to yer bed this vera meenit!"

"Macgreegor," said Mr. Purdie, "here, an' I'll gi'e ye a guess. If a herrin' an' a hauf cost three bawbees, hoo mony wud ye get fur eleevenpence?"

"Ach, that's an auld yin! I ken it fine. Gi'e's anither, Granpaw."

"Ye sudna speak to yer Granpaw like that," said Lizzie.

"Whit wey, Maw?"

But Lizzie, feeling affronted, left the room to join her mother in the kitchen.

Mr. Purdie then repeated the old rhyme:

Come a riddle, come a riddle, come a rote-tote-tote!
A wee, wee man in a rid, rid coat!
A staff in his haun', an' a stane in his throat —
Come a riddle, come a riddle, come a rote-tote-tote!

"Och, that's anither auld yin. It's jist a cherry. Gi'e's anither, Granpaw," said Macgregor.

Mr. Purdie scratched his old head. "Dod, I doot I canna mind ony mair. John, gi'e Macgreegor a guess," he said, appealing to his son-in-law.

"I ken a' Paw's guesses," said Macgregor before his parent could open his mouth.

But just then arrived relief for the elders. Old Mrs. Purdie entered smiling. "Are ye a' ready fur yer suppers?"

"Ay!" replied Macgregor so promptly, that the assents of the others were mere echoes.

"Weel, ma dearie," said his grandmother, "come awa' wi' me an' help to cairry the plates."

He followed her to the kitchen, and there cried in triumph: "I kent it wis a pie!"

"Aw, Macgreegor," sighed his mother reproachfully.

A few minutes later there was not a cheerier little year-end party in Scotland. Perhaps the old people missed their son Robert, the grocer in Glasgow, to assist in bringing in the New Year, but they knew he would arrive with his wife early the next day, and they pretended not to hear when Macgregor whispered to his father:

"I'm awfu' gled Aunt Purdie's no' here!" For, as those who have met her know, Aunt Purdie was inclined to play the grand lady with her plain relations, and, also, to treat Macgregor even more sternly than was necessary.

Grandfather Purdie laughed to his spouse across the table, as he flourished a large knife and fork. "This'll no' be yer first Hogmanay pie, auld wife!" he cried.

She smiled. "Ask a blessin', auld man," she said softly.

"Dod, I near furgot!" he muttered apologetically, laying down the knife and fork; and, resting his right elbow on the table, he covered his eyes with his wrinkled hand...

"Macgreegor gets helpit first fur bein' the youngest," he said presently.

"Dinna gi'e him a' that gravy, fayther," said Lizzie.

"But I like the gravy, Maw," protested the boy.

"Ay; but I'm feart ye mak' a splutter on yer Granmaw's fine braw table-cloth."

"I'll be rale canny, Maw."

"Weel, weel. See an' no' mak' a mess."

It was a plenteous repast, seasoned throughout with benevolence and merriment. Mr. Purdie told stories and chuckled; Mrs. Purdie listened and beamed; John laughed and winked pleasantly at his wife; and Lizzie, having somehow relaxed her watchfulness over her son, enjoyed herself more than she usually did in company.

And what if Macgregor ate and drank more heartily than was perhaps good for him? What if he did splutter some gravy on to the cloth? What if he boasted rather often about sitting up to welcome the New Year? What if he insisted on pouring half his lemonade into Mr. Purdie's tumbler, which contained a little whisky, and so touched the old man that the latter drank the sweet mixture although he loathed it? What if he nearly wrecked the whole feast by sliding off his chair under the table, all but clutching the cloth in his descent? What if—

But no matter! The feast ended as happily as it began, and once more there was a gathering by the hearth to while away the two hours that remained to the Old Year.

But now Macgregor was content to sit on the hassock while his grandfather gave one more reading. And when the reading was ended he did not demand another. And ere long the elders paused in their grown-up chat, and nodded, smiling, to the hearth-rug where the boy, having slipped from the hassock, had fallen sound asleep.

"Puir daurlin'," said his grandmother gently.

"He'll be wearit wi' the journey, nae doot," said Mr. Purdie.

Lizzie remembered she had forgotten to bring the family bottle of castor oil, but looked sympathetically on the sleeper. "John," she said, "wud ye no' pit him ower on the sofa?"

"'Deed, ay," replied John, and Macgregor, without protest, allowed himself to be carried to the temporary couch.

The old couple and the young talked, and talked, and talked, – sadly, gladly – of days gone by and of days to come – sighing or laughing quietly, but sympathising always. Now and then there fell a silence, and they would glance separately at the sleeper, and back to one another, smiling gently, Lizzie as gently as any. What would they do without him? ...

"Mercy me!" cried Lizzie pointing suddenly. "It's twal' o'clock!"

The long hand of the old clock in the corner was only a minute from the hour.

"I maun wauken Macgreegor," said John. "He wud be sair disappintit if–"

"Ay; he maun hear the 'oor strikin'," said Mr. Purdie starting up. "Haste ye, an' wauken him, John."

But the boy was sleeping very sound.

"Macgreegor, Macgreegor, the New Year's comin' in!"

Macgregor grunted drowsily.

"He wudna furgi'e us if we let him sleep past the time," said Lizzie, and she joined her husband in attempting to rouse the boy.

Sounds rose in the street, and a voice bawled, "A guid New Year to yin an' a'!"

"Whit a peety! He'll be ower late," sighed Mrs. Purdie as she joined the parents.

The jovial sounds from the street increased. A church clock boomed midnight.

"It's ower late," sighed Mrs. Purdie, John and Lizzie as Macgregor at last sat up blinking.

"Is't the New Year?" he asked.

"Ay, but – but – "

A chuckle came from Grandfather Purdie. "Na; it's no' ower late. It wants near hauf a meenit to twal'." And he pointed to the face of the old clock in front of which he was standing.

Macgregor rubbed his eyes and gazed.

"Listen," said Mr. Purdie, "D'ye hear the Auld Year tickin' away'? ... Noo, it's jist gaun to strike!" ...

"A guid New Year!" cried everybody to everybody else, and much handshaking ensued.

"Did ye like bringin' in the New Year, ma mannie?" enquired the old man a little later.

Macgregor, now fairly wide awake, replied: "Ay, fine! But did the New Year come oot the nock, Granpaw?"

"Eh?"

"Whit wey is the wee door o' the nock open, Granpaw?"

Mr. Purdie stared helplessly. "I thocht I had shut it," he muttered feebly.

"Whit wey," began the boy again.

"Macgreegor, come to your bed, dearie," Lizzie interrupted.

"But whit wey–"

"No' anither word! Ye maun ha'e a guid sleep noo, and be ready fur yer presents in the mornin'." And she led him away.

"I wis near catched that time," said Grandfather Purdie to himself. "I wudna ha'e liket onybody to ha'e seen me haudin' the pendulum." Mrs. Purdie and John were talking together by the fire, and he went over to the clock and cautiously closed its door.

"Ay, ay, John," Mrs. Purdie was saying a little sadly, as he joined them, "anither year bye! Time waits on nane o' us."

John shook his head solemnly, but as the old woman continued gazing into the failing fire, he turned and winked gaily but sympathetically at his father-in-law.

Heart's Desire

MACGREGOR had slept in, but he entered his grand-parents' kitchen without hesitation or apology, for he knew the lenient ways of the old people.

They had finished breakfast and were seated on either side of the hearth, Mr. Purdie beaming gaily at his spouse, and she smiling back at him happily, though with wet eyes. Mr. Purdie held a letter in his right hand and telegram in his left, and as the boy appeared he was saying:

"Dod, ay, auld wife; I'll read them again to please ye."

"Oh, here Macgreegor?" said Mrs. Purdie, hastily wiping her eyes. "Come awa', dearie. I thocht I wud let ye get yer sleep oot, so I didna wauken ye."

"Ay, here he comes wi' as mony feet's a hen!" cried the old man jovially. "Guid mornin' to yer nicht-cap, Macgreegor!"

Greetings over, Mr. Purdie drew his grandson close to him and, smiling broadly, said:

"I've a fine bit o' news fur ye, ma mannie. Whit dae ye think it is? Eh?"

"I'm to get an egg to ma breakfast, Granpaw?"

"'Deed, ay; ye're gaun to get an egg, dearie," put in his grandmother. "I'm jist gettin' yer breakfast ready fur ye. But yer Granpaw's got some rale nice news fur ye." And Mrs. Purdie, tremulous with partly suppressed excitement and emotion, set about preparing the youngster's place at table.

"Whit is it, Granpaw?" enquired Macgregor. "Am I to get the wee dug hame wi' me?" He referred to a puppy which a friend of the Purdies had offered him a couple of days before, the offer being subject to his parents' approval, for which his grandfather had promised to write. "Am I to get the wee dug?" he repeated eagerly. "Dis Paw say I can tak' it hame to Glesca?"

"Ah, we'll see aboot the wee dug anither time," said the old man. "It's faur finer news that I've got fur ye the day. Ye've got a wee brither, Macgreegor!" Mr. Purdie chuckled with delight and lay back in his chair to watch the effect of the announcement.

"I hivna!" said Macgregor, not understanding.

"Ay; but it's true, laddie. Ye – ye jist got him yesterday. Here a letter frae yer Paw tellin' us aboot it, an' at the end yer Paw says: 'Tell Macgreegor he's got a wee brither noo.' "

"Is't a new baby ye mean?" asked Macgregor at last.

"Jist that – a baby brither," Mr. Purdie replied.

"A baby brither," echoed Mrs. Purdie in a voice of softened jubilation. "Ye'll be a prood laddie noo, Macgreegor!"

The boy did not reply immediately. He broke the silence with the curt question: "Is't an awfu' wee yin?"

His grandfather laughed. "I suppose it'll jist be the usual size, ma mannie."

"Usual size!" cried Mrs. Purdie, suddenly indignant. "Did John no' say in his letter that the doctor said he never seen a splendider baby?"

"So he did," admitted her husband humbly. "He's a fine big yin, yer wee brither, Macgreegor," he added, as if to reassure the youngster.

"Hoo big?"

"Aw, I canna tell ye that. But yer Granmaw's gaun to Glesca the day, an' she'll be comin' back the morn's nicht wi' a' the news aboot yer wee brither."

"I hope it's bigger nor Jeannie wis when she wis new. She wis awfu' wee – an' when she grat, she wis jist like a wee monkey wi' a rid face."

"Ye wis like that yersel' yinst," interposed Mrs. Purdie, endeavouring to conceal her annoyance at her grandson's lack of sympathy. "Come awa' an' tak' yer breakfast noo, fur I maun get ready fur the road."

"Did ye bile ma egg hard?" enquired Macgregor, as he seated himself at the table. "I dinna like egg when it's driddly."

"Ay; I biled it hard. Are ye no' gaun to ask a blessin' afore ye tak' the tap aff?"

Macgregor continued tapping the top of the egg with his

spoon until the fragments of shell could be removed. Then he dug out a spoonful of white and peered in at the yolk.

"Ay; its hard," he observed in a tone of satisfaction, and bowing his head, remained still and silent for about ten seconds. Looking up, he enquired, "D'ye think I'll get takin' hame the wee dug, Granpaw?"

"We'll see, we'll see," Mr. Purdie returned evasively.

His grandmother looked at him reproachfully ere she left the kitchen to make some preparations for the journey from Rothesay to Glasgow. "I thocht ye wud ha'e been thinkin' mair o' yer wee brither nor a bit dug, dearie," she said gently.

Macgregor looked uncomfortable, but continued eating, casting an occasional glance at his grandfather, who had taken up the morning paper.

"Granpaw," he began at last, "did Paw no' say onythin' aboot the wee dug in the letter?"

Mr. Purdie shook his head.

"Nor in the – the telegraph?"

"Na, na, laddie. Ye see yer Paw wud be that tooken up wi' yer wee brither, he wudna be mindin' aboot the wee dug. Ye can speir at him an' yer Maw aboot it when ye gang hame."

"But I ken they baith like dugs. I wis to ha'e gotten yin last year, but it got rin ower when the man wis bringin' it to the hoose."

"That wis an unco peety," Mr. Purdie remarked sympathetically, from the midst of reading a violent letter to the editor on the fiscal question. "An unco peety," he repeated, absently.

"D'ye no' think Paw an' Maw wud be rale pleased if I wis takin' the wee dug hame wi' me? It wud gi'e them a nice surprise, an' it wud gaird the hoose fine. Eh?"

"Whit wis ye sayin', ma mannie?" said the old man without impatience, laying the newspaper on his knee.

Macgregor put a spoonful of egg in his mouth and repeated his query and argument, adding, "An' I wud ca' it Joseph."

"Efter Maister Joseph Chamberlain," said Mr. Purdie, looking amused.

"Wha's he? I dinna ken him. I meant Joseph, him that's lyin' badly. He's the laddie that thocht there wis monkeys at Rothesay an' wantit me to bring him hame some partins frae the shore. D'ye no' mind aboot him?"

"Fine, fine. An' is the puir laddie nae better yet?"

"Naw. But he wud be gey prood to ha'e ma wee dug ca'ed efter him. He yinst ca'ed a wheen white mice efter me. But I wisna heedin' muckle aboot that."

"It wis maybe no' jist complimentary."

"Whit?"

"I said it wis maybe no' jist complimentary, Macgreegor. But never heed that. Ha'e ye had plenty to eat?"

"Ay; I'm done noo," Macgregor replied, leaving the table. "Are we gaun ootbye noo?"

"Rest ye a wee, an' then we'll gang an' see yer Granmaw awa' in the boat."

"An' efter that we'll gang an' see the wee dug. Eh, Granpaw?"

Before Mr. Purdie could reply, his wife returned and set to work to tidy the kitchen. "Mistress M'Tavish'll luk efter the hoose till I get back," she said to her husband. "Leave yer checkkey wi' her at nicht, an' she'll come in in the mornin' an' licht the fire an' mak' the breakfast."

"An obleegin' neebour's a mercy," remarked Mr. Purdie. "Macgreegor an' me'll mind aboot the key."

"See, dearie," said Mrs. Purdie to her grandson, who was busy twisting out the button of a hassock on which he sat by the hearth, "ye micht cairry the dishes frae the table to the jawbox, fur it's gaun to tak' me a' ma time to catch the boat."

Macgregor sprang up, and did his best to assist his grandmother, for he had a feeling that he had offended her in some way. Moreover, he was going to ask a favour of her.

But, somehow, when, half-an-hour later, he was bidding her good-bye on the pier, he could not manage to put his desire into words, and she sailed away without the urgent message he had intended sending to his parents.

"Weel, whit wud ye like to dae noo?" enquired Mr. Purdie

as they moved shorewards. "It's ower cauld the day fur sittin' ootbye, but we micht tak' a wee walk afore we gang hame. In the efternune we'll hap wursel's weel, an' tak' a ride in the caur to Port Bannatyne. Wud ye like that, Macgreegor?"

"Ay, Granpaw. But wull we no' gang an' see Joseph noo?"

"Wha?"

"Joseph – ma wee dug."

"Toots! laddie, ye're gaun ower quick!" said the old man good-humouredly.

Macgregor slackened his already easy pace. "I furgot ye wisna as soople as me," he said kindly.

"I didna mean *walkin'* ower quick, ma mannie," returned Mr. Purdie, touched by the youngster's consideration. "I meant ye wis makin' up yer mind ower quick aboot the dug."

"Whit wey that?"

"Aweel, ye see, I'm no' jist shair ye can get takin' the beastie hame wi' ye. Wud it no' be best to wait till ye get word frae yer Paw?"

"But I want to gi'e him an' Maw a fine surprise. I tell't ye they liket dugs. An' if they didna want the wee dug they wud ha'e pit it in the letter."

"Weel, weel, that's dootless yin wey o' lukin' at it," admitted Mr. Purdie, feeling rather helpless. "But – but, ye see laddie, ye – ye've got a wee brither noo."

"But he's ower wee to hurt the dug, an I wudna let Joseph bite him, Granpaw."

"I'm shair ye wudna. But a' the same, I doot it wudna dae to ha'e a beast in the hoose the noo."

"We had a cat when Jeannie wis new."

"Had ye?"

"Ay; had we!"

"But a cat disna mak' a noise, laddie," said Mr. Purdie, groping for arguments. "An' ye canna keep a dug quate – can ye?"

"A dug disna mak' near the noise a new wean dis. I'm shair I wud keep Joseph quate, Granpaw. Wull we gang an' see him noo?"

"Aweel, we'll gang an' see him fur twa-three meenits; but, mind, ye mauna set yer hert on the beastie, laddie, fur I doot ye'll no' get takin' him hame to Glesca."

"Wait, an' ye'll see," confidently returned Macgregor, to whom a happy thought had just occurred. "I'm gaun to write a letter to Paw."

"'Deed, ay. He'll be prood to get a letter frae his big laddie," said the old man heartily.

"Wull ye help me to spell it, Granpaw?" the other asked at the end of a longish silence.

"I'll dae ma best, but ma spellin' 's no' whit it used to be."

In a little while they reached the house of Mr. Purdie's friend, and Macgregor fell deeper in love than ever with the puppy, being quite convinced that it answered to "Joseph."

Whenever the obliging Mrs. M'Tavish had cleared the kitchen table of the remains of the simple dinner, Macgregor perched himself on a chair and laid several sheets of paper before him.

"Are ye gaun to write it wi' a pincil?" asked his grand-father.

"Ay. I've got a bew pincil. Paw'll like that fine. The last time I wrote to him, I done it wi' a rid yin. It wis when I wis bidin' wi' you yins. But I can write faur better noo, an' I dinna need to kneel on the chair. Hoo dae ye spell *fayther*? I ca' him that in writin'.' "

Mr. Purdie spelt that word and several others to the best of his ability; and the boy, whose tongue made nearly as many movements as his fingers, completed – after several abortive attempts – an epistle which gave him the highest satisfaction, and caused his elderly companion to pat him on the back and to say, in the kindliest voice, "Weel dune, weel dune, Macgreegor."

Omitting the address and the date, the letter read as follows:

My dear Father,

I am very well and hope you are well and so is mother and Jeeny and the litle new baby. There is a we dog. I want it.

Can I get takeing him home. It is a beutifull dog and he will gard the house for theifs. It is a fine day. He ansers to Joseph. Please right soon.

Your dear sun,

MACGREGOR ROBINSON.

As speedily as Macgregor could hurry Mr. Purdie forth – the old man missed his accustomed nap – the letter was taken to the post, after which the twain took the car to Port Bannatyne.

Next evening Mrs. Purdie was home again, full of thankfulness for her daughter and overflowing with pride in her new grandson.

"They're baith jist daein' splendid," she exclaimed again and again, while her husband nodded his head and beamed his satisfaction.

Macgregor, waiting for the evening post – for his grandmother had delivered no message, save that of love, to him – listened patiently to the eulogies on his newest near relation, and promised half-a-dozen times to be a shining example and unwearying protector to the latter.

But when the post came at last, there was no letter for him.

It was not until bed-time that Mrs. Purdie recollected that she had another message from his father after all.

"I'm unco vexed I furgot to teel ye it the first thing, dearie. Yer Paw wis rale pleased and prood to get yer letter, but he hadna time to write back. He's gey thrang the noo. But ye're to gang hame the morn, so ye'll see him then, dearie. Ye're needit to help them in the hoose, an', furbye that, they're missin' ye sair. Wee Jeannie's wi' Mistress M'Faurlan. So yer Granpaw'll tak' ye to Glesca the morn's mornin'. Noo, it's time ye wis in yer beddy-baw – or, wud ye like a piece first?"

Macgregor shook his head. "Did – did ma Paw no' say onythin' aboot Joseph?"

"Wha, dearie?"

"Joseph – ma wee dug?"

Mrs. Purdie looked at her husband for help.

"Macgreegor, ma mannie," said Mr. Purdie gently, "I'm near as vexed as ye can be yersel', but yer Paw says ye mauna tak' the beastie hame wi' ye."

The youngster restrained himself – at any rate, until he was alone.

Mr. Purdie had a decidedly sulky travelling companion the following afternoon, and was genuinely grieved as well as surprised, when the latter refused his offer of a bottle of lemonade on board the steamer.

"Never heed, Macgreegor, never heed," he repeated frequently, but the boy did not seem to hear him.

After a dismal journey they reached the Robinson's abode, and, it being the dinner hour, John himself opened the door to them.

Possibly Macgregor remembered his home-coming after the first appearance of his little sister Jeannie, but on that occasion he had returned very homesick and without a regret after an absence of several weeks, and had dropped into the free arm of his mother with a sob of relief. But now, he had been away but a few days, and –

"Weel, Maister Purdie! Weel, Macgreegor!" said John cordially, but not boisterously. "Come ben, come ben. Yer Maw's wearyin' fur ye, laddie," he whispered to his son.

"Whit wey–" began the boy crossly, and halted, for there seemed to be something unfamiliar about his father. "Whaur's Maw?" he asked suddenly, as he caught a glimpse of a strange elderly woman walking across the kitchen with a white bundle in her arms. "Whaur's Maw," he repeated anxiously.

John whispered something to his father-in-law, who nodded gravely and stepped softly into the kitchen.

"Come wi' me, Macgreegor, ma son," said his father, taking his hand.

And presently Macgregor was in the parlour, which now looked so queer as a bedroom that he clean forgot everything else and stared amazed till he saw somebody on the bed smiling and beckoning very gently to him.

"Canny noo, ma mannie," whispered his father, "canny noo."

With a sore lump in his throat and a half-choked cry at his lips, Macgregor reached his mother's arms.

"Are ye no' weel, Maw?" he sobbed. Never in his life had he felt so sad.

"Ma dear wee laddie," murmured Lizzie, and began to comfort him.

John tried to smile on his wife and first-born, but failing miserably, stole noiselessly from the room.